A Matter of Perspective

Other Stick Foster Mysteries by Kevin Robinson

Split Seconds
Mall Rats

A Matter of Perspective

A Stick Foster Mystery

Kevin Robinson

Walker and Company
New York

First published in the United States of America in 1993
by Walker Publishing Company, Inc.

Published simultaneously in Canada by Thomas Allen & Son
Canada, Limited, Markham, Ontario

Library of Congress Cataloging-in-Publication Data
Robinson, Kevin
A matter of perspective / Kevin Robinson.
p.   cm.—(A Stick Foster mystery)
ISBN 0-8027-3242-9
1. Foster, Stick (Fictitious character)—Fiction. 2. Journalists—Florida—
Orlando—Fiction. 3. Orlando (Fla.)—Fiction. I. Title. II. Series: Robinson,
Kevin. Stick Foster mystery.
PS3568.O2892M38   1993
813'.54—dc20   93-15674
CIP

Printed in the United States of America
2 4 6 8 10 9 7 5 3 1

This book is dedicated to Stephen Epstein. Not because he is a Renaissance man, a gambler, an observer of the female form, or a soldier of fortune . . . though he is all of those things. And not because he is a lawyer . . . I try not to hold that against him. But because he is, and has been, my friend. Thanks for being there, Steve.

Acknowledgments

I am *not* a lawyer. (Praise God from whom all blessings flow!) But in order even to attempt this story, I needed help from more lawyers than one person should have to talk to in a lifetime. To a shark, they were responsive, patient, and able to explain the legal mumbo jumbo in terms that at least I *thought* I understood. Any inaccuracies in legalese are most definitely my fault, and not theirs. My special thanks to them, and to the others whose expertise gave my concept wings:

Bob Albright, first reader and friend, whose ear for subtlety and eye for scene sometimes make me feel deaf and blind.

Larry Weimer, an old friend who knows firsthand that the only thing worse than a lawyer is a paralegal with an attitude!

Greg Vleisides, Esquire, a new friend and a longtime mystery fan.

Jim Jarrow, Esquire, a good cop gone bad, and all his compatriots at Baker, Sterchi & Cowden, especially Chuck, Phil, Mitch, Brian, Becky, and Randy.

Dr. Robert Cohon, of the Nelson-Atkins Museum of Fine Art in Kansas City.

Dr. Kevin Kuebler, a heart surgeon with heart.

Wayne Sarosi, for his circuit wizardry.

Sid Brechin, for the L.I.M.

Harold Hutchinson, for spelling *ibrat al-maut*.

Claire Israel, for the encouraging smile I've seen only over the phone.

A Matter of Perspective

THE LAW OFFICES OF
Ketchum, Latham & Bennet, P. A.
221 Lake Eola Drive
Orlando, Florida 32801
(407)555-1975 - FAX (407)555-1999

Rodney J. Ketchum	Charles D. Young
Rosemary I. Latham	William P. Graham
Robert G. Bennet	H. Russell White
Bernard R. Ketchum	Robert W. Albright
Rebecca H. Forest	Samantha Wagner-Foster
Stephen B. Epstein	Paul W. Kilpatrick

1

I HATE CORPORATE dinner parties, so I never go unless I have to. Wearing my only suit and rolling around a crowded room in a wheelchair while trying to juggle appetizers and club soda on my lap is a pain . . . especially while slick-haired men in pin-striped suits with suspenders and stiff-looking women in tight black dresses and jewelry worth more than my classic '86 Monte Carlo SS vie for position in the most portentous conversations. The lively mannequins posturing around me were my wife Sam's fellow workers, the lawyers and staff of Ketchum, Latham & Bennet, one of Orlando's most prosperous firms.

The annual party is a required social function; in fact, I think it's the company's *only* social function—although it could easily be argued that the true purpose has far more to do with the politics of looking like a family than with real people and genuine fellowship. Rodney Ketchum, Rosemary Latham, and Robert Bennet are the Three Rs, and the successful partnership they founded in 1969 has nine additional attorneys on staff, along with three paralegals (I call these the Apostles, the three "lesser" and the nine "greater"), eight secretaries, one receptionist, and a part-time runner named Clarence "Gross" Grosse.

The firm primarily handles worker's compensation and personal injury cases and, if Sam's reports are to be believed, the Three Rs seldom lose. "Sometimes," she's admitted to me, "I think winning and losing are more important to some of them than the client's real needs, but fortunately the one usually takes care of the other."

Rodney "The Old Man" Ketchum must be almost seventy, a handsome white-haired chronic smoker whose pacemaker-controlled heart has been bypassed more times than downtown Miami. Still, The Old Man's very name strikes fear into insurance carriers and their legal representation throughout the Sunshine State. He has a reputation for wanting nothing less than the best for his clients . . . and almost always getting it. He also has a reputation as an avid gambler; if there's a big money poker game in town, for instance, odds are good that The Old Man has a seat at the table. It's said that he frequently makes important decisions based solely on whether or not he feels the "luck."

He is, Sam says, quite proud of the fact that he recently "stole" his eldest son, Bernard, from another central Florida law firm. "Great luck for the firm!" he'd assured his cohorts, but Bernard "Silverspoon" Ketchum, by all accounts, is a snobbish, condescending brat who cares far more about his imported sports car (Daddy gave it to him as a "signing bonus") and his twelve-hundred-dollar suits than he does for the firm's broken and needy clientele.

It is common knowledge that Silverspoon and his father never got on in the first place. Needless to say, the prospect of having them in the same building wasn't something that the others found particularly lucky at all . . . to say nothing of the ramifications any lateral insertion within a law firm has on the all-important letterhead ladder. As apostles go, I already had Bernard cast in the Judas role.

This was my second Three Rs party, and I came only after a second-rate spat with Sam.

"You know I *hate* these things."

"That's too bad. If I have to suffer through it, so do you."

"But you *like* lawyers!"

"Watch it, bub! You're coming as my husband and as my escort . . . and you're *not* bringing your computer."

"It's still in the shop."

"Good."

So, I went. But computer or not, I went prepared to entertain myself while Sam chummed the shark-infested waters. When I had finished my requisite munchies and ditched the cut-glass predinnerware, I pulled my old Minolta 5000 out of the backpack hanging behind me on the wheelchair and looked for a good vantage point from which to shoot the well-groomed crowd until the dinner call came. The northwest corner, near a window and behind an antique lamp table, seemed the perfect place for a paparazzo wallflower.

Even with its long mahogany table, the conference room was more than spacious enough to accommodate the firm and its extended family. The expansive west wall behind me consisted mostly of designer-draped windows, each looking out across Lake Eola Drive toward the scenic downtown park with its green domed fountain glistening in the warm colors of the waning sun. Though the room was chic and hospitable on the inside, the windows were fitted with black wrought-iron bars on the outside. As I looked closer, I noticed that each windowpane was framed with clear security-alarm tape. The north wall to my left, and the south wall at the far end of the room, were actually floor-to-ceiling bookshelves brimming with important-looking tomes . . . the kind I've always suspected every law firm has but no self-respecting barrister is ever caught reading.

On the remaining wall, about six feet in from either end, were two doors leading to the firm's main hallway. Between these doors, surrounded by additional hardwood book shelving, hung a framed picture that looked for all the world like an original J. M. W. Turner oil painting . . . the Bridge of Rialto, I guessed, on the Grand Canal in Venice. Surely it was a print or a reproduction. The bronze bust on a waist-high pillar to the right of the south door was that of a regal-looking Roman woman clad in a draping garment that was clasped on her left shoulder and covered only her right breast. Her bronze mate, sitting just to the left of the north door, was clearly a great Roman leader, though he lacked the customary laurel crown. Back in the far corner, next to the golden lady, stood an elaborate portable TV/video center, costly enough, I reasoned, to justify the high-security windows.

When I slid the ON switch forward, my old computerized camera lit up and displayed *Program* across its tiny screen, presumably announcing that the "mind of Minolta" was still relatively sane, ready to do my bidding. I'd recently talked my editor at the *Orlando Sentinel,* Ben "Good News" Dawson, into pitching an ongoing feature to the newspaper's *Sunday Magazine* for me. He sold it, and I was reacquainting myself with my 35mm autoeverything camera. The (tentatively) monthlong series of weekend photo stories was called "Take This Sitting Down," and in it I endeavored to humorously portray Orlando as it might be seen from the eye level of someone in a wheelchair. Of course I worked hard to exaggerate the unusual perspective, and my somewhat tunnel-visioned shots assumed little or no vertical scanning.

At Sam's company soiree, for example, my 28–85mm lens would focus in on that straight-ahead landscape that stretched from the ladies' pearl-and-diamond-draped décolletages to the equatorial latitudes of the gentlemen's vest-covered midsections . . . a veritable panorama of wineglasses, hors d'oeuvres, boobs, and bellies. Taking journalism to new heights has always been a life's priority for me.

"Why, hello, Mr. Foster," said Rosemary Latham, partner and stunningly dressed cohostess.

"Please," I said, "call me Stick. Even my dad never put up with 'Mr. Foster.' "

"As you wish," she said, extending a jewel-encrusted hand. "I wanted to say how much we appreciate having Samantha with our firm. It's just over a year now, and she's made a real place for herself here. She's doing a dynamite job on the Fraiser case, and I look forward to many big things from Sam."

"She thrives on competition," I said, carefully disengaging my hand from Ms. Latham's sparkling glass cutters. "And as near as I can tell, nothing short of the NBA offers more intense one-on-one confrontation."

"Yes," Rosemary said with obvious satisfaction, "I've always appreciated a good full-courtroom run and gun myself—the bloodier the better."

Mmm.

"Speaking of shooting," she went on, "I thought the *Sentinel* had a staff of photographers . . . or are you a hobbyist?"

"Mostly a hobbyist," I said, rather than explain my new project. "This is just a little excursion, hopefully a fun one."

"Well," she said, smoothing her form-fitting black designer dress over near-perfect post-middle-aged hips that had already smoothed the material to its limit, "I hope you'll capture my best side!"

"Can't miss from any direction," I said as she moved off with the pleased and confident air of royalty.

"Foxy old tart, isn't she?"

I turned left to see a looming, lopsided figure lumber up beside me in one of only two suits in the room cheaper than mine. (The other, Clarence Grosse, was, at that moment, slipping appetizers into the pockets of his.) The big man had made no attempt to lower his voice.

"You must be Rick Scully," I said. "Sam told me they hired another gimp."

"Straight on!" said the leaning tower with the bad case of five o'clock shadow. "Friends call me Scully. Someone's got to keep these slimy crooks on the up-and-up!"

Richard Scully, a six-foot, five-inch, 220-plus-pound paralegal with stiff and unruly brown hair and wild-looking blue eyes, slapped my shoulder for emphasis and nearly knocked me out of my wheelchair. I clutched at my camera to keep it from bouncing off my lap. While his left leg and arm were clearly gimped up by what I assumed had been some con-

genital disorder, his right side suffered from no such defor-
mity. I felt certain that Scully had a serious right cross at his
disposal.

"So you're the famous Nick Foster, aye?" he said. "I like
your reporting style . . . but I *really* like your wife! What a
babe!"

Sam had said that young Scully was a little rough around
the edges, but she hadn't added "like a steamroller."

"Why thanks, Scully," I said. "Just call me Stick, okay?"

"Sure, Stick," he said, clutching my shoulder with fervor.
"I hear you earned that wheelchair during Operation Desert
Storm. I'll have to hear the tale sometime."

"You've been listening to Sam," I said, shaking my head.
Tall, varied, and straight-faced fairy tales about how I became paralyzed were my wife's idea of a wonderful running
joke. In a year's time, I'd lost track of how many phony
stories had come back to me. There were at least four going
around at church, and another even made the paper. "Don't
believe everything you hear, Scully. I fell off a garage roof."

"Bummer," he said, looking genuinely disappointed.

"Yeah, I know. How do you like it here at the Three Rs so
far?"

"It'll do till I finish school and pass the bar, Stick. Between
you and me," he said loudly, "most of these clowns are so anal
retentive, it'll take this high-dollar Cheese Whiz a month to
reach the swirling blue waters in the old porcelain pond!"

"I'll take your word for it, Scully," I said, laughing at the
metaphorical picture that I suddenly hoped to capture with
my camera. "Sam says you've been on the road a lot lately.
How's the Fraiser case coming?"

"Careful, Stick," Scully said, glancing from side to side.
"Didn't Sam warn you about using the 'F' word in mixed
company?"

"Well, I know the case is supposed to be qt."

"That's true," he said, straining to keep his booming voice
at what might pass as a whisper. "But there's some mighty
bad feelings in this room, and it all has to do with who The

Old Man did and didn't choose for the F-word team."

"I didn't know."

"What're you taking pictures of—besides pucker-butts?" Scully said with a knowing nod, his ringing voice back in full force.

I told him.

"Well, to each his own," he said, shaking my shoulder before motioning across the room with his good hand. "I'd better mingle. Wouldn't want to go home without annoying as many people as possible, aye?"

"Certainly not," I said, bracing myself for the farewell shoulder pounding. "Nice to meet you, Scully."

The needle on some inner truth meter wavered slightly, but appearances and behavior notwithstanding, something about the limping behemoth actually appealed to me.

Sam and her hot-pink, ultralight wheelchair kept rolling in and out of the frame, her sparkling blue-gray eyes and long blond hair in sharp contrast to all the dark material in my chosen focal range. She reorganized the conversational cliques wherever she went, well able to hold her own with anyone and everyone in the room. Despite her welcome interference, I shot several interesting, but not particularly amusing, photos of the crowd's midsection before catching a doozy.

Halfway down the long room, a man's hand, sporting a bulky gold wedding ring, was deftly depositing an olive in the pumped-up and packed-in décolletage of a woman who could only be Victoria Mann, the firm's buxom and vivacious receptionist. The hand was withdrawing as my shutter tripped, and the olive sat there, high and proud, like a green golf ball ready to be driven down the fairway. By the time I looked up to see who was teeing off, the gallery had shifted enough to block my view.

"Putting together a company yearbook, Mr. Foster?"

"Hi, Mrs. Ketchum. Call me Stick, please. No, I'm working on a humor piece for the *Sunday Magazine*."

"Okay, Stick, but you must call me Anna. I'm not sure I

understand what could be very amusing about this bunch," she said, the tone of her voice and the rolling sparkle of her bright green eyes making it clear that she was bored.

"You should see it from down here," I said, "especially when I frame out the highs and lows."

Anastasia Ketchum was Old Man Rodney's third and youngest wife. According to Sam, the former dancer-model still liked to jet to Miami or New York to boogie with the in crowd at all the hip clubs. My best guess put Silverspoon and his latest stepmother at very nearly the same age.

Anna hiked up her tight dress far more than was necessary and sat down on the carpeted floor beside me. "I see what you mean," she said. "It's kind of like being a kid again!"

I laughed with her, enjoying the good-natured, nonstuffy personality that seemed out of place in the highbrow assembly.

Moments later, after Anna moved on (only the lingering essence of her perfume remaining in her wake) I was shooting a promising composition built around a gold Rolex watch down at the south end of the room when the Minolta slipped out of my hands. It bounced once on my lap, and I caught it just before it could get farther away, accidentally tripping the shutter in the process. I found my subject again and resumed shooting pictures, but one of the extras in the frame had the ill manners to collapse—just as the shutter sucked in the picture with a faint click.

By the time my whining autoadvance finished setting up the next shot, the far end of the room was in turmoil. The crowd and the table proved impassable; I exited by the north door, passing the bronze Roman leader on my way out, and turned right down the hallway before I learned the nature of the disaster. Sprawled in the conference room's south doorway, lay the firm's senior partner. He thrashed for several seconds, clutching his chest, before his body seized up like a rusty robot.

Robert Bennet tore open his partner's vest and shirt—exposing an interesting collection of scars—bent closer to The Old Man's nose, and motioned one of the nearby paralegals to join him on the floor. I knew the firm made all its employees take the American Red Cross CPR course, but before the young woman in the black dress could hike up her hemline and kneel beside her bosses, Rodney's chest rose violently and then went still again. The accompanying sound was totally unnerving, a noise that no human—dead or alive—should ever make.

Bob Bennet and the young woman worked valiantly until the ambulance arrived, but it was clear to everyone that The Old Man was dead.

THE LAW OFFICES OF

Ketchum, Latham & Bennet, P. A.

221 Lake Eola Drive
Orlando, Florida 32801
(407)555-1975 - FAX (407)555-1999

Rosemary I. Latham	William P. Graham
Robert G. Bennet	H. Russell White
Bernard R. Ketchum	Robert W. Albright
Rebecca H. Forest	Samantha Wagner-Foster
Stephen B. Epstein	Paul W. Kilpatrick
Charles D. Young	

2

"I SUPPOSE IT was inevitable," Sam said as she piloted her red Mustang convertible through the warm Florida night toward our new lakefront home on Shorecrest Drive in Maitland. "The Old Man might as well have lived on intravenous cholesterol, and he was always shouting at somebody. His face turned beet red sometimes. I can't imagine what those little outbursts did to his blood pressure."

"Rodney always struck me as the ultracontrolled type," I said.

"Oh, he was controlled whenever he wanted to be—like in court—but some people just tripped his switch . . . like the new guy, Rick Scully. The Old Man went at it with Scully almost every day about something."

"But didn't fire him?"

"Oh, no. I actually think he liked it. Even when he argued with his son, Bernie, the kid had all the hostility. The Old Man just loved to get in your face . . . a theatrical thing almost."

"A heart attack just waiting to happen," I said. "Why would a new paralegal mix it up with the senior partner, though? That doesn't seem very expedient to me."

"There isn't anything expedient about Rick Scully. Having him around is like having a loaded harpoon cannon poised over a tankful of helpless sharks! Ah, Stick," Sam said, chuckling, "sometimes I just crack myself up!"

I love it when Sam laughs. Her face lights up like the sun, moon, and stars, and only an ogre from a deep mountain cave could resist laughing along. She drove north up the dead-end street to where the pavement turned to pine needles, swung into our blacktop driveway, and parked next to my classic black '86 Monte Carlo SS. Our double carport overlooks a sloping backyard that includes 150 feet of Lake Martha shoreline. Reflections from the pole lights at the now quiet private school across the lake to the northeast glistened on the surface of the water, while across to the east, the wildlife refuge was dark but not silent. Beasties of every tone and timbre joined their voices to those of the lake's resident loons and welcomed us home to a nightly cacophony we had already grown to love.

Finding and buying the long, ranch-style, red-brick house was a traumatic and exhilarating experience. Dad's life insurance was just enough for the down payment on the small Melbourne house I had purchased after his death, and the monthly cost was only $318. Almost three years later, when a terrorist destroyed it with a car bomb, my home owner's policy had reimbursed me almost $75,000 with which to have it rebuilt. Sam and I had put nearly all *that* much *down* on our Orlando area lakefront villa. And if that weren't scary enough, we were in the midst of a major remodeling project—the supreme test, they say, of a marriage. It was, at least, nice having a *real* breadwinner in the family to pay for it.

"I can't help wondering about the bereaved widow," I said. "Or the bereaved son. I doubt that either one of them will have a whole lot of trouble getting over their tragedy and getting on with their lives. What do you suppose The Old Man was worth?"

"You are nasty, babe, but the answer is: a bundle. Anna Ketchum never struck me as the ever-faithful type anyway; but then, neither did her randy husband."

"Liked the ladies, did he?"

"He could afford to," Sam said as she transferred into her colorful folding wheelchair. "He was probably hitting on someone at the party when he keeled over."

We rolled into the disaster area we now called home and saw a note taped to the foyer wall.

The two hundred amp service is in and you can use the new oven and microwave now. The washing machine is functional, but the 220 line for the dryer's not hooked up yet. Tomorrow. The tile you want for the kitchen counter will take two weeks or more to order. What about this?

A pencil line ran down off the note and plummeted across the unpainted drywall before turning into an arrowhead just above the floor.

This stuff costs a little more, but there's plenty of it in stock. BTW, Bill and Wallace were a big help with the living room ceiling . . . good kids, couldn't have dry-walled it without them! —Danny

P.S. The computer shop called. It's ready.

Danny Kincade is a full-time handyman whose reputation keeps him constantly in demand. How Sam finagled him away from whomever was *supposed* to get him next, I didn't exactly know . . . and it was probably better that way. The man was Bob Villa, Norm Abrams, and Isaac Bashevis Singer all rolled into one. His ability to create beauty out of chaos was extraordinary, both in home remodeling and in story-telling. Sam often scolded me for encouraging the latter as it was usually guaranteed to set back her timetable some, but I couldn't help myself. Danny was a remarkable student of human behavior, and his discerning tales were filled with insight, pathos, and good humor.

"I'm getting tired of all this drywall dust," Sam said for the hundredth time. Her wheelchair left two sets of tracks as she rolled across the pressed board subfloor, one from the inflated and cantilevered high-pressure rear wheels, and one from the tiny black rubber casters up front.

"It's better than that blown-in insulation we had all over when Danny pulled down the old ceiling," I said as I rolled into the living room and looked up at Danny's latest Sheetrock project. The taped seams and screw heads had all been covered with a light coating of mud, most of which was already dry. Only in the corners where the ceiling met the walls did the slightly darker shade of gray give evidence to the fact that Danny had worked late.

When the portable phone rang somewhere nearby, I searched the living room rubble only briefly before giving up and heading for the kitchen wall extension. The temporarily buried telephone had come in the mail a couple months back, a free premium from someone, a credit union or some such, I think. It was a high-dollar deal and actually quite handy . . . when it wasn't lost. By the time I made my way past Danny's portable workbench and turned toward the kitchen, Sam had already picked up the phone in the bedroom.

"It's for you, babe!" she shouted from the far end of the house.

"Got it! Hello?"

"Nick? This is Joe O'Donnel. You got a minute?"

"Sure, Doc. What's up?"

Joe O'Donnel was my first physician at Florida Hospital when the ambulance crew hauled me into the ER with a broken back and no feeling in my legs. We got along fine until a state rehab nurse said I needed the kind of rehabilitation available only at an institution like Craig Hospital in Denver. From then on there was always a tinge of the betrayed in his voice, but he'd never failed to help me when I asked. But Joe had *never* called me.

"It's about your wife's late boss, Nick, but you've got to

swear not to repeat what I'm going to tell you until it's been confirmed. Deal?"

"Deal, Joe. Sounds serious."

"Maybe. Maybe not. But Jessie Sanderlin's hunches are seldom wrong. Jessie's the best heart mechanic in the southeast, maybe in the country."

Joe hesitated and I waited.

"They called her in tonight because Rodney Ketchum is—was—her special patient, and, well, she thinks he was murdered. I thought you might like a head start . . . just in case."

"You're right, Joe. Will she talk to me?"

"More likely you than the police," he said. "This kind of thing makes us look really stupid if we stir things up but can't come up with any solid evidence. Can I tell her that you'll keep it quiet?"

"You bet."

"Tomorrow then."

"Tomorrow. Thanks."

THE LAW OFFICES OF

Ketchum, Latham & Bennet, P. A.

221 Lake Eola Drive
Orlando, Florida 32801
(407)555-1975 - FAX (407)555-1999

Rosemary I. Latham	William P. Graham
Robert G. Bennet	H. Russell White
Bernard R. Ketchum	Robert W. Albright
Rebecca H. Forest	Samantha Wagner-Foster
Stephen B. Epstein	Paul W. Kilpatrick
Charles D. Young	

3

My 8 A.M. appointment with Dr. Jessica Sanderlin was squeezed in just before a bypass operation. The tall, platinum-haired surgeon swept into her outer office and motioned for me to follow her back to an examination room. She wasted no time closing the door and slapping an X ray into place on the wall-mounted light box.

"Mr. Foster," she said efficiently, "you've got a reputation for this kind of thing. How about we play detective, you and me?"

I felt the urge to make a crack about playing doctor instead, but I held my tongue.

"Call me Stick," I said. "What have we got?"

"Cardiac arrest. Plain and simple heart failure, in a patient who's been asking for it all of his life. Except for one thing," she said, pointing to the X ray for emphasis. "Mr. Ketchum's pacemaker failed somehow, but it was humming along perfectly last week when he had his physical."

"Is that unusual?" I asked, looking at one of two obviously nonorganic devices on The Old Man's chest film. "Does the pacemaker just keep ticking, even after its owner stops?"

"Of course. I've installed hundreds of them, Mr. Foster. The batteries eventually go, yes, but the pacemaker slows down as the battery fades, it doesn't just die. The patients usually notice a growing sense of fatigue, difficulty breathing, and sometimes profuse sweating for no apparent reason. Rod, I mean Mr. Ketchum, was running on nearly new batteries."

"Don't you get rejects sometimes, manufacturing defects and that kind of thing?"

"That's exactly what the police would say—if I were foolish enough to tell them what I'm telling you. It does happen, yes, but every recorded case is a *total* failure. And, mind you, that's *very* rare. And this pacemaker," she said, stabbing the X ray with her pointer finger, "checked out perfectly. If the cars we drive were built with half the quality control and pretested half as much as these little electronic thumpers, half the used-car salesmen in the country would have to get real jobs."

I laughed, but Dr. Jessie seemed startled by my response. "We're talking about a man's life here." she said. "And even if the pacemaker did quit all at once, it's highly improbable that the patient would just keel over and die that violently—at least from that alone."

"I'm sorry, the car salesman thing was funny," I said, "but I really think the police could help—"

"No!" she said. "You can't go to the police, but I do want to know who did this. I'll pay you," she added, looking at her watch, snatching down the X ray, and sweeping out of the examination room. There was vehemence in her voice— and if I wasn't mistaken, dampness in her eyes.

"Call me if you have any questions," she added as the door slammed behind her.

My first question was why anybody not in the publishing business would offer to pay a newspaper reporter to follow a story. My second question was why The Old Man apparently had two pacemakers in his chest, but I deduced by the echoing door slam that I wasn't going to get an answer to that right away.

*   *   *

On my way home I dropped my film off at a "one-day" drive-up photo booth on Semoran Boulevard. Normally the paper would develop them for me, but I wanted first crack at the party pictures. Next I ran by the computer store.

"I got her cleaned out like new, and she's up and running again," said the thin man wearing a white shirt and horn-rims, "but I still say you should replace the case."

I smiled and inspected the man's work. The dark gray case, with its tip-up lid-screen, was fast becoming a diary of my career as a newspaper reporter. The top was scarred by a four-inch slash mark, the result of a Middle Easterner's razor-sharp, curved blade—which had been, by the way, plunging straight toward my heart at the time. Additionally, both top and bottom were now perforated, hole-punched like a lunch ticket, twice on each side. I had the late Ruffus T. Alligator to thank for those.

"What did you put in there?" I asked while inspecting the gator's entry in my electronic diary board.

"Silicone adhesive," he said proudly. "I know you wanted the ghastly holes to stay as is, but I tried to restore the integrity of the case as much as possible. The goop will remain flexible for years and should seal out both water and dust."

"You done good. What do I owe you?"

"Well, I had to replace the motherboard and the LCD display," he said, nervously pulling a yellow billing sheet out from under the counter. "And the hard drive motor was trashed, but I managed to run the head on another unit and save most of your stuff!"

"Great. What do I owe you?"

"Well, the internal fax-modem had a hole right through it, so I had to replace that too."

"Thanks," I said to the young techno nerd. "I said fix it, and I'm sure you did a fine job, but now it's time to pay the pipe fitter. How much?"

"Well, our bench rates are—"

I sighed and motioned for him to hand me the bill. He slid

it across the counter, wincing slightly and looking away. I laughed and wrote a check.

"The extra twenty is for you," I said, putting my precious companion in my wheelchair backpack with the Minolta before rolling out the front door. What a day, I thought. It's sunny and perfect outside, my laptop computer, which was dead, is now alive, and, for the moment, I've got Sam's checkbook. Life is good!

I rolled in my front door to find Danny Kincade outfitted like an alien from outer space, with goggles and an elaborate dual-filtered-breathing face mask. Covered with white dry-wall dust, he was running an orbital sander against the living room ceiling, singing a muffled version of "Frosty the Snow-man," and doing an abbreviated two-step as he worked his way across the riser platform he'd built for the occasion.

Most of the swirling cloud of white dust was being pulled out of the room through the box fan Danny had set up in a living room window. The rest was depositing itself in a thin, relentless, and all-encompassing layer on everything in the house. I suspected that my already slurring answering machine would never be the same; I checked it, certain it was running more slowly than ever. After a cursory look at what passed for progress, I escaped back into the fresh warm Florida air and drove to the Palmetto Plaza Mall.

While writing a recent running feature about mall life, I'd laid claim to a second-floor window in the food court. It faced south, overlooking a parking lot and affording me a panoramic view of Colonial Drive and the Herndon Airport. It was a great place to work, warm and sunny despite the mall's perpetual air-conditioning and surrounded by life-affirming sounds ranging from old folks to young mothers pushing strollers. School was in session, so the only mall rats who showed up during the day were playing hooky, something not altogether uncommon.

On this morning, there was no sign of the pubescent youngsters, but Luigi Leone, the food court's resident pizza man, had coffee on, and there was a selection of fresh-baked danish on his stainless steel counter.

"Good morning, Louie."

"Hello, Stick. How's that fantasy novel coming?"

"Slowly."

It began as a fanciful idea about lost books, a dying culture, and the old magic that once gave it life. The thinking turned to tinkering, the tinkering turned to typing, and the typing was turning slowly into a sizable manuscript. Among serious journalists and literary types, it just doesn't seem to be fashionable to be a fan of J.R.R. Tolkien, Steven Donaldson, and Elizabeth Moon. But no one ever accused me of being fashionable, and, as the Buckaroo Banzai T-shirt my mall rats gave me says across the front: "No matter where you go, there you are."

"Not much excitement around here," Louie said, "but we still get lots of tourists. You know, folks who never shopped the old mall before but just want to come see where it all happened."

"That was then and this is now, Louie. I think I may be starting all over again, though. Know anything about lawyers?"

He snorted and went back to spinning pizza dough. I told him there was a chance Sam's big boss had been murdered and asked him what he knew about pacemakers.

"Only that I used to have to post a 'Microwave Oven in Use' sign, and now I don't have to anymore."

"Mmm. Thanks, Louie," I said taking coffee and a cinnamon roll to my table by the window. I pulled out the battered old laptop computer to start the article that would accompany my latest collection of photographs. Usually the quips came while I was shooting, and I made it a point to write them down soon after. My routine had been interrupted at the Three Rs party, and the wit what was was gone. I could almost hear Garth Brooks singing "Witless" instead of "Shameless." Perhaps the old magic would return when I saw the developed film.

In the meantime, I considered again the possibility of murder at the big-money law firm where my wife was only two rungs up a potentially treacherous corporate ladder. Sam and I rarely discussed the nuts and bolts of the firm's hierarchy, but I knew enough to know that one's prestige, pay, and power were related directly to one's position on the firm's letterhead. Exactly how and why one did or didn't move up was a study I now felt compelled to pursue in detail.

The concept of a shark feeding frenzy wasn't a pleasant one, but it was time to chum the waters.

THE LAW OFFICES OF

Ketchum, Latham & Bennet, P. A.

221 Lake Eola Drive
Orlando, Florida 32801
(407)555-1975 - FAX (407)555-1999

Rosemary I. Latham	William P. Graham
Robert G. Bennet	H. Russell White
Bernard R. Ketchum	Robert W. Albright
Rebecca H. Forest	Samantha Wagner-Foster
Stephen B. Epstein	Paul W. Kilpatrick
Charles D. Young	

4

As IT TURNED out there was no reason to cast my bloody fish upon the waters. The sharks were already circling and, murder aside, the spectacle was mesmerizing.

"Okay, Sam," I said, dumbfounded at my wife's answers. The more often I thought I was beginning to figure out my new bride, the more often I was reenlightened as to the extent of my ignorance. "You mean to tell me that The Old Man isn't in the ground yet, and they're fighting already?"

"Of course."

"Who's fighting with whom?"

"It's mostly Silverspoon and the partners at this point, but everyone has a stake in the outcome and they're choosing sides even as we speak."

"You too?"

"Me too."

"Mmm."

"Newcomers actually have more to lose than the partners—college loans, mortgages, car payments, families to feed, not to mention extensive home-remodeling projects. Think of the firm as a lifeboat where everyone standing in the front wants to be in charge, while everyone sitting huddled in the back plots who to push overboard if they don't

sit down by themselves. If they back the wrong partner, or if
the firm sinks as a result of the fight, it's a dismal job market
out there. Shark meat is cheap this year."

"Not a pretty picture."

"This is the big leagues, babe."

"What's Silverspoon want out of this? Partnership?"

"That's a given. The Old Man brought him in as the top
associate, laterally. I told you about the bad vibes whenever
associates on their way up the vertical path lose a turn when
someone is brought in above them from the outside?"

"Yeah," I said. "The pie can only be cut into so many
pieces."

"Until the pie gets bigger. Right. And depending on both
the economy and the efficiency of the firm, that might take
a year . . . or it might take ten. The three Rs has about an
eight-year career track to partner. Rosemary made it in five,
Bob Bennet made it in six, and the two guys who left just
before I was hired and started their own firm in Titusville
took about eight years each. But when Bernard came on
board he got the fourth rung automatically—one away from
a partnership. That means Becky Forest, who would normally have made partner next, maybe even this year, got
bumped, along with all the rest of us.

"But that's all to be expected," my barrister bride went
on. "The deal was that Silverspoon would make partner
whenever the income he generated equaled that of Bob Bennet. You know, a bigger pie. It's also called 'developing power,'
and the buzz is that he brought nearly enough of a client
and referral base with him to equal Bob and Rosemary com-
bined. If that's true, Silverspoon would probably have made
partner at the next firm meeting anyway, but he wants his
father's spot on the letterhead too. He wants to take over as
the senior partner."

"Isn't there a vote on stuff like this?" I asked, as it occurred to me that there was a miniseries or at least a "Hard
Copy" episode in this real-life drama.

"Sure, in a big firm, among the partners; with only two

living partners, our decision will be more of a test of wills
and expediency."

"Politics. Why doesn't that surprise me? You'd vote against
the kid if you could, wouldn't you?"

"Good question. I'm not sure yet."

"Sam!" I was shocked by my wife's blunt answer, and she
laughed at the mortified look on my face. If I'd thought
deeply enough about it, I should have known Sam was capable of such cold, calculated logic, but that's a side of her
I'd chosen to pretend did not exist.

"Think about it, babe. The firm was founded by Rodney
Ketchum. I mean, he was already very successful when he
talked Bob and Rosemary into joining him as associates in
nineteen sixty-nine. Nearly every hospital staff in the state
knows about The Old Man, and when some injured Joe
Public starts asking where to find a good lawyer, you can bet
that the name Ketchum comes up pretty quickly. Some of
his cases are Florida legend, and he practically wrote the new
worker's compensation law."

"But Silverspoon is the personification of what everybody
hates about lawyers . . . no offence."

"Cheap shot," Sam said with a laugh. "But maybe that's
one reason why he's developed so much power in such a
short time. That, or maybe it's just the name Ketchum."

Mmm.

I picked up the party pictures on my way to the paper and
shuffled through them briefly while I drove my Monte Carlo
SS west on Colonial Drive. The classic Chevy had taken
quite a beating when one of my stories crossed paths with a
drug gang, but the hoodlums were now in jail, and the old
'86 Monte looked as good as new. I know muscle cars aren't
politically correct, but the way I figure it, driving the Monte
sort of makes up for not being able to walk. Besides, the
optional 350-cubic-inch fuel-injected engine gets almost fifteen miles to the gallon when I take it easy, more than a
wheelchair van any day of the week.

Somehow my screwball photography always looks better after it's printed than it did through the viewfinder. Added to the shots in the mall, the grocery store, and at the library that I'd taken the week before, I had enough stuff for my first article—if I ever got around to writing it. Writers are easily distracted and masters of procrastination. That's why God created deadlines.

"You want to what?" Ben Dawson said. His expression was hurt, not angry. "I pitched that feature hard for you, Foster. The *Sunday Magazine* has already cleared a spot for it."

"I know, Ben, and thanks. But I've got a lead on a story that could be really big."

"Who died?"

"Now what would make you say that, Ben?"

"Call it a hunch. Follow your murder theories anywhere you want, but have that 'Take This Sitting Down' installment on Betty's desk by Friday . . . or else."

Touché.

Everybody who hates doing detail work needs a Peter Stilles, especially lazy writers who still feel somewhat overwhelmed in the reference section of the library. That's why the next thing I did was telephone him. Peter was an archivist for IBM and lived in Endwell, New York, before moving to Melbourne, Florida, and taking over his brother's blue crab fishing business. The man's a walking encyclopedia anyway, but prompt him for research data on a subject he's not up on, and he'll go like a hound on a rabbit, just for the fun of it. The list of resource data bases into which Peter and his 9,600-baud modem can tap his personal computer is a long and undoubtedly somewhat questionable one.

"Peter! How's the yacht coming?"

"Hi, Stick. Great! As a matter of fact, I had her out last weekend!"

"Out, as in out in the Intracoastal Waterway?" I said, shocked that Peter's WW II vintage Chris Craft rehab project might have actually left its mooring in the south Melbourne marina.

"You bet! One engine is still running a little rough, but the old thirty-five-footer really hauls keel! When are you and Sam coming over for a spin?"

"Ah, soon, Peter. Real soon."

"Great! We'd love to have you."

"We?"

"Oh yeah, I guess you and I haven't talked in a few weeks. Bice moved in last Thursday!"

"Well, I guess that answers my next question. Things must be going okay."

Bice Wathan owns and operates a high-dollar electronics shop in Melbourne and is reputedly a wizardess of wiring— everything from stereos to alarm systems. As I was responsible for introducing Peter and Bice, I was delighted to hear that the romance was flourishing.

"You bet. What are you up to, Stick?"

"I need a research assistant, Peter. Know anything about pacemakers?"

"Not much, but that sounds like a downer subject. What's going on?"

"I'll know better when you get back to me, but I need to know anything you can find about how someone might break one without cutting open the patient."

"Break a pacemaker?"

"Well, you know, stop it, short it out, anything like that. They used to say that microwave ovens were a hazard for people with pacemakers, but supposedly that's not true anymore. Why and why?"

"One reason might be that the microwave doors seal better nowadays," Peter said. "I think I read somewhere, though, that they program pacemakers with microwaves of some sort. I take it you're snooping into another suspicious death?"

I told him about the party at Sam's firm and made him promise to keep it quiet until we had something more substantial to go on. He loved my rendition of Sam's "life in a law firm" lecture and was as amazed as I had been at the ramifications of the in-house infighting.

"Pretty high stakes indeed," Peter said. I could picture him shaking his head from side to side. "But it's kinda fun to think about all those sharks attacking their own kind for a change!"

Before we hung up, I told Peter about Rodney Ketchum's strange X ray and asked him to find out why a patient might have two pacemakers in his chest at one time.

THE LAW OFFICES OF

Ketchum, Latham & Bennet, P. A.

221 Lake Eola Drive
Orlando, Florida 32801
(407)555-1975 - FAX (407)555-1999

Rosemary I. Latham	William P. Graham
Robert G. Bennet	H. Russell White
Bernard R. Ketchum	Robert W. Albright
Rebecca H. Forest	Samantha Wagner-Foster
Stephen B. Epstein	Paul W. Kilpatrick
Charles D. Young	

5

WEST ORLANDO CEMETERY doesn't look all that big any-more, what with the city's continuing westward expansion and developments on three of the graveyard's four borders, but they always manage to find room for one more hole in the ground. Rodney Ketchum's graveside service wasn't much like the others I'd attended there in recent years; the wind-driven afternoon shower had come up suddenly, and those in attendance seemed far more distraught by the effect of the water on their expensive clothing then they were by The Old Man's interment.

Wind whipped the canvas roof flaps of the green graveside tent while Sam huddled with the rest of the well-paid corporate mourners. Her shockingly bright wheelchair stood out in the soggy gloom, and she used the standing bodies around her to block a good deal of the blowing rain. Despite Sam's parting look of ire, I remained warm and dry in the Monte, studying the firm's new letterhead. Rodney's body could hardly have been cold when the phone call to the print shop was made. Rosemary Latham now headed the all-important list of names, but if Sam's summation of the ongoing power struggle was accurate, someone might be calling the printer again in the very near future.

I knew the names, had at least shaken hands and ex-
changed greetings with most of them, but in light of a possible murder, I didn't really know anything about any of
them. Rosemary Latham was a hotshot, a highly capable
woman with a flare for high fashion and courtroom fire-
fights. Bob Bennet struck me as the reserved, conservative,
but extremely competent type. I didn't even like the look of
Bernard "Silverspoon" Ketchum, and shaking his hand had
been a lot like touching a snake. Becky Forest was married,
and she and her husband, Tom, seemed like nice folks. Sam
and Becky got on well at work, and we'd recently been invited
to the Forests' Winter Park home for an evening of barbecue
and mah-jongg. Becky is every bit as competitive as Sam and,
if possible, even more intense.

The rest of the listees were more or less just names Sam
had mentioned in passing. Paul Kilpatrick, for example, was
the new guy, hired about the same time The Old Man
brought Bernie on board. Like Sam and all the other bottom
rungers before him, Paul was kept extremely busy doing research for the higher-ups. Epstein, whom I'd never met, was
a high quadriplegic; that is, a neck-level spinal-cord injury
kept him in an electric wheelchair with limited use of his
arms and hands. He seldom used his office during the day,
according to Sam, but worked mostly at home. Despite his
physical restrictions, Steve Epstein was supposed to be gang-
busters in the courtroom.

"I trust you're still warm and dry," Sam said when she
opened the passenger door, transferred in, and began folding
up her wheelchair.

"Why, yes I am. Thank you for asking. So did you and
your befinned predator friends manage to get The Old Man
buried okay without me?" I asked, reaching over to pull
Sam's chair in next to mine—where the Monte's backseat
would normally have been bolted to the floor—as she leaned
forward, tipping the back of her bucket seat out of the way.

"He's gone but not forgotten," Sam said. "And at least no
one spit on his casket."

"I didn't think anyone looked too broken up."

"No, but there was one thing. Scully seemed unusually bummed."

"Mr. Brash?"

"Go figure," Sam said. "I'd almost have expected grave-yard wisecracks from Scully."

"Mrs. Sulla."

Rick Scully startled me. First because he'd come up from behind and caught me staring up at the bronze bust's bronze bust, and second because of his subdued and serious tone of voice. The semiofficial wake in the firm's conference room had gone on around me while I worked my way over to the pedestal near the room's south door. One of my party pho-tographs seemed to suggest that the Roman lady's naked left breast was shinier than the rest of her truncated body. Closer examination proved that the prurient mind of Minolta had been thinking clearly, even from the far end of the room.

"Hi, Scully," I said, trying without success not to look embarrassed. "Mrs. Who?"

"Commander Lucius Cornelius Sulla," he said, pointing his gimpy left arm toward the other bust near the north door. "One thirty-eight to seventy-eight B.C."

"Okay, I'm impressed."

"The Old Man told me. Sulla was known as a believer in, and a man of, great luck. A leader of the aristocratic conser-vative party, his rivalry with populist-democrat General Gaius Marius led to the first of the civil wars between various military leaders that ultimately resulted in the collapse of the Roman Republic as it existed before the emperors. After defeating Marius, Sulla made himself dictator of Rome, with what he called 'special powers.' He assumed the name Felix, or 'fortunate one.' Sulla's the guy who looted Delphi."

"Oh yeah," I said.

"He was also the sole patron of the famous Roman actor Quintus Roscius Galus," Scully went on quietly. "Felix the

Lucky retired the year before he died of old age. The Old Man said he was hoping to retire next year."

The silence was one of those awkward voids that I can't help trying to fill.

"I, ah, well . . . one of my photos from the party seemed to suggest that Mrs. Lucky here was, ah, slightly more, ah, *polished* on one side," I said, nodding at her gleaming left breast. "Odd, isn't it?"

Scully chuckled softly. "The Old Man bought this pair of statues in Italy right after the second world war. He told me that when he heard the story about the Roman leader and his wife, he just had to have them. Every time he left this room, The Old Man rubbed her bare breast for good luck. He thought he was subtle about it, but I think everybody knew."

"That would certainly explain the shine," I said.

"Nobody knows who sculpted them, but Roman artwork was often anonymous. The Old Man never told me what he paid for these guys, Stick, but I did a little research on my own," Scully went on, his voice dropping even lower. "A pair of original bronzes like this, near as I can tell, are likely to be worth between one and a half and two million dollars, give or take."

"That would certainly explain the building's security system," I said.

"Yeah, it would," Scully said, passing his right hand gently across the lady's lucky breast on his way to the door. "See you around, Stick."

As he lumbered out of the room and turned left in the wide corridor, something across the hall caught my eye. The Old Man's office was the last and the largest in a line of four in the building's south wing. This upscale stretch of corporate real estate was what Sam and her fellow associate firm members referred to as Power Alley. All four offices had east windows that looked out over the firm's back parking lot, but of course The Old Man's also had a window facing south.

His private secretary's desk sat behind a counter at the end of the hallway, between the south end of the conference room and her boss's wall.

The conference room's southernmost door faced The Old Man's across the hallway, and I could see his east window, part of his imposing mahogany desk, and the brown leather soles of a pair of shoes that sat crossed atop one another on the blotter. Fools and reporters tend to rush in where a more upright sort knows enough not to go and so, before I had time to let common sense prevail, I'd rolled though the open door and sat facing the impressive desk.

"Trying it on for size?" I said. Silverspoon looked up from the extensive file he had balanced across his thighs.

"Mr. Foster," he said with almost no expression at all. "What can I do for you?"

Bernard Ketchum looked casually back at the file, his tone and manner suggesting that he was far above doing anything for the likes of me.

"Nothing much," I said, taking the opportunity to survey the prestigious office where The Old Man had presided only days before. Perhaps he had been on his way there on the night he collapsed.

"Most people call me Stick," I said, looking back at the disinterested attorney. "I'm sorry about your dad. I know a little about his past heart problems, but did you notice that he was having particular difficulty recently?"

Reporters can send signals too.

"What do you mean?" he said, looking up at me more earnestly.

"Well, nothing, except that he seemed to be doing so well. I thought maybe you'd know more about whether his pace-maker was acting up or maybe if the batteries were getting weak. Anything out of the ordinary."

The self-possessed young lawyer studied my face warily, his eyes shifting ever so slightly from side to side like a cobra watching a mongoose. Apparently satisfied, he shifted the bulky file onto the desk top, removed his feet from the leather-framed blotter, and leaned toward me, his elbows on the desk and his hands together.

"Can't say that I did," he said smoothly. "We haven't talked about his health in years . . . not since the last time I told him to quit smoking. After that little tiff, I decided that if he wanted to kill himself, it was his business."

I nodded. "Sam says you're taking on the partners," I pushed on. As long as the shovel was out anyway . . .

"Knowing what is and isn't one's business, Mr. Foster, is one of life's toughest lessons. Some folks catch on right away. Others learn too late."

The manner in which he returned his attention to the file was as clear a dismissal as I could ever hope to be issued. I had to hand it to him—even if begrudgingly—Silverspoon had honed condescension and arrogance to an art form.

"That may be," I said, thinking that while Jessica Sander-lin didn't want it known she was suspicious, I had no such inhibition, "but I'm a nosy reporter, and I have reason to believe that your father may have been murdered . . . and that makes it my business."

I watched him stare at his desk for a second, then as I spun my chair to leave, I felt him glaring at the back of my head as I rolled away. I didn't wait around to see if he would respond. I glanced into the conference room door on my way back down the hallway and smiled with some satisfaction. I've been around, and I know a little something about tit for tat. Except, to be perfectly honest, I've never been quite sure where to find the one, or how much of the other is needed in order to trade out successfully. Or, for that matter, why one would want to make such a trade in the first place.

THE LAW OFFICES OF
Ketchum, Latham & Bennet, P. A.
221 Lake Eola Drive
Orlando, Florida 32801
(407)555-1975 - FAX (407)555-1999

Rosemary I. Latham	William P. Graham
Robert G. Bennet	H. Russell White
Bernard R. Ketchum	Robert W. Albright
Rebecca H. Forest	Samantha Wagner-Foster
Stephen B. Epstein	Paul W. Kilpatrick
Charles D. Young	

6

THE RAIN VANISHED as suddenly as it had come, and the late-afternoon sun made the wet blacktop steam. I rolled around the firm's back lot, making semieducated guesses about which automobiles belonged to which legal eagles. The black Ferrari belonged to Silverspoon. Even I knew that. Sam's Mustang was home under the carport, and I'd seen Becky Forest's silver BMW before, in the driveway at her house, so that one didn't really count. The battered four-wheel-drive Ford pickup that was leaving when I'd rolled outside to wait for Sam was driven by Rick Scully, and the red Mercedes with vanity plates that said STILHOT was probably Rosemary Latham's. The top-of-the-line Volvo wagon had Robert Bennet written all over it.

The rest of the vehicles ranged from a rusty and sad-looking Triumph ragtop to a tidy black Jeep Laredo. The once proud British sports car would likely belong to the new guy, Kilpatrick, but all my other guesses were pure speculation. Chuck Young, I decided upon closer examination, owned the Jeep. There was a miniature soccer ball hanging from the rearview mirror in a white mesh net, and a "Soccer is a kick in the grass" bumper sticker on the back. According to Sam, you couldn't get away from Chuck without hearing the latest story about his sons and their respective teams.

I liked the Laredo, though if I ever bought one, it would have to be a two-door; otherwise there'd be no way to get my chair into the backseat. As I backed my wheelchair out from between the Jeep and the electric blue Mazda MX6 on its right, it occurred to me that every car in the lot had a cellular phone antenna, even the old Triumph. Time was money, and money was everything. The blue Mazda, as it turned out, had two phones. One was an AT&T rig mounted on the console, and it was similar to the ones Sam and I had in our cars. The other looked just like the Sony walk-around phone currently buried somewhere under the tarps in our dusty living room at home. Upon reflection, that realization made sense; ours, it seemed to me then, had been a Christmas freebie from the firm rather than a premium as I had thought.

"Window shopping?"

At first I didn't see the man who went with the deep, resonant voice, but after Chuck Young opened the door on the opposite side of the Laredo and got in, he electrically lowered the passenger window and stuck out his hand.

"Hi, Chuck," I said, shaking the offered hand. "I'm Sam's husband. We met last year."

He laughed pleasantly and rested his right arm on the Jeep's seat back. "Everybody in this town knows Stick Foster," he said. "Sam said it hasn't registered with you yet, but I didn't believe her."

Mmm. Who am I to blow against the wind? "Well," I said with a shrug, "at least everybody who takes the *Sentinel* and manages to hang in past the A section."

The associate lawyer laughed again. "You like Bob's little Mazda?"

"Too small," I said, "but I wouldn't turn down a free two-door Laredo."

"Trade you a four-door for your Monte Carlo Super Sport."

"No deal."

"I thought as much," Chuck said. He slipped the Jeep into gear and started out the parking spot. "It's sure enough a cherry set of wheels. Anyway, later, Stick. Joey's got a soccer game in Longwood at five. His team is eight and oh!"

Sometimes, I thought briefly, even lawyers seem like real people.

"There are probably too many ways to bugger up a pacemaker," Peter said. "Electronics failure, contact failure, battery failure, and so on. I never realized how much was involved in pacemaker technology, Stick. I was right about the microwave programming. The doctor can speed up or slow down the device without opening up the patient, so, theoretically, someone could make the user feel pretty bummed by raising or lowering the tempo too much, but it probably wouldn't be deadly . . . at least not right away. As far as breaking, stopping, shorting out the thing, microwaves—at least at doses readily available—just aren't enough."

"Well, so much for that theory," I said, hugging the car phone with my shoulder and pushing my Traveling Wilburys cassette into the Monte's tape deck. "What about electricity? Couldn't you shock someone hard enough to foul up the pacemaker's circuits for a couple of minutes?"

"Oh sure, but you can kill someone without a pacemaker that way too, and maybe not the person you intended."

"Good point, Peter. Well, The Old Man was definitely right next to a potential booby trap when he died. It was even a great conductor. My suspicion, at the moment, is that by touching a bronze statue in the conference room at Sam's firm—you know, maybe like those brass lamps with no switch—Rodney Ketchum triggered some device deliberately rigged to kill him. But there were several dozen people there, any one of whom could easily have touched the same statue first. So you're right, electricity wouldn't be the way to go if The Old Man was the intended victim."

"Hmm," Peter said. "And you're sure he was the intended victim?"

"No, I'm not sure of anything—except that he's dead and nobody at the firm seems to be pining away in the wake of his passing."

"Well, Bice is the resident expert, Stick," Peter said. "I'll ask her what she thinks when she gets home. About the other thing, it probably wasn't another pacemaker you saw on the X ray. They just don't install them in pairs like the mufflers and pipes on your Monte Carlo."

I thought as much.

"It was an Implanted Cardiac Defibrillator. And you can't tell anyone that." Dr. Sanderlin's voice left no doubt about the importance of my silence.

"What does it do, and why is it a secret?"

"Its purpose is to jump start the heart should the patient experience an arrest. As long as the heart beats along like it's supposed to, the ICD just sits there minding its own business, but if the heart fails, for any reason, the device automatically discharges a strong enough electric shock to— hopefully—get things going again. That's why I feel certain someone killed Rod," she said. "Even if he'd experienced heart failure naturally, *and* the pacemaker coincidentally failed for some reason at exactly the same time, the ICD should have saved his life. It was fully discharged."

The look on Jessica Sanderlin's face and the growing strain in her voice were puzzling to me. Either this second electronic wonder toy killed her patient and she was trying to cover up or she was genuinely disturbed about The Old Man's death. If the latter were true, she was in the a minority.

"So why the secrecy?" I said, holding her gaze and trying temporarily to control a woman used to being in control. "Don't you think you should have told me about this gadget in the first place, especially if it might just have backfired and killed Rodney Ketchum?"

"It did no such thing!"

"No? Well, then, you shouldn't be so concerned about letting the police conduct a real investigation."

"You don't understand," she said. "I wasn't supposed to implant the ICD at all. I could now, of course, but we weren't approved by the FDA when Rod—Mr. Ketchum—had his bypass surgery."

In the silence that followed, I watched tears form in Jessie's eyes and then looked away when she wiped at them angrily.

"I wanted him to live," she said, almost desperately. "I couldn't get him to quit smoking, I couldn't get him to change his diet, and I couldn't get him to leave that disco-queen tramp who married him for his money . . . but he told me that he loved me. I *had* to do something."

Good night, nurse.

" 'Oh, what a tangled web we weave,' " I said softly.

"Don't quote Scott to me!" Jessie Sanderlin said, the fire coming back into her eyes. She leaned back in her chair and closed her eyes. "I loved him, Stick Foster," she said, her face radiant in its forlorn beauty. "More than the law. More than my fear of being sued. More than my license to practice medicine."

It was after 10:30 P.M. when Sam and I returned to the offices of Ketchum, Latham & Bennet. After unrigging the security rigmarole, Sam ushered me into the nearly dark building.

"I still find it hard to believe that anyone would go to all this effort to kill Rodney Ketchum," Sam said as we rolled into the conference room. "And even if they did, who'd be stupid enough to leave the murder weapon here for us to find?"

"Probably no one," I said. "I told you it was a long shot."

We studied the shiny-breasted Roman lady from every angle and tried unsuccessfully to pry her from her perch. The brass rivets that secured Mrs. Sulla to her neo-Romanesque display pillar were very real, and nothing short of a chisel or a drill would make them let her go. The pillar felt so solid, I suspected it would take a jackhammer to uproot it from the floor.

"Sorry, babe. I hate to say I told you so."

"Well, we haven't proved anything yet . . . only that if someone did plant a gadget inside here, they went to a lot of trouble to put everything back where they found it. Brass rivets and a pop-rivet gun can be purchased at almost any hardware store. Hey! We need Danny!"

"Oh no," Sam moaned. "Now you want me to pay him to tell you stories at night too. Haven't you seen enough?"

"Not quite. Here, look at this reject picture."

Sam took the screwball photograph and scrunched up her gorgeous eyebrows. "Getting a little surrealistic, weren't you?"

"An accident. I dropped the camera, grabbed at it, and tripped the shutter without meaning to. Look, here by the statue. Do you see something shiny, glinting in the light, maybe?"

Even though the picture was actually framed all gee-ward, and the focus was blurred, Sam turned it so the room looked the way it was supposed to and stared at the spot I had pointed to.

"Maybe," she said, "like one of those bogus flying saucer photos. That's it, isn't it? Aliens! The Old Man was killed by aliens! Why didn't I think of that before?"

Smart aleck. I handed Sam two additional photographs and backed away from the bronze good luck charm. I bent over and surveyed the carpeted floor, at the base of the pillar, under the big video cart, and along the baseboard. Nothing.

"There!" I said. "What's that in the air duct under the bookshelf?"

"Yeah," Sam said, bending down to look at the opening under the bottom shelf. "I think there is something in there. Another murder weapon, babe?"

"We should be so lucky."

At two different spots along the hardwood bookshelves at

the south end of the room, the kick board had been customized to allow air-conditioned or heated air to flow out into the room. The narrow wooden slits were wide enough to see through, but neither of us could get our hands to fit through or slip underneath. It had to have been a pretty funny sight: two gimps trying to help each other reach into the narrow openings along the floor.

"Wait!" I said. "I've got an idea!"

I rolled across the hall to The Old Man's office and tried the door. It was locked.

"I don't suppose you have—"

"Right here," Sam said. "What do you need in there?"

When she opened the door, explaining that everyone working on the Fraiser case had access to the "holy of holies" at the end of Power Alley, I pointed to the fishing rod on the shelf beside The Old Man's great mahogany desk. It was almost too high, but not quite. I steadied Sam's wheelchair while she grabbed the shelf, pulled herself up, and retrieved a top-of-the-line Bass-Buddy 5000, complete with the latest treble-hooked Big Mouth Jiggler.

"Go fish," Sam said. And I did.

But my jigging skills were pretty rusty, and it was ultimately Sam's more deft touch that hooked the suspicious object and dragged it out from under the bookshelves in the conference room.

"Deadly," she said, when the petite stainless steel hors d'oeuvre fork slid out onto the carpet. "Well, I think you've pretty much wrapped up this murder, Stick Tracy. Want me to dial nine-one-one now?"

"Cute." I used a handkerchief, picked up the utensil, and turned it over several times. It still had bits of dried food on it; and for the life of me, I couldn't imagine why it would be under the firm's bookshelf. Wouldn't the caterers have counted their paraphernalia before they packed up and went home? A cursory search of the floor should have revealed the missing item . . . but then Sam and I have a lower perspective than most folks. Thinking about that sent me back to the photographs Sam had looked at and then placed on the end of the conference table.

"Fish here often, do you?"

The distinctive New York accent caught Sam and me totally by surprise—she with her fishing pole, I with my hors d'oeuvre fork. We turned our wheelchairs back toward the room's northern door and faced the late-night intruder.

THE LAW OFFICES OF

Ketchum, Latham & Bennet, P. A.

221 Lake Eola Drive
Orlando, Florida 32801
(407)555-1975 - FAX (407)555-1999

Rosemary I. Latham
Robert G. Bennet
Bernard R. Ketchum
Rebecca H. Forest
Stephen B. Epstein
Charles D. Young

William P. Graham
H. Russell White
Robert W. Albright
Samantha Wagner-Foster
Paul W. Kilpatrick

7

"Whatcha using for bait . . . bookworms?"

"You're in good form," Sam said with a laugh. "What brings you out of your lair tonight?"

The soft hum of Stephen Epstein's electric wheelchair accompanied him into the room. "You, my love," he said smoothly. "My heart told me you would be here, and I couldn't stay away. Unfortunately," he added with a sigh, "my heart did not tell me that you would be with *him*."

"Stick," Sam said with a wink, "this is Stephen B. Epstein, Esquire, the man who would gladly save me from my folly and sweep me off to a life of bliss and good fortune. It was bliss and good fortune, wasn't it, Steve?"

"Actually," he said, taking Sam's hand and kissing it dramatically, "it was bliss, good fortune, and incredible sex."

"Oh, yeah," Sam said. "I forgot. And incredible sex."

"And the folly?" I asked innocently.

"That—well, that would be you," Sam said.

"Everybody's got a part to play," I said. "And 'provided a man is not mad, he can be cured of every folly but vanity.' Nice to meet you, Steve."

The grinning quadriplegic took my hand firmly in both of his nearly useless ones. "Rousseau, right? Let me see . . . 'I have entered on an enterprise which is without precedent, and will have no imitator. I propose to show my fellows a man as nature made him, and this man shall be myself!' "

"Bravo!" I said. "And was this man born free?"

"Yes, and everywhere he is in chains!"

"Ah, excuse me boys," Sam said, "but wasn't I being wooed and worshiped here?"

" 'A man says what he knows,' " I said to Steve with a roll of my eyes, " 'but a woman says what will please.' "

"Enough! What *are* you doing here, Steve?"

"I asked you first," he said. "And when I came in, as I recall, you were saying something about murder?"

"Ask Sherlock here. He thinks somebody killed The Old Man."

"With that?" Steve asked, gesturing at the little fork on the handkerchief in my left hand. "I can't wait to read about this one, Stick!"

"Well, the theory still needs a little fleshing out."

Moments later, Sam and Steve were gone. Oh, they were still in the firm's conference room, six or eight feet away, but they were discussing the hottest shop topic of the hour. Hotter, as it turns out, than the possibility that Rodney Ketchum had been murdered. They were part of the firm's Fraiser Team, and the Fraiser case was, Sam had assured me, going to make international headlines. But I was not supposed to know—let alone write—about it . . . yet.

Headlines or not, the Fraiser case was a blockbuster. The Old Man himself had handpicked the team, and Sam had showed me the pretrial video she, Stephen Epstein, and Richard Scully had prepared in expectation of the upcoming settlement conference. I was learning more about the legal system from Sam than I ever thought I'd want to know; but in this instance, the case was fascinating. Sad . . . but fascinating.

A man named Anthony Fraiser, an executive on the way up with SunBank, was taking a spin on one of the new exercycles at one of Orlando's premier downtown health clubs: The Hardbody Shop. While he was pedaling his way up Pike's Peak on the stationary bike's computerized Colorado landscape, the right pedal crank sheared off its spindle. There was no place for the poor man to go but down, and the resulting injury to his genitalia was only the beginning in a long line of medical complications that led, ultimately, to his demise at age thirty-seven.

A settlement conference, I learned, was to be a meeting between the respective counsels for the plaintiff and the defense and a judge. Despite my preconception to the contrary, Sam assures me that an out-of-court settlement is nearly always preferable. And the days when tall stacks of tedious depositions and detailed research were piled in front of the judge by both parties are very nearly gone. Somewhere along the line, lawyers discovered MTV, and the legal process will never be the same.

The video produced by the Fraiser Team was so slick it made the hair on the back of my neck stand up. The professional announcer followed a script right out of television's best investigative magazine shows. After introducing the victim briefly (while the video showed still photographs and family videos of Mr. Fraiser with his wife and his three children), she went on to talk about the internationally recognized company that manufactured the exercise machine (serial number 0671-50397 mentioned prominently) on which the young family man was injured.

While the camera took the viewer down a woodsy northeast country road, into a quaint New England town (I kept waiting for Charles Kuralt to step into the frame) and up to the gates of a chain-link-enclosed factory, the announcer chronicled a day nearly two years before, the day number 0671-50397 came down the assembly line.

"I stopped the line," a long-haired young woman said matter-of-factly, "and called for the line foreman." Behind her, the living room of her house was decorated for Christmas; the tree lights were on.

Scully's deep voice replaced that of the professional announcer, and while the video camera caught every expression on the former factory worker's face, he interviewed her about the events that led her to stop production.

"It was pretty obvious," she said simply. "The crank arm didn't fit on the spindle right."

"How did you know this?" Scully asked her.

"It's my job to know. I press the crank arm on and tighten down the nut that holds it in place . . . seventy-eight pounds of torque. That's spec. But the crank arms weren't going on right, and I couldn't hardly get the nuts on, let alone torqued right."

As damning as the young woman's testimony was (the foreman called the shop supervisor, the shop supervisor called the plant manager, and the plant manager—a nephew of the company's owner—ordered the assembly line to be restarted and the part to be pressed on as best as possible and covered up with the black plastic cap used to finish off the process), it was only the beginning. Four line workers, including the ex–line foreman, were all similarly interviewed in their own homes. Their stories varied not a whit, and the announcer's voice came in at crucial intervals to show on various drawings and photographs exactly what the plant workers were talking about.

As the astounding video moved forward in time, and that particular model of exercycle continued to roll off the line (complete with safety memos, quality-control inspections, letters from consumers and dealers, and a reported injury in California), the announcer periodically noted exactly where number 0671-50397 was at the moment; from the factory shipping department to the regional warehouse to the Orlando-area dealership, and finally (three weeks before Anthony Fraiser's ultimately fatal accident) to its delivery to The Hardbody Shop.

The step-by-step details (including obviously perjurious video interviews of the company's owners and upper management) were outlined so meticulously that even the most cynical observer would be convinced beyond all doubt that

(from the failure to heed all warnings by the assembly workers to the dismissal of their own quality-control reports to
the suppression of the earliest complaint information to the
denials by the owners that any problem existed) the company was negligent. But, despite the overwhelming evidence
that this was a no-lose case, Steve had just informed my
lovely barrister that the manufacturer had no intention of
accepting a settlement. They would, one of the defense attorneys told Steve that afternoon, "not roll over."

Even sitting on the fringe of that fast-breaking news, I was
still trying to figure out how the little fork got into the duct
work under the shelf. Life is, after all, just a matter of perspective. I couldn't do anything for Anthony Fraiser, and
maybe I couldn't really do anything for Rodney Ketchum
either . . . except figure out whether he was murdered. The
road to building any case begins with one clue. The Fraiser
team had a drop-dead video. I had an hors d'oeuvre fork.
Everybody has to start somewhere.

I spread my thirty-one party photographs across the end
of the conference table and separated out the two I'd shown
Sam before Steve Epstein rolled in on us. One—taken just
before the other two—showed one of the catering company's
waiters. His left hand deftly balanced the hors d'oeuvres tray
as he wove his way through the crowd at the south end of
the room. There, resting demurely on the edge of his goodies
tray, was the tiny fork. The next picture was my drop shot;
and in the one after that—though the subject was actually
a gold watch—most of the waiter's tray was still in the
frame . . . without the fork.

In a matter of those few seconds, it was clear that at least
two things had happened: The Old Man keeled over, and the
little fork jumped ship and went AWOL. What, if anything,
the one had to do with the other was at least one question I
would have to answer. I carefully wrapped the fork up in the
handkerchief and placed it in my backpack and, as I mulled
over the options, decided to wash my hands thoroughly.

THE LAW OFFICES OF

Ketchum, Latham & Bennet, P. A.

221 Lake Eola Drive
Orlando, Florida 32801
(407)555-1975 - FAX (407)555-1999

Rosemary I. Latham	William P. Graham
Robert G. Bennet	H. Russell White
Bernard R. Ketchum	Robert W. Albright
Rebecca H. Forest	Samantha Wagner-Foster
Stephen B. Epstein	Paul W. Kilpatrick
Charles D. Young	

8

MY DAD WAS a man who believed in something bigger than himself—a sovereign creator who expects each of us to be honest and responsible in the way we treat one another and the world in which we live. From Genesis to Revelations, my dad saw the Old and New Testaments of the Judeo-Christian scriptures as a completely plausible and highly practical world and life view. He studied his Bible daily. He believed it. And he lived it.

But nothing in my father's life resembled that of the stereotypical Christian that seems to be the norm in the public eye today. He denounced the bombastics and the buffoons who waved their Bibles and shouted their "join my giving throng or die" messages. He used to say: "Jesus was first and foremost a servant. He came to give his life—the ultimate sacrifice—for a willful and self-centered world."

My dad gave me advice (most of it from his Bible) that reflected on nearly every area of life, including sexual conduct. The only notable exception was marriage. My mother died when I was young, and my memories of her are somewhat vague. Between the lines, as I look back on it, I think I always sensed that my dad's sadness about my mom had to do not only with her early death but also something to do with their relationship never having been quite what he had hoped. Oh, he surely loved her, and would, like the Christ, have given his life for her in an instant, but even as a youngster, I sensed that hidden echo of loss and disappointment. That returning sound of disenchantment is further enhanced for me when I recall what seemed perfectly normal at the time but strikes me as very odd now: my father, a handsome man in his early forties, never dated after my mom died, never showed the slightest interest in romance again.

Perhaps that faint echo of disillusionment is part and parcel of every marriage. My own marriage to Sam was the source both of great potential and joy and of great fear and sadness. When we clicked, it was as if no power on earth could stand against us. That feeling of being part of a winning team was far better than any like experience with high school athletics; it was life. When Sam and I didn't click, it was like opening a window just a crack, only to discover that instead of fresh air coming into the room, all of the oxygen was suddenly being sucked out. We always managed to slam the window shut before we both suffocated, but the experience—though infrequent—was profoundly unsettling.

The night that we found the hors d'oeuvre fork was one of those open-window experiences. Sharing love with Sam was undoubtedly the most life-affirming phenomenon of my haphazard existence. When she came to me, her devoted abandon was a miracle of giving and taking that I was always loath to see come to an end. I did my best not to think about how many men she had made love to before giving up the fast lane for a life with me, but on the night we came home late from the offices of Ketchum, Latham & Bennet, I couldn't think of anything else.

It was as if I weren't even there. Sam pursued some climax that seemingly did not include me—fighting, groping, struggling to conquer or seduce some reluctant lover that I could not see but whose presence was as apparent as the thinning air. All of my attempts to help, to become a part of whatever was happening, were futile. When it (whatever *it* might have been) was over, Sam, if not satisfied, was totally exhausted. She rolled away from me and fell promptly into the sleep of the dead. Even my brown Tonkinese cat, Butkis, sensed something different and curled up next to me instead of Sam for the first time in many months. After an hour of staring at the ceiling, listening to the lonely call of the loons out on Lake Martha and trying not to think about what advice my dad might have given me about marrying an "experienced" woman like Sam, I gave up trying to sleep and went to our dusty office to work on my fantasy.

My desk is tucked into a corner where Danny the handyman removed the former bedroom's closet. To my left is a west window, looking out across the pine needle–strewn path that separates our house from several others built just north of where Shorecrest Drive's pavement came to an end. It was as if we lived on the edge of civilization . . . in the middle of America's fastest-growing metropolitan area. Central Florida had the Magic Kingdom. I was creating the "Land of Life." Fantasy is, after all, the highest literary form of escapism. I gave myself to my epic manuscript and followed my intrepid wood-carving protagonist as he searched for the lost magic that—on that night, at least—Sam and I had misplaced as well.

"You've got to be kidding."

"Come on, Stan. Humor me."

"Humor is the right word, Stick. This is a joke, right?"

"Okay, so it's a little farfetched. What can it hurt to check it out?"

FBI Agent Stanley Fredericks shook his head and sighed. "I'll ask the crime lab folks to go over this—obviously dangerous—fork, but I'll never hear the end of it."

My friendship with Stan was built almost entirely on mutual respect. The difference in our ages made hanging out a little awkward (he is a few years away from retirement), but we were kindred spirits. Both of us were bulldogs, whether it meant tracking down a bad guy or a newspaper story, but we also shared a tendency to flounder from time to time in our own best intentions. Neither of us lacked the zeal and the commitment to do our jobs well, but somehow things just never seemed to go the easy way for Stan and me. We never talked about it, the occasional teasing aside, but we both knew that we were relatively successful—despite ourselves.

"Thanks, Stan," I said, putting away the three photographs that I had hoped would impress him more. "I owe you."

"You always have."

What is friendship? There are many answers, but at its root, the concept has to do with devotion and selflessness, the willingness and the ability to put another's needs and desires before one's own. I've always made friends easily and don't usually mind getting the short end of the friendship stick. But whenever I reflect on my truest friends (those individuals who both know and accept me as I am, flaws and all) Eleanor Algretto always tops the list. And that scares the crap out of me.

Almost two decades ago, Ellie and I were in whatever state of love high school sophomores are capable of achieving. It seemed like the perfect friendship long before it became the perfect dating relationship. Unfortunately, my sixteen-year-old ego rose up in hurt and pride and walked away from both when one of Ellie's old boyfriends tried—unsuccessfully—to win her back. When I finally grew up enough to realize how stupid and hurtful I had been, it was far too late. There are some things in this life that we just can't take back or make right. We often (along with those we have wronged) just have to live with them.

Ellie never gave up on me, though, literally. She made her decision at the tender age of sixteen and has never wavered. Today she owns Little Oak Books, a quaint shop in a west Orlando strip shopping center, and her office walls are lined with Nick Foster memorabilia. She is, she tells me without rancor, just "waiting."

"We were made for each other," she said the last time I saw her. "And it's only a matter of time before we get the chance to prove it."

The woman not only attended Sam's and my wedding uninvited but helped me solve the murder that occurred during the ceremony. As scary and illogical as the whole relationship between us seems to be, in my heart of hearts, I feel certain that both her love and her friendship are as pure and genuine as they get.

That is one reason why, sometimes, when I'm feeling sad and insecure about my relationship with Sam, I drive out to the west Orlando shopping center and park under the great spreading oak tree at the top of the parking lot near West Colonial Drive. From this relatively safe and distant spot I can look down across the vast parking lot at the book shop Ellie runs. I can speculate about what's happening to my relationship with Sam, what might have been with Ellie, and what questions about "girl stuff" I'd ask either or both of them if I weren't so afraid of the answers.

Occasionally I'd see Ellie leave the shop and walk to one of the neighboring businesses. Sometimes I'd see her get into her black short-bed Chevy pickup and drive away. Most times, I'd never see her at all. But somehow, she was always with me in spirit, a phenomenon I would rather not try to analyze too closely. I knew instinctively that she would be perfectly willing to listen if I chose to pour my heart out and verbalize my insecurities. I knew that she would listen and respond with empathy and with love. I also had a pretty good idea how much the experience would cost her emotionally, and so could never consider actually seeking out her ear. Instead, I sat a hundred yards away and tried to sort out my feelings as best I could.

Life is like that sometimes. Unless you stand back and ask yourself all the hard questions, out in the full light of day, they're apt to sneak up on you in the dark. "If God wanted life to be easy," my dad once told me, "He'd have never put that tree in the center of the Garden of Eden. It's the tests that make or break us, son . . . and thank God we don't have to face them alone."

That sums up the difference between my late father and his sojourning son. As far as I could tell, his claims about God's presence held no trace of rhetoric. Something about his relationship with his Creator was so tangible, even the skeptical and intellectual newspaper reporter couldn't explain it away. For my part, though I had come to respect his theology, though I had finally made an effort to link myself to it by joining the quaint congregation on the corner of Broadway and Livingston Avenue, I still felt alone.

Not always. I have a wife I adore, friends I cherish, and acquaintances who fill my life with warmth and fellowship . . . most of the time. It's those shaky in-betweens that get me, those dark moments when the edges of life's security blanket start to come unraveled. Oh, there's enough of the soft comforting material to last for months yet, maybe years, but to notice the dangling threads is to know that nothing lasts forever. *That's* when I become jealous of my father's unshakable faith.

"Something you wanted to talk to me about, Nick?"

I nearly snapped my head off my shoulders and ripped the steering wheel off the column at the same time, so startled was I by the voice coming in the passenger window from my blind side. Eleanor Algretto laughed, opened the Monte's door, got in, and told me to drive to Burger Man.

Yes, ma'am.

THE LAW OFFICES OF

Ketchum, Latham & Bennet, P. A.

221 Lake Eola Drive
Orlando, Florida 32801
(407)555-1975 - FAX (407)555-1999

Rosemary I. Latham
Robert G. Bennet
Bernard R. Ketchum
Rebecca H. Forest
Stephen B. Epstein
Charles D. Young

William P. Graham
H. Russell White
Robert W. Albright
Samantha Wagner-Foster
Paul W. Kilpatrick

9

"I, AH, WAS just, well . . ."

"Smooth, Nick," Ellie said, tuning my stereo to the country station. "Look, it makes you uncomfortable to think that I'm still hanging in there on you. I know that. And it makes me look pretty flaky, doesn't it?"

Shut up, Stick. Don't answer that. Don't even blink your eyes.

"You can relax," she said with a soft laugh, "I won't bite you. But regardless of what happened between us, you and I go deep. We can't make that go away, and we both wonder what it could have been like . . . maybe what it *will* be like."

That gentle smile. It wasn't a threat; it was a promise. Sweat from my palms soaked into the Monte's black leather steering wheel cover. It took me all the way to Burger Man to get any semblance of control.

"What'll you have, El?" I asked, looking out at the B Man's bright plastic face and trying to breathe a little more deeply.

"Two Cheese Man Specials, two fries, one cola, one lemon-lime," she answered with a smirk.

Right.

We parked and ate under the old oak in West Orlando Cemetery, and I tried to cover my embarrassing predicament by telling Ellie about the possible murder investigation I was getting more deeply involved in with each passing day. As an ardent mystery fan, Ellie was easily drawn into the tale and only rebuked me mildly for being hesitant to "consult" her. I didn't tell her about all the memories her perfume was resurrecting in my mind and in my heart.

"I *love* this!" she said, already analyzing the brief data I had given her. "Can I have that copy of the firm's letter-head?"

I didn't think all that much about the peck on the cheek I received from Ellie when I dropped her off in front of Little Oak Books until the next day . . . when I received a black-and-white snapshot of it in my mail at the paper. It was obviously telephoto stuff but more than clear enough. Typed on the back was a simple yet perplexing cliché: "A picture is worth a thousand words."

Mmm.

Sam and I were meeting for dinner that night at Angelo's Italian restaurant on Semoran Boulevard in Altamonte Springs, and I hadn't particularly been looking forward to going there *before* the photo arrived. We'd avoided one of our favorite eateries for almost a year, partly because it was the scene of our first real newlywed spat and partly because we were both certain the scene we created had become a legend among the employees. It was Sam's nature, in the end, to insist that we face our embarrassment and stop denying ourselves the pleasure of Angelo's cuisine. When Sam wanted something, she always went for it—and usually got it. For my part, I would just as soon have kept eating Italian at Lorenzo's down on Orange Avenue; it is very nearly as good, and half as expensive. At any rate, on this night, the newest topic of controversy between Sam and me would not come up (at least from me) until after dinner. Then, God help me.

I stopped at home to check on the answering machine, the bills, and Danny the handyman. No, there were no threat-

ening messages, and only one puzzling bill (several unfamil-
iar-looking long-distance phone calls); and yes, Danny could
still meet me later that evening. On the way to Handy City,
I called Butch Grady and got the same answer. At The Palmetto Plaza Mall, I hunted down the head maintenance
man, Ernest Boyle, and talked him into making it a four-
some. Senior Agent Stanley Fredericks called me back just
as I was passing the jai alai fronton on Route 441, just south
of Semoran Boulevard, in Altamonte Springs. He clearly enjoyed giving me the entire rundown of appetizer residues and
worthless partial fingerprints the lab folks had (at public
expense) found during their thorough analysis of my tiny
stainless steel hors d'oeuvre fork. By the time I made it
through the busy intersection and pointed the old black
Monte east toward Angelo's, he was winding down.

"Well, Stick, I considered locking this baby up in the evidence vault, but I didn't want to take the chance that some
unsuspecting agent might impale him or herself while innocently rooting around down there for something harmless."

"Thoughtful of you Stanley," I said, with as much good
humor as I could muster. I'd spent the afternoon watching
my rearview mirror, hoping that my years of watching "Rock-
ford Files" reruns would serve me. Nothing. "I'll come get
the fork tomorrow and return it to the caterer with the official blessings of the FBI."

"Leave us out of it."

"Got any tips on catching a tail?" I asked, interrupting
Stanley's laughter.

"I'm a happily married man, Foster," he said promptly. "I
don't know anything about that sort of thing!"

"You're such a pip, Stan. Look, I'm being followed by someone with a camera and a telephoto lens. Any suggestions?"

"I have to ask. How do you know?"

"I just got a sample black-and-white glossy in the mail."

"Well, that would convince me. Were you trying to catch
tail at the time?"

More laughter. I waited.

"Sorry. I'm sorry. I couldn't help myself. What *were* you doing?"

"Actually, I was getting a completely innocent peck on the cheek from Eleanor Algretto."

"The book woman? I warned you about her, Stick. That kind of obsessive behavior is nothing to take lightly."

"I know, Stan, but how do I find out who's dogging me?"

Stanley Fredericks's comedic routine was forgotten. He didn't mind giving me a hard time (after all, I seldom left him unscathed), but he was extremely proprietary about his family and friends. Fortunately, I was one of his friends. "How have things been with Sam?"

"What?" His question caught me completely by surprise; and, of course, dragged itself along a considerable area of exposed and painfully raw nerves. "What does that have to do with anything?"

"Maybe nothing . . . unless Sam's having you followed."

I turned off the Monte's 350-cubic-inch, fuel-injected engine and sat staring at the soft red neon cursive writing that spelled out "Angelo's" on the side of the popular restaurant. How many times had I driven out to west Colonial Drive and just parked under the old oak tree? Four? Maybe five? How many times did Sam know all about it? What would she have to say about it? The picture, I thought wryly, might be worth a thousand words . . . at least.

"You still there, Stick?"

"Yeah, Stanley. I'm still here, wishing I wasn't. I gotta go, but thanks."

"Hey—"

I watched Sam's red Mustang convertible swing into the parking lot and whip into the handicapped space next to me, and I thought about how unhungry I was. Sam rolled down her window and spoke without turning off her engine.

"I couldn't get you on the phone," she said, with more than a tinge of irritation in her voice. "I've got to go right back to work . . . it's serious."

"Sam, I—"

"Save it for later."

In a heartbeat, the red classic ragtop was lost in the early evening traffic on Semoran Boulevard, much like a night nearly a year before. I couldn't help thinking about the elderly and inadvertent practitioner of Déjà Voodoo. Caught up short, he was reportedly overheard saying: "Haven't I sacrificed this chicken before?"

The ducks had long since crawled away under whichever bushes the homeless transients had left for them, and Lake Eola Park was quiet in the shadows of the city streetlights. The fountain was doing its thing, and the lights in the great fiberglass dome changed colors slowly. It was nearly eleven o'clock, and the Orlando police officer assigned to the park on that night would not likely ignore us if we were still sitting on the grass when he came around the sidewalk perimeter a second time. There's nothing particularly threatening about a man in a wheelchair, and perhaps he thought we were residents of the boardinghouse across Lake Eola Drive on the corner, but any closer examination of our little party could not help but expose a varied and highly suspicious array of tools.

"They're gonna be in there all night," Butch Grady said flatly, "and I'm not too keen on losing my license anyway. Let's get out of here."

Brenda "Butch" Grady is a Melbourne-based private investigator who's never met a lock she couldn't pick. In this case, however, she'd simply cut us keys from the wax impressions I'd made while Sam was sleeping. A well-built, powerful, and strikingly blond short-haired young woman who moonlighted as a bouncer, Butch Grady had helped me several times before.

"It doesn't look good, so to speak," Ernest Boyle added. "I mean, I don't mind helping or anything, but we're asking for trouble if we just sit where we are."

Of course he was right. The mall's scrawny "environmental engineer" was a classic case of a book easily misjudged because of its cover. Sergeant Ernest "Soda-speak" Boyle was, before being falsely accused of fragging a superior officer in Vietnam, one of the most highly decorated Green Berets in the United States Army. He joined us in the northeast corner of the park, only after thoroughly reconnoitering the lake one bush at a time. Had we cared, I'm sure he could have told us exactly where the ducks and the vagrants were sleeping and which ones were nursing eggs and/or bottles. Neither ducks nor drinkers, he had assured me, were packing cameras on this night.

"They're leaving," Danny said. "Look."

Our friendly handyman was right. The new Fraiser team was apparently finished with their emergency meeting, and we could see them filing out of the conference room one by one; first Sam, then Rick Scully. Bernie Ketchum held his hand on the light switch until Stephen Epstein motored out of sight into the hallway. Bernie and Rosemary Latham glared at each other momentarily before she left the room and he threw the switch. Moments later, five vehicles rolled out of the firm's parking lot, Bernard's Ferrari leading the way, followed by Sam's Mustang, Scully's pickup, Rosemary's red Mercedes, and Epstein's wheelchair lift–equipped van. Operation Bronze Bust was a go.

We broke up casually and moved out in different directions, but by the time I arrived at the firm's back entrance, Butch and Ernest had opened the door and disengaged the alarm system.

"I'm sure glad we had a key and knew the code," Butch said flatly. "This alarm system is state of the art. I know I couldn't have gotten past it . . . and I'm *good*."

"I could probably figure it out, so to speak," Ernest said, shaking his head, "given enough time, but I'd have to be in here looking at it. I'm glad we had a key too. We wouldn't have known how badly we'd screwed up until the police showed up!"

Danny went right to work hanging dark silky pieces of fabric from the valances in the conference room while Butch

and Ernest patrolled the perimeter. Once it was safe to turn
on my flashlight, Danny took out a center punch and went
to work making indentations on the brass rivets holding
Mrs. Sulla to her pedestal.

"Great invention, these cordless drills," he said, settling
the drill's bit squarely in one of the rivet's newly formed
dimples. "We'll have her off here in a minute or two. Here,
hold this."

I took a miniature hand-held vacuum, held it up over my
head, and pointed it where Danny indicated. The tiny whir-
ring motor neatly sucked up all the gold colored filings and
stashed them in its invisible "bag of holding" within. In the
world of fantasy, a bag of holding is imbued with the magical
ability to carry an almost infinite supply of booty. In the real
world, we have Dustbusters.

By the time Danny Kincade got to the fourth and last rivet,
Ernest had returned to the conference room and was looking
on with interest. "What if there's nothing in there, Stick?"
he said, tapping lightly on the fake marble column with his
gloved right hand.

"It won't be the first time I've been wrong," I said. "But
I'd be really surprised."

I wasn't to be surprised on this night. Danny tapped out
the remaining rivet scraps, and Ernest helped him lift the
bronze lady.

"Hold it!" I said when they'd raised her an inch or two
into the air. "She's wired. There."

Both men looked under the bust where I pointed the flashlight beam.

"Here," said Ernest, "let me have a look-see, so to speak."
He took my light and explored the innards of both the statue
and the display pedestal. "It's a professional wiring job," he
said, "and the stuff up here's probably a touch switch, like
those lights with no on-off button. Good thing we're wearing
gloves."

"I watched Rick Scully touch it," I said, "and Sam and I
both touched it. Nothing happened to us."

"As far as you know," Danny said with a grin. "You could both be sterile and just not know it yet!"

"Thanks," I said. "What's down there, Ernest?"

He pointed the light downward and peered into the column and shook his head. "Nothing I've ever seen before. Wait, there's an ID tag on it—if I can read it."

THE LAW OFFICES OF

Ketchum, Latham & Bennet, P. A.

221 Lake Eola Drive
Orlando, Florida 32801
(407)555-1975 - FAX (407)555-1999

Rosemary I. Latham
Robert G. Bennet
Bernard R. Ketchum
Rebecca H. Forest
Stephen B. Epstein
Charles D. Young

William P. Graham
H. Russell White
Robert W. Albright
Samantha Wagner-Foster
Paul W. Kilpatrick

10

WE WROTE IT all down, but that wasn't much help. None of us had ever heard of Shortshire Ltd., and the fact that the enigmatic device was clearly labeled as an L.I.M. Propulsion System left us clueless.

"Probably designed to run on batteries or capacitor power, and it's all pooped out," Ernest said. "Maybe that's why nobody else was affected."

"No, it's live," Danny Kincade said as the tiny light bulb on the end of his handy pocket circuit tester lit up. "Whatever this gadget does, it's still juiced up and ready to do more of it."

"Well," Ernest said, looking up at me, "what about it? Do we try and take it out of here, or are you content just knowing where it is?"

"I draw the line at being dragged in here against my will after the rest of you broke and entered," I said, smiling as their eyebrows rose together. "I won't be party to a burglary."

Retorts were interrupted by crashing sounds from somewhere down the hall. I recognized Butch's distinctive karate exclamations, and the unseen battle was over before the rest of us could move out into the hallway. I was looking forward to seeing whom Butch had waylaid but instead found her in the entryway near the firm's back door, looking angrily down the barrel of a Glock 9mm automatic.

"A friend of yours, Stick?" said the hulking figure holding the pistol.

"Yeah, Scully," I said. "Take it easy. Meet Butch Grady, black belt. I'd put some ice on that eye if I were you."

"Shut up," he said testily. "What's going on here anyway?"

"An investigation of sorts. And as long as you're here," I said, "I've got something unusual to show you. Come on back."

When I turned around, Danny was there in the hallway behind me, but Ernest was nowhere in sight. I considered calling him off but decided that there was more to Rick Scully than I knew anything about, and since he was holding the equalizer, I'd hold out my other ace in the hole. Danny and I headed back down the hall to the farthest conference room door, with Butch, Scully, and his gun in tow. As I turned to go through one conference room door, Ernest Boyle came silently out of the other behind Rick Scully. I just stopped and watched in amazement. The element of surprise aside, Scully had nine or ten inches and at least a hundred pounds on Boyle, but in an instant, the big paralegal was on his knees with his good arm farther up his back than God ever intended, his own weapon pressed against his neck.

"Scully," I said, trying hard not to smile. "I forgot to introduce Sergeant Ernest Boyle, U.S. Army Green Berets, retired."

"What else did you forget," Scully said angrily, "the pungi sticks in my office?"

"No booby traps," I said. "Just Danny Kincade, my handyman. Danny, this is Rick Scully, one of the firm's paralegals and, unless I'm badly mistaken, one of the few real friends of the deceased."

"You got that right," he said. "Now are you going to let me up or shoot me? Jeez, Stick, this is all pretty melodramatic . . . even for you."

* * *

Sam was asleep when I arrived home in the wee hours of the morning, and I was certainly not about to wake her up. I went instead to our office across the hall, closed the door most of the way, and pondered the ill-fitting puzzle pieces of my immediate existence. Because I was feeling alienated and insecure, I had left Sam out of the raid on her firm's offices. In light of the fact that someone was following me with a camera, it was a good bet I'd soon be feeling considerably more isolated from my spouse . . . with more than some of the responsibility resting squarely on my own over-developed shoulders. Someone had clearly installed something in The Old Man's favorite bust, though precisely what it was remained a mystery. To say that Rick Scully appeared genuinely angered was an understatement, but I'd done some fine acting myself, so who could know?

Scully had, perhaps, cleared up one matter. Sam's temperament was probably related as much to the Fraiser case as to anything I might have done. First Stephen Epstein tossed the grenade about the defendant's law firm refusing even to talk settlement (even in light of the Fraiser team's drop-dead video); and then, during their late-night meeting at the firm, Bernard Ketchum had unleashed the real bomb. Not only had the firm's videotape literally dropped dead, but all three copies on the cart with it had been discovered to be totally blank, destroyed, worthless—almost on the eve of their pretrial settlement conference with the judge. No wonder she was (how shall I say?) distracted.

Scully had taken it upon himself to watch the office that night, determined to discover the "scummy traitor" who "sold us out" should said perpetrator be foolish enough to return. Starting in the morning, he said, the Fraiser team members would be working around the clock until the original footage was reedited and remixed with the taped interviews and professional narration. If the studio and/or the original producer-editor were not readily available, Rosemary Latham had authorized whatever dollar figure would free up those respective schedules. To say that this disastrous technical snafu overshadowed Rodney Ketchum's mysterious death was an understatement—even, to some degree, in the case of Rick Scully. That bothered me.

I tried linking the two problems but couldn't make the connection. The real work of the Fraiser case had all been done by associates and a paralegal; sure, The Old Man's name was primary on the case file, but it was clearly the tape, the evidence, and not the Ketchum name, that would win the day. Industrial espionage—if that's what the video debacle really was—was one thing, but I couldn't see that murder was a logical tool, no matter how many millions were at stake. On the other hand, the two events might well be related in another way. Assuming that the level of disgruntlement among those not chosen by The Old Man for the Fraiser team was as high as Scully and Sam had suggested, it was conceivable (though, I hoped, unlikely) that a disgruntled someone might have been overly anxious for a new name at the top of the letterhead ladder. That thought left me determined to find out something about which piqued ladder climbers had the most to gain by a change of corporate venue.

"I'm sorry."

The firm but gentle kneading of Sam's fingers in the knotted muscles of my weary shoulders felt like heaven. The words were warm but unexpected. It was probably safe to assume that whether she had commissioned the candid photographs or not, Sam had not yet seen them. I immediately wondered how much money the shooter intended to "request" in order to keep it that way.

"Before you apologize," I said, pulling the black-and-white picture out of my shirt pocket, "you might want to see this."

Let the chips fall where they may.

"Why are you showing me this?" Sam asked after several long seconds of silence.

"Because it just showed up in the mail at the paper. And because I don't like being threatened—or followed, for that matter."

I turned to face her, but before I could muster the courage to ask Sam whether she had hired the shooter to follow me, she answered my unspoken question with a question of her own.

"Who is the woman?"

"Eleanor Algretto."

"Your old girlfriend at the bookstore?" Sam said uneasily. "Then this must be, what, a year old?"

"Ah, well, not exactly."

Okay, it wasn't much fun to explain, but ultimately Sam chose to believe me. She was more concerned, I was relieved to discover, with her behavior in the wake of the Fraiser case going temporarily south and the idea that someone was tailing me. That did wonders for my sagging self-image and led me further, to confess my night's adventure with Foster's Raiders at her office. She would hear it from Scully in a few hours anyway, though he had agreed not to mention it to anyone else until further investigation could be conducted.

"You were right after all," Sam admitted when my abbreviated tale petered out. "Wait! That's it! Whoever put that thing in the statue probably did something to the videotapes while they were at it . . . a real one-two punch. We've got to figure out who did it and nail them."

I said nothing but was more than mildly disturbed by the obvious fact that Sam was referring primarily to the damage done to the Fraiser video, not to the death of Rodney Ketchum; but, like much of what she had taught me about our justice system, sometimes "the one takes care of the other."

"Why," I asked, "would someone knowingly risk instigating a homicide investigation when all they needed to do was destroy the tapes?"

"I don't know," Sam said, "but The Old Man, while he made us do all the legwork, would have been the one handling the courtroom action had it come to that. And if the legends are to be believed, he'd only lost two big cases in his life."

Mmm.

THE LAW OFFICES OF

Ketchum, Latham & Bennet, P. A.

221 Lake Eola Drive
Orlando, Florida 32801
(407)555-1975 - FAX (407)555-1999

Rosemary I. Latham	William P. Graham
Robert G. Bennet	H. Russell White
Bernard R. Ketchum	Robert W. Albright
Rebecca H. Forest	Samantha Wagner-Foster
Stephen B. Epstein	Paul W. Kilpatrick
Charles D. Young	

11

AGENT STANLEY FREDERICKS shook his head slowly while I spoke, occasionally muttering "I'm not hearing this," mostly to himself. Naturally he didn't like the idea of our little break-in, but I assuaged his agitation by assuring him that we'd entered with Sam's key—true, not only because it was Sam's key we copied but because I'd just given her that copy to cover this very contingency.

"You're nuts! Have I ever told you that?"

"On several occasions, Stan. But so are you, and we both muddle along pretty well despite our mental handicaps. So how do we pursue this thing?"

"Which thing? The stalking photographer? The killer hors d'oeuvre fork? The bronze statue? What? Stick, this whole thing is beyond bizarre, and if you expect me to get officially involved, you've gone beyond nuts to the fringes of true mental ill health. But," he said with a glint of rising curiosity in his eye, "if you want my advice, I might have a suggestion or two—not that you'd listen."

"I always listen to you, Stan."

"Right. Okay, you're gonna have to interview everyone at the firm, or get someone else to. Doing them all simultaneously would be best, but the idea is to avoid having one you've questioned chat with any of the rest of them before you get to them. It was an inside job, Stick, at least partially."

"You sure about that?" I said, not having made up my own mind about it at all. "Just because Butch and Ernest Boyle thought they couldn't handle the alarm system doesn't mean a pro couldn't bypass it."

"Oh, you're right about that. There are definitely pros who could get past the security system, but why bring in an outsider when everyone who works there has equal access to the building? No, Stick, even if Sam's right about the other law firm being desperate enough to plan something like this, there's an even better reason to believe that they had help from inside the Three Rs. Think about it."

I hate it when Stan does that, the old pro using the Socratic method to teach the student at his feet. Of course, he never quizzes me like that unless he's pretty sure of himself; and that meant the answer was probably something obvious.

"Wait," I said, my pride getting the best of me. It took me longer to run through the steps than I'd like to admit, but after all it was obvious. "The bust! Who else would know that The Old Man felt up his lucky statue every day?"

"Right! You get a gold star. And if there are as many disgruntled associates as you say, and as many millions at stake in the Fraiser case as Sam says, dropping a couple of hundred thou to get one of those associates to let you in and look the other way would be a relatively small investment in light of the potential return. Then again," the veteran FBI man said with a smile, "maybe one of the associates offed him just for spite, and it has absolutely nothing to do with any lawsuit at all!"

"I've been thinking about that," I said, glad for the chance to make what I hoped was an original contribution. "If you were an angry but intelligent associate here, and you planned this elaborate execution, what's the first thing you'd have done when it was over?" Touché.

"Yes, I see. Taking the gizmo out and getting rid of it couldn't be any more difficult than getting it and installing it in the first place. Except why wouldn't the same be true of someone from another firm?"

Mmm.

Stan's threefold plan of attack was as solid as the senior agent himself. First, find out what the gadget was and how it killed The Old Man, of course. Next, find out where it came from. Finally, establish a link between the device and a suspect, be it an associate at the Three Rs or someone connected with Brown, Nealy, Howser & Columbine, the defense counsel in the Fraiser case. No sweat.

"I've never heard of an L.I.M., " Peter Stilles said. I could tell, even over the telephone, that he was intrigued. Peter might not know *everything* about everything, but I think he secretly prides himself in knowing *something* about *almost* everything. "But if I can find Shortshire Limited, the answer can't be far behind. I know a half-dozen corporate data base listings, Stick. Give me a day or two."

"Thanks, Peter," I said. "I knew you'd be there for me."

Next I called Scully and set up a three-way meeting: Scully, Sam, and myself. It was as difficult to arrange as I had thought it would be; the Fraiser team was running at a pace somewhere between frantic and frenzied, well on their way to hysteria. See the sharks. See the sharks swim. See the sharks swim *fast.*

"Make this quick," Sam said while taking a bite of her hot dog.

"No kidding, man," Scully said, mustard fighting its way out of the corner of his mouth. "This better be *really* important."

"It is." We sat under a colorful umbrella near the hot dog stand at the northwest corner of Lake Eola Park. The ducks and the pigeons were out in full force, knowing from long experience that there always seemed to be just a little more bun than hot dog in the world and that good crumbs come to birds who wait. "We need to work together and interview everyone at the firm. I've written up a list of questions—"

"Are you out of your mind?" Scully said sharply. I guessed that meant I'd have to scratch both the young paralegal and the old FBI agent off the list of personal references to testify to my mental health. "Okay, so something's rotten in the law world, what else is new? You get paid to investigate news, we get paid to practice law—*if* we win. Our jobs are on the line here, Stick, and we're way behind the eight ball." He looked at his watch as if to punctuate his tirade.

"He's right, babe," Sam said. "We're swamped here, playing catch-up and, quite frankly, it doesn't matter who did it, only whether we can recover in time."

"I know, I know. You're overworked and underpaid, and there's never enough time. But consider how your stock would rise if you not only won the Fraiser case but caught The Old Man's killer and nailed the industrial saboteur, probably Brown, Nealy, Howser & Columbine themselves. I could feature you both in one heck of a story, and you could write your own tickets."

Okay, so I was appealing to the darker side of the legal force, but when they stopped chewing and looked at each other, I knew I'd nailed them.

"Look," I said, handing them each a slip of paper with four questions scribbled in my less than artistic hand. "We want this to be fast, as fast as possible. We'll divide up the firm, decide when to hit, and question everyone before they have a chance to compare notes. What do you say?"

Rick Scully looked up from the list of questions in his hand and smiled. "You'd make a sharp lawyer, Stick. What about tomorrow morning, Sam?"

"As good a time as any."

"Great!" I said as they left the remnants of their rushed lunch and started east down the lakefront sidewalk together. "Don't say anything. We gotta hit 'em cold."

Scully just waved me off as he lumbered along, struggling to keep up with my wife's ultralight chair. Sam was, I guessed from behind, bending his ear about what a persistent pain in the butt I could be. Everybody's good at something . . .

*   *   *

I don't know what time it was when Sam came home that night, but I enjoyed the way she woke me up. Maybe things were okay after all. Over breakfast she briefed me on the plan of attack she and Scully had discussed. They'd discreetly checked everyone's desk calendars while working late with the rest of the Fraiser team and had a pretty good idea where people would be and when there would likely be holes in their schedules. Between them, they'd even come up with a half-decent excuse for me to be rolling unannounced into the various offices. Last, they divided up the firm, deciding who best to put the moves on whom. Scully had taken it upon himself to hone my questions slightly, and the result was excellent. Project Rubber Hose was a go.

As I sat in the old black Monte Carlo, waiting for Sam to back her red ragtop Ford Mustang out of the driveway, I was still aware that someone wished me no good. The black-and-white photograph was not forgotten by either Sam or myself, merely displaced by the presence of more demanding matters, and whether that someone had anything to do with the goings-on at Ketchum, Latham, & Bennet was well beyond my ability to deduce. (I'm generally partial to some kind of clue.) If I'd had to bet one way or the other, however, the odds seemed to be not only with the firm but specifically with the lawyer's lawyer, the shark among sharks, the sleaziest of the sleazeballs. Silverspoon Ketchum struck me as a young man so filled with pettiness and conceit that he'd think nothing of paying a photographer just to take a shot at screwing up someone's life. If I was right, of course, his actions might say nothing about guilt or innocence in the death of his father, only something about his ire in the wake of being talked back to by an inferior being. Oh, the shark bites, with his teeth, dear . . .

I followed Sam west out to Semoran Boulevard, then south to Colonial drive, then west again as we headed into Orlando. Whoever was behind the candid snapshot certainly didn't know me very well. That thought came to me as we passed a boarded-up building that had, until only recently, housed a topless bar. What had the snoop thought? It was likely—given the statistics in our society—that I might have been having an affair. Given our trip to Burger Man's, of course, it must have appeared that my torrid affair with Eleanor Algretto was a pretty weeny one. That I would automatically attempt to hide my apparent indiscretion, or at least bend to some higher will to avoid being exposed, was not the reasoning of anyone who knew much about me. I just don't lie well—my father always loved that about me. The only other individual I could think of who might wish trouble on my relationship with Sam just wasn't that kind of person, at least I wanted desperately to think not. Still, the vision of that particular photograph framed and hanging on the wall in the back office at Little Oak Books wasn't all that big a stretch.

Ketchum, Latham & Bennet was coming alive as we joined a string of punctual firm members pulling into the rapidly filling parking lot—all but one associate, that is.

"He's dead! He's dead!"

It was difficult to zero in immediately on what Victoria Mann was screaming, such was the lively and provocative bounce of her ample breasts. She ran across the parking lot with all the swiftness her high heels and tight skirt would permit, and the effect was mesmerizing. Certainly no such low-cut garment could be expected to contain the kind of kinetic energy on display there in the early morning Florida sun. How did it go? *Force = Mass × Acceleration*? The woman's bra, I decided, must be constructed of nothing less than high-tech carbon fiber. Amazing.

"Mr. Epstein's had a terrible accident!" she bellowed, turning this way and that, sweeping the disembarking firm members toward the back door with urgent arm gestures that only enhanced the eruptive potential of her swelling bosom.

By the time I transferred into my wheelchair and crossed the asphalt parking lot, everyone but Sam was already inside the long brick building. I followed her chair through the door, even as police and ambulance sirens could be heard approaching from the west. Someone with less bounce and more presence of mind had undoubtedly called 911. The ambulance, unfortunately, was far too late to do anything but haul Steve's lifeless body away when the police were finished with him, nearly an hour later. Fortunately, as gruesome as it seemed to those who might have noticed, I snapped several photographs of the dead quadriplegic even before the crime lab team was summoned.

Everyone was detained for questioning and, needless to say, Scully, Sam, and I had to scrap our interrogation plan. We sat, huddled together at the north end of the conference room, trying to make something of the sad but ridiculous scenario surrounding the young associate's death. Sam and I just looked at each other, keenly aware of the farce, but Scully had to verbalize what he thought. His voice was uncharacteristically low.

"Ain't no damn way! Look at me, you two!"

We looked.

"What kind of jerkface thought anybody'd buy that frame-up? Jeez! Can you believe it?"

We assured the agitated young paralegal that we didn't for a second believe it. The problem was: what were we going to tell the police?

THE LAW OFFICES OF

Ketchum, Latham & Bennet, P. A.

221 Lake Eola Drive
Orlando, Florida 32801
(407)555-1975 - FAX (407)555-1999

Rosemary I. Latham
Robert G. Bennet
Bernard R. Ketchum
Rebecca H. Forest
Stephen B. Epstein
Charles D. Young

William P. Graham
H. Russell White
Robert W. Albright
Samantha Wagner-Foster
Paul W. Kilpatrick

12

"KNOW ANYTHING ABOUT that statue, Mr. Foster?"

I told the young detective what I'd learned from Rick Scully, watching his eyes as he listened. He whistled through his teeth when I was finished.

"Good enough motive for a burglary, wouldn't you say?"

I didn't know the rookie gold-badge whose name was James Henderson, but I refrained from dressing him down. This was probably his first big investigation since coming in off the street, and I'm sure he wanted to look good in the eyes of the other Orlando detectives and uniforms who were asking similar questions throughout the building. The distant echo of Rick Scully's booming voice gave evidence that he was not exercising the same restraint with the steel-eyed woman who'd led him off to an unused office moments earlier.

"James," I said, as kindly as I could, "you can do this by the numbers and we can tick each other off, or you can lose the TV cop attitude and we'll see if we can't make some sense out of this fiasco. I'm going to break this story with or without you, and it's not about robbery. There have been two murders in this firm now, and if you want to be the cop who brings the bad guys down, you can work with me. What about it?"

The young black man studied my face intently. There was no test of wills; I just smiled and waited for him to make up his mind. I know why people instinctively trusted my dad but have never quite understood why it works for me. That's certainly not to say that I haven't used it to my advantage on any number of convenient occasions. I saw the answer in the detective's eyes long before he spoke.

"You've got a rep, Mr. Foster," he said slowly, "and I want one. I asked Agent Fredricks about you once, and he says you're okay. I'd love to have your help . . . I'll even return the favor in any way I legally can. Is that good enough?"

"Only if you call me Stick," I said. "Can you spring my wife and the big paralegal named Scully so we can all have a talk?"

"I know who your wife is, Stick, but not Scully."

"The loud one."

"Ah."

After introductions, the four of us wandered across the street, and while Rick Scully and James Henderson sat next to each other uneasily on a Lake Eola park bench, Sam and I pulled our wheelchairs up on the grass in front of them and got comfortable. I started things off before the young detective had time to give in to the innate compulsion to take charge that many law officers seem to be born with.

"First, James, although I don't doubt your lab crew will find Stephen Epstein's prints all over that bronze bust that he seems to have conveniently dropped on his own skull, I'm going to give you a little lesson about quadriplegics. I don't mean to be patronizing, but the general public, at least, knows little or nothing about the difference between a quad and a para. Sam and I are paraplegics; that is, our legs are paralyzed, but we have full use of our upper bodies—arms and hands. Steve was a quad. More than that, he was a high quad—C5 to be exact." I was delighted to see that James was listening intently, taking notes with no hint of being put off by my lecture or ill at ease about the subject.

"His spinal cord injury was two vertebrae up from the

sharp one that protrudes at the base of your neck." I motioned to the large bony knot on my spine, and the young detective reached back and felt his way down his own neck to the same spot. "That's C7, or the seventh cervical vertebra. Screw up below that point and you're a para. Above, and you're a quad. That means your hands and arms are affected, the severity of which depends on how high up the injury is. C5 means no functional use of your fingers, and so little triceps that you'd be unlikely to raise your arm over your head like this." I let my right forearm drape across the top of my head, and then lifted my hand skyward, moving the arm only from the elbow up. "Steve Epstein's fingers were curled up like this," I said, bending all my fingers slightly at the joints, "and he couldn't open or close them on his own, let alone reach up, remove four brass rivets, and lift down a bronze bust of Mrs. Lucius Cornelius Sulla. Doctor Joe O'Donnel over at Florida Hospital—or any M.D. for that matter—will verify all of this, but you've got to get past the stupid little exhibition left for us at the firm this morning before we can head in the right direction."

"You should know," James said with a shrug, "but you aren't giving us much credit. If Epstein was that limited, don't you think we'd figure that out? We may not be experts on spinal cord injury, but we know who to ask."

"Fair enough. And you're right," I said. "I've no doubt your buddies will figure it out given time. But why not see if James Henderson is willing to cut through that crap right now and help us get to the heart of the matter?"

Now that we had his full attention, we took turns filling our new friend in on the strange goings-on at Ketchum, Latham & Bennet, including the now missing L.I.M. propulsion unit, a device James unfortunately knew no more about than we did. To give credit where credit is due, Detective Henderson was a quick study. He knew enough not to ask how we knew what we knew, but he was clearly arranging puzzle pieces faster than a smart kid at a big card table on a rainy day.

"Okay," he said, looking up from his notes, "what about Epstein's work habits? Would it be unusual for him to come in at night?"

"Not at all. He worked more often at night than he did during the day," Sam said. "Liked having the run of the place—and the quiet."

"So," the detective went on, "Epstein shows up while whoever installed the gadget is in there taking it out, and they decide to ace him and make it look like a bungled burglary?"

"Go, man, go!" Scully said, slapping the cop soundly on the shoulder.

James blinked hard but smiled at the looming paralegal beside him on the park bench. "And the gadget may or may not have trashed the videotapes and/or the head of the firm—hey! Electromagnetics! Think about it! That's what the studios use—bulkhead erasers. They're just strong electromagnets! Stick, that might explain your flying fork as well. You've got to call The Old Man's doctor and ask her about pacemakers and magnets."

Yes, sir!

"It's all electronic, Mr. Foster. There are no moving parts, nothing that a small magnet could affect, at least not that I could imagine. I'll call the company technician, but I'm sure that's what he'll say."

Jessica Sanderlin sounded confident.

"What about those new magnetic scans?" I asked. "Can a person with a pacemaker get one of those?"

"You mean Magnetic Resonance Imaging? No, it's not recommended, but that field probably would stop a pacemaker. The MRI's electromagnet is the size of a room, and the force field it creates is about as bad as the field created by those superhigh power lines. Did you ever see the photo of that little girl holding up two fluorescent light bulbs under a set of high power lines? Both bulbs were lit, just from the electrical field in the air around her. Also, that strong a magnetic field could, conceivably, rip anything with metal in it right out of a patient's body. But there's probably not enough metal in a pacemaker to make that a problem."

Mmm.

Later, when Peter Stilles and his live-aboard electronic wizardess, Bice Wathan, both gave me the same answer, I really started to get optimistic. Detective James Henderson's brilliant theory would, if correct, certainly explain the damage done to the videotapes, but now we had some real reason to tie The Old Man's death to the same turn of events.

"So it just might fly, eh, babe?" Sam looked up from the desk in our dusty home office. "Now all we've got to do is find the gizmo and figure out whodunit."

The Orlando police sent everyone home so that the crime lab team could give the firm's building a thorough going-over. Silverspoon and Rosemary Latham let it be known that they weren't budging from the parking lot until the cops were through, but no one else showed any interest in hanging around.

"No sweat," I said, "it's just a matter of time now."

"Sure," Sam said. "It all boils down to time in the end, doesn't it?"

"It's the propulsion business that gets me," Danny Kincade said from the doorway. He stood holding an air-powered finish nailer in his right hand, and he scratched his head with his left. "A 'propulsion unit' ought to propel something. A car motor, a steam locomotive engine, those are propulsion units. They drive a cam or a shaft or a chain or something. Even the compressor on this old nail gun pushes something. What kind of engine has no discernable moving parts and doesn't go anywhere?"

"I don't know, Danny," I said as he wandered back toward the living room and the oak molding Sam had picked out for the ceiling trim. "I just don't know."

"Did you call Hawaii?"

"What?" Sam's question came from so far afield, I was sure that I'd heard her wrong.

"Did you call Hawaii—or Cancún for that matter?" She held the phone bill, reminding me that I'd forgotten all about asking her the same question.

"No, as a matter of fact, and I saw those too. We'll just call Ma Bell and tell her she's got her fiber-optic wires crossed again."

Somehow, I was not too surprised when Sam and I drove our cars into Ketchum, Latham & Bennet's lot the next morning . . . right behind a blue-and-white FleetPrint delivery truck. As we transferred into our respective wheelchairs, we watched the van's driver load a dozen or so ream-sized boxes of letterhead stationery onto a hand truck and wheel them into the firm's back door. And then there were ten . . .

THE LAW OFFICES OF

Ketchum, Latham & Bennet, P. A.

221 Lake Eola Drive
Orlando, Florida 32801
(407)555-1975 - FAX (407)555-1999

Rosemary I. Latham	William P. Graham
Robert G. Bennet	H. Russell White
Bernard R. Ketchum	Robert W. Albright
Rebecca H. Forest	Samantha Wagner-Foster
Charles D. Young	Paul W. Kilpatrick

13

Bᴇʀɴᴀʀᴅ Kᴇᴛᴄʜᴜᴍ ʜᴀᴅ reluctantly agreed to see me. He was now, in addition to being arrogant and condescending, notably surly. This was—like the arrival of the firm's newly corrected letterhead—to be expected.

"I don't like you, Foster," he said, leaning across his desk with a perfectly polished sneer on his face. I continued pushing aside one of the two padded leather chairs that faced his father's huge mahogany desk and was just backing my wheelchair along in front of him when he went on . . . just a little too far. "But I'd lay your wife down in a second."

I'm not a violent guy, though I've been forced to commit a number of very violent acts in my lifetime. This act was purely instinctual, and if my late father were there to observe it, he would have seen it as totally uncalled for. We would have agreed to disagree. I reached across the desk with my left hand while I clutched my right wheel with the other, and before Silverspoon had the opportunity to enjoy his crudeness, I had his silk tie and his $100 tailored shirt collar firmly in my left fist. With my chair trapped under the leading edge of the desk, it was almost too easy when I jerked him straight out of his chair and dragged him across the paperwork laid out between us.

"I've at least been trying to like you, Bernard," I said, digging my right fingers into the soft of his neck, just behind his left jaw, and pressing my right thumb firmly against his left eye, "but it's just not nice of you to taunt a poor helpless cripple boy like me. Mmmm, you seem to have a mote or something stuck in your eye. Do you know what a mote is, Bernard? Should I help you get it out? Just nod one way or the other."

I used to know how much pressure it took to pop the human eyeball—one of those fun facts they taught me in the army. I couldn't recall the figure just then, but I knew that Bernard was probably wondering about the very same thing himself. When he moved his head carefully from side to side, I eased up slowly, let go of his face and his collar, and tidied up his tie. I breathed deeply while the adrenaline rush began to fade. I wasn't proud of myself, but, at the moment, I wasn't sorry either. Silverspoon had a startled and frightened look on his face that was almost comical.

"Money's a great insulator, Bernard," I said as I resumed backing into the spot where the big chair had been, "but sometimes even the kind of money you have won't protect you in the kind of battles that occasionally take place outside of the courtroom."

His eyes were narrowing as he eased back off the desk, and he looked as if he were about to respond.

"I'm not finished, Bernard," I said as calmly as I could, "and I'm not in the mood to be interrupted by a spoiled, preppy brat."

Bernard closed his mouth and sank back farther into his father's oversize swivel wing chair.

"Good. Now you may not recognize anyone besides lawyers, doctors, and CEOs as being professionals, but there are a good number of us out there in the real world, and some of us are pretty good at what we do too, even though we don't make as much money as you do. You and I can communicate like two professionals, or you can continue to sit in your ivory tower and look down your nose at me . . . and let the publicity chips fall where they may. I'm writing this story, and at the moment you look like the perfect villain to me. Orlando would eat it up, believe me, and it wouldn't do the firm or your standing in it a bit of good. So what will it be?"

There was a momentary, silent test of wills, and I figured that the desk probably didn't seem like quite the fortress it once had. "Damn, you're strong," he said, blinking his watery left eye, loosening his tie, and unbuttoning his shirt collar, all the while watching me warily. "The crack about Sam was out of line. She's a damn fine lawyer."

It was probably the closest thing to either respect or an apology any commoner ever got from Bernard Ketchum. Of course I didn't trust him for a minute, but I smiled and said, "I know."

"Look," he went on, "I know Stephen wasn't stealing Dad's statue, and if whoever killed him was any kind of decent thief, they would never have hit him with a million-dollar bronze bust, let alone left it on his lap. They left both of them," Bernard said, shaking his head. "And an original Turner worth nearly as much."

My eyebrows rose on their own.

"That's right," he said, almost laughing, "it's real too. I told Dad he was nuts leaving that stuff around here, but telling my father what to do was like telling the ducks to quit shitting in the park."

Like father, like son.

Our meeting was profitable but somewhat disappointing. I hate to lose a prime suspect. Silverspoon may or may not have been capable of killing his own father, but I left fully convinced that he'd rather lose his left eye than lose the Fraiser case. Partnership was a given, but winning that one, he admitted, would almost certainly guarantee that a majority of the associates would back him if he bypassed Robert Bennet and unseated Rosemary Latham. If he thought he could get away with it, though, I was relatively certain that he'd be tempted to kill whoever destroyed the videotapes. So, if the tapes and the death of The Old Man were indeed related, it appeared far less likely that Bernard was our man.

"What if they're not related at all?" Stanley Fredericks said over the phone. "Would he off his dad for a chance to head the Fraiser team?"

"I don't know, Stan. I don't think so. He just let a gimp push him around in his own office. I doubt he has the stomach for it."

"For a fair fight, maybe not," the FBI man pushed on, "but from what you've told me, he's the back-stabbing type anyway."

"Could be, I suppose—oh, crap!"

"What's the matter?"

"I should have asked him whether he was having me followed when I had my thumb in his beady little eye."

When I called James Henderson, the young detective was not as gung ho as when we'd spoken with him in Eola Park. The reason, however, was a fair one. There wasn't a shred of hard evidence that there had ever been any kind of device inside the beautiful Mrs. Sulla and her faux-marble display stand—no fingerprints, no wires, no gluey residues. There was nothing in there but brass filings and demolished rivets.

"How many?" I asked.

"Well," he said, "that, at least, might back up your story. It's most likely the remains of twelve rivets, four of them unlike the others but matching the set at the other end of the room. You were right, of course, about Mr. Epstein. His disability—or should I say physical challenge—aside, nobody here's buying the scenario. No tools, no gloves, and no motive. The guy's worth a fortune anyway, maybe more even than Ketchum. It was an insurance settlement of some kind when he was injured as a kid, and it apparently aged rather well until he turned twenty-one."

"What about Shortshire? Anything on it?"

"Nothing."

"Okay, thanks, James. If I turn up any more, I'll call. Keep in touch."

"You got it, Stick. You know," he said, lowering his voice, "I *want* this one."

Me too.

After dropping off my hastily written "Take This Sitting Down" piece and its accompanying photos at the paper, I drove several blocks south, parked the old Monte SS, and braced myself. I don't exactly hate libraries, but I am intimidated by them. People like Peter Stilles are apparently born perfectly at home in the great information warehouses, but I have always felt overwhelmed. Just going in the front door feels oppressive, as if I might be buried in an avalanche of data if I touched the wrong tome or made too much noise. Fortunately, I discovered Jennifer Creacy shortly after moving to Orlando.

"Well, it's Mr. Library!"

"Funny."

"No camera this time . . . must be serious. Should I tie you to the reference desk with a long string, or did you bring bread crumbs with you?"

I swear, librarians can read the insecurity on your face— like pit bulls smelling fear. Jennifer knew I was lost the first time I rolled into the downtown branch, and every time thereafter. She always razzes me but has never failed to help me find whatever I was looking for, even when I wasn't exactly certain what that was. I had a secret fantasy about Jennifer and Peter Stilles facing off on "Jeopardy"; and not only did Jennifer win but she did so in the nude. Whatever stereotypical image one might have of a librarian, Jennifer Creacy would dash it on the rocks. Oh, to be sure, she was intelligent, witty, and a master of such details as most of us would never care to know, and she dressed like a proper Republican, but there was a sensuousness about her that was so provocative it almost frightened me, especially when we were side by side in one of those long, dark aisles in the basement.

"I need to locate a company and find out what they do," I said, "but all I have is a name."

"No problem. Follow me."

We ended up in a section of the library I wouldn't even have considered entering alone. The shelves were lined with volumes in paperback, hardback, and loose-leaf binders, all of them enormous. An avalanche would certainly be fatal. Surely only Gulliver or Paul Bunyan actually read books like these.

"Name?" Jennifer said, her hand poised by a green, four-volume set with *Ward's Business Directory* embossed on the spines.

"Shortshire, Limited."

"Do you mind if I use you as a desk?" she said, placing the appropriate volume on my lap and beginning to flip through without waiting for an answer. "Hmmm. Nothing here. You sure about the name?"

"Yup."

The next anvil-sized book to cut off the circulation to my toes was *The Directory of Corporate Affiliations,* a massive red paperback that shed no light on Shortshire, Ltd.

"If it's American, even a subsidiary," Jennifer said, "it should have been in there."

"Maybe it's not American," I said, noticing the obvious. "I just thought the founder might be a Tolkien fan . . . you know, the Shire, Hobbits, Bilbo Baggins, and all that. But it could just as well be a British company, I suppose."

"That would be here," Jennifer said, replacing the red book with a large dark tome entitled *Kelly's* something or other. "Nope," she said, her full lips only inches from mine, her smile so innocent and sincere. "No dice."

Why did the Orlando library always seem warmer when I was scouting around with Jennifer Creacy?

"What about Canada?" I said, trying not to think any more unseemly thoughts about my local librarian.

"We can do Canada."

She swept up *Kelly's* and replaced it with *Fraiser's*, one paperback volume from a set of three.

"Bingo!" she said.

Fraiser's? Where have I heard that name before?

THE LAW OFFICES OF
Ketchum, Latham & Bennet, P. A.
221 Lake Eola Drive
Orlando, Florida 32801
(407)555-1975 - FAX (407)555-1999

Rosemary I. Latham	William P. Graham
Robert G. Bennet	H. Russell White
Bernard R. Ketchum	Robert W. Albright
Rebecca H. Forest	Samantha Wagner-Foster
Charles D. Young	Paul W. Kilpatrick

14

I'D NEVER BEATEN Peter Stilles to the research punch before and could hardly wait to get on the car phone and rub it in his face. Jennifer photocopied the sketchy page I needed from *Fraiser's,* and after thanking her profusely, I returned to the Monte. I finally knew what an L.I.M. was, but until I actually called Shortshire, Ltd., in Ottawa, Canada, I had no idea what a "linear induction motor" did. As it turned out, handyman Danny Kincade would be delighted; the little engine drove commuter trains, but only in select cities around the world. Shortshire was the only manufacturer on record, and the United States, apparently, has not yet been sold on the benefits of this compact, nearly maintenance-free engine that literally pulls the cars along the tracks by turning on and off a powerful electromagnet that is built into the underside of the train.

"No," said the Shortshire representative, "our normal engines are much larger than what you describe, but we've built a number of smaller L.I.M.s for demonstration purposes."

"Could you tell me whether there might have been one delivered to a Florida customer? I'd love to see one up close."

"Let me check the computer. Yes, as a matter of fact," she said seconds later, "we shipped a small L.I.M. to Orlando several months ago, to a John Dough."

She spelled out the bogus last name but didn't seem the least bit aware of its absurdity.

"Could I please have the address and phone number? Maybe Mr. Dough will give me a demonstration."

"Certainly," she said, probably smelling a possible sale.

I took down the box number address and the Orlando telephone number, thanked her, and hung up. The description of John Dough I got at the Mail Boxes R Us location would fit fifty percent of America's white male population, and the young woman who answered the phone when I dialed the local number told me firmly that she knew nothing about either John Dough or linear induction motors. Surprise, surprise. She also refused to tell me who she was, inviting me to call again and discuss the matter with her husband, who, by the tone she took with me, was not a man to mess with lightly. Visions of a big biker-type guy with tattoos for sleeves came immediately to mind.

Detective James Henderson was shocked and pleased when I rolled into his office with my gold mine of information. Of course I bargained with it some before I gave it to him.

"We have a deal then?" I said.

"The phone number, yes. I'll run it and let you know whose it is," he said quietly, "but getting the phone records for everyone at both firms, Stick, that'll take a court order. I don't know . . . "

"You can do it," I said, patting him on the shoulder, "for a murder investigation. We need to know who ordered that electromagnet and who at the Three Rs has been in touch with friends at Brown, Nealy, Howser & Columbine."

"Then I was right?" The light in the young detective's eyes came on like Main Street in the Magic Kingdom. When I grinned, James leapt to his feet and shouted, "Yes!"

"Having trouble pushing that theory around here?" I asked with a laugh.

"Lots. Boy, am I gonna rub some noses in it if we can nail this down! Whatcha got?"

He took notes, pausing to whistle from time to time. When he had everything down, he sat back and smiled.

"We might just get these guys," he said, "but what about your friends, will they all testify that they saw this thing?"

"Sure. Especially since we were all there with Rick Scully."

"Right. Look, be careful what you do in the paper, Stick. We don't want to send anybody packing before we can do the legwork and pin them down."

"Wouldn't think of it," I said, even though I was thinking quite seriously about using an article to stir up the shark tank and see which dorsal fins broke water first. I had a sudden vision of Roy Scheider's face while he watched Robert Shaw disappear into the Great White's toothy maw and decided that I could wait a couple of days. Besides, there might be another way.

Clarence Grosse is hardly a quiet, unassuming man, but he takes his job seriously. Some would call him a gofer, but in strict legal firm lingo, he's a runner. Chewing tobacco and poor dental hygiene have taken their toll on the short, heavy-set man's smile, and it's easy to see why those at the firm who call him Grosse to his face are spelling it *gross* to themselves and to each other. If Clarence had a clue, he didn't let on while chatting with me over a hot dog at Lake Eola. By all counts, including his own, he is a stickler for details; so much so, in fact, that he tends to get on some firm members' nerves. "You have to tell him *everything*," Sam reported shortly after starting at Ketchum, Latham & Bennet. "Somebody's dumped on him for making a bad decision somewhere along the line, and now he's bound and determined that it will never happen again. Even a trip to the courthouse requires specific instructions . . . and he goes there several times a day."

"It's their game," Clarence told me with a self-satisfied grin. "I ain't got no college degree like them high-dollar shysters, but I can play their games. Lawyers want to work every stinkin' thing to their advantage, so no matter what comes

down, it'll slide off 'em slicker than shit down a plastic crap-
per. Know what I mean?"

Strangely enough, the unusual metaphor was perfectly
clear and I nodded my head. Clarence's brown-and-yellow
grin grew and his dark eyes sparkled.

"They love to twist everything back on somebody else, see,
so I pin 'em down, exact. Then if they don't like what I fetch
'em, they got nobody to blame but their darn selves!"

"Who's who, Clarence? I mean, between you and me, tell
me about the sharks at the Three Rs."

"Well, I like your wife, Stick, but I wouldn't want to get
on her bad side!"

Mmm.

"Most of 'em are thataway," he went on with a patented
grin, "but still decent enough. Epstein was pretty coarse, like
Scully, but I liked him 'cause he was a straight shooter. No
bullshit when it mattered. You think somebody killed Steve
and The Old Man, don't you?"

"Yes, I do."

"One of our guys?"

"I doubt it, Clarence," I said with a shrug, "but who
knows these days? Maybe an accessory. What about Bennet?
What about Young and the rest of the Back Alley guys?"

The Back Alley was the firm's nickname for that tail-end
stretch of hallway at the far north end of the building—not
even shouting distance from Power Alley where the partners'
offices were. Sam and Paul Kilpatrick shared a secretary at
the Dead End of the Back Alley, and something about the
long walk was supposed to keep them humble. I've never met
a humble attorney, so don't put much stock in that particular theory.

"Bennet don't say much," Clarence said philosophically,
"but he's always seemed okay enough to me. Never loses it like
Latham sometimes does, or like The Old Man did most every
day. Chuck Young and Bob Albright are pretty real—for lawyers—but Graham, White, and the new kid with the old Triumph are hard cases. Cut your throat to win a case. Sore losers,

for sure. I get *real* specific instructions from those guys!"

Clarence grinned again, and I gave up trying to eat my hot dog. "Has anyone outside the firm ever approached you about getting into the building after hours, Clarence? Maybe offering you money to look the other way?"

The firm's runner straightened up as if a steel rod had just been run up his spine. His mischievous eyes turned stormy, and his voice suddenly sounded threatening. "I ain't no lawyer, but I'm good at what I do," he said, leaning in close enough that his breath made my eyes water. "I ain't *never* been fired off a job, and I ain't never screwed over anybody who put bread on my table. Somebody treats me bad, I walk, an' nobody's treated me that bad at the shark tank. If you're thinkin' of goin' somewhere with that question, just watch your damn self!"

"Easy, Clarence," I said, holding up my hand to ward off any further defensiveness. "I'm not accusing you of anything at all. But what if another firm is behind all this? They might have sounded out several people before they found somebody sore enough to help them get in. Subtle hints maybe. See what I mean?"

"Oh yeah," he said, leaning back and away as the idea sunk in. I took the opportunity to inhale the newly available Florida air. "I never thought about any of that. Hmm, no, nobody never said nothin' to me."

"Do you hear much unhappy talk from the associates who didn't make the Fraiser team, Clarence? I mean, Sam and Scully say that there was some bad blood over that."

"Ha! You got that right! Several of 'em was pissed about that business," he said, rolling his eyes and shaking his head. "Ms. Rebecca darn near spits whenever the F word comes up. And if looks could kill," Clarence went on, pointing east across the park with a chubby forefinger, "well, there'd be several murderers in that old shark tank."

By the time Sam arrived home that night, I'd reorganized my own letterhead suspect list, called Brenda "Butch" Grady to arrange for her to try intercepting my picture-taking fan, and convinced the phone company that no one had used my phone to call either Hawaii or Cancún. Sam rolled into our home office with a less than joyous look on her beautiful face.

"You love to stir things up, don't you?" she asked.

"Sure, just as much as you do, but to what stirrings, specifically, are you referring?"

"Did you really tell Gross that one of us at the firm was a traitor?"

"Not in those exact words."

"Well, your exact words are academic at this point, babe. The Gross Man seems to think that Orlando's famous Stick Foster is about to expose this traitor—maybe even Steve's murderer—and there suddenly seems to be a lot of paranoia going around at the office. Everybody's looking suspiciously at everybody else. If it weren't so serious, it might be funny."

"Where there's smoke," I said with a shrug, "there's fire."

I never realized how true that was until about five hours later. The smoke *and* the fire were in the hallway just outside our bedroom door.

15

IT WAS AN odd crackling sound that woke me from a disturbing dream about Hemingway's *The Old Man and the Sea*. I shook Sam awake and started pulling on the blue jeans I'd left hanging over the back of my wheelchair. It had never really bothered me all that much that getting dressed took considerably longer than it had before my spinal cord injury . . . at least not until I woke up in a burning house.

"What is it?" Sam asked sleepily.

"Fire!" I said, rolling back and forth to pull the jeans up over my bony hips. "Call nine-one-one and then get dressed fast! We'll grab what we can and go out the patio door."

The sliding glass patio door that afforded our bedroom its wonderful view of the lake had just taken on a new and much appreciated virtue. With the flickering red glow of live flame visible through the door to the hallway and the acrid smell of a six-inch layer of smoke that curled and hovered in the dancing light on the ceiling over our heads, the front and back doors were suddenly a very long way away, both being at the other end of the long ranch-style home. As I hopped into my wheelchair, I thanked God for the former owners who had torn out the room's east windows, built the decorative cinder-block garden patio, and installed the triple-pane sliding glass door.

"Phone's dead!" Sam said, throwing down the handset and snatching up the gray slacks that hung over the back of her hot-pink ultralight. "And so's the electricity. It's really going great guns out there. I wonder what happened. I didn't hear the smoke alarm, did you?"

"No."

The view from her side of the king-size water bed afforded her a better look down the hall, but I rolled over and peeked myself before closing the bedroom door. It wasn't an encouraging sight.

"What are you doing?" Sam asked as I pushed into our very dark bathroom and ran water on one of the bath towels.

"Sealing us up a bit before I open the patio door and let in a new batch of oxygen. No sense giving that beast any more life than it's already got."

"Where'd you get so smart?" Sam asked. She transferred hurriedly into her wheelchair and pulled a sweatshirt out of her bureau.

"Did a weeklong story on the Melbourne Fire Department a few years back." I placed the soggy towel along the floor at the foot of the door and turned back toward the big glass slider. "Crap!"

"What?"

It took a house fire to make me realize that there are only two or three possessions that I'd really become attached to. One was in the carport, fifty feet from the house, and one was in my backpack. The other should have been in the bedroom with us but wasn't. "Butkis."

"Oh, Stick! We've got to get him!"

"We get us first," I said firmly, unlatching the patio door, removing the security stick from the track along the floor, and pulling on the sturdy aluminum handle.

Good night, nurse. I'd used the door that morning for a breath of fresh air and an appreciative perusal of Lake Martha along with coffee. It had opened easily then. Now it felt like it was set in concrete. I nearly pulled myself out of my wheelchair when I yanked on it a second time. Somebody started the fire intentionally, I realized suddenly, somebody who didn't want us to get out.

"What is it? What's the matter with the door?" Sam had swept a three-foot-high stack of lawyer clothes off the closet bar and was sitting behind me expectantly with the costly costumes piled on her lap.

"I don't know." Adrenaline might make you stronger, but it also makes it harder to be calm and coolheaded in a crisis. I looked around the bedroom for something heavy but manageable. The TV on my bureau was too big to throw, and the green glass bedside reading lamps were too small and fragile.

"Here," Sam said, divining my visual quest and handing me a sturdy wooden hanger from one of her business suits. "Try this."

Though I wouldn't want to be hit over the head with the hanger, our patio door turned it into kindling on the first blow. It wasn't much comfort to know that a potential burglar would also have found the eight-foot aperture forbidding. We both looked instinctively at the north window. It was more than half blocked by the big bed's bookshelf-headboard and would provide no escape—at least not without our draining and disassembling the water bed first.

"What now, bub?"

Sam was, like her gimpy husband, trying to fight back the rising panic in her voice. "Maybe a drawer," I said. "Back up, toss that stuff on the bed, and help me pull out my jeans drawer."

When we'd managed to get the heaviest of my bureau drawers out, we swung it back and forth between us, agreeing to launch it on the count of three. The count went well, as did the launching, and the sound of breaking oak and pine was most impressive . . . as was the thick glass door, which remained quite intact. My blue jeans lay scattered awkwardly along the floor by the nonsliding door, like one of those acrobatic Levi's commercials run amuck. What an odd comment on our lives, I thought, that all our knickknacks were small. Neither Sam nor I was into tacky, overstated bric-a-brac, but as we scanned the dark, smoky room in desperation, I think we both thought belatedly about the value of collecting some good old American garage sale junk—big, heavy junk. What I wouldn't have given just then for a brass Buddha clock or a Franklin Mint pewter Elvis.

"This is *not* good," Sam said.

We were both scanning the puny books on the headboard shelf. In the dim light I couldn't read the cover, but as much as I was enjoying William Love's Bishop Regan/Davey Goldman novel *Bishop's Revenge*, I couldn't help wishing that the ex-priest, ex-banker turned author had written a few thousand extra pages. The good bishop's library, I thought with chagrin, now *there* was some heavy reading. A copy of the *Collegeville Bible Commentary*, for example, might have just done the trick.

"I always meant to read *War and Peace*," I said, squeezing my chair past Sam's and rolling back toward the bathroom. "You keep working on the door. I'm going out the other way."

"You can't be serious!"

"No? Well, unless you've got a hammer on you, we appear to be out of other options."

After I slipped on my old door-ramming penny loafers, I pulled the spread off the bed and took it with me into the roll-in shower.

"Someone will come," Sam said. "The fire department's probably already on their way."

"You willing to bet our lives on that, counselor?"

I used the hand-held shower nozzle to soak myself down before covering my lap with the remaining bath towel and drenching it too. When the bedspread was completely sodden, I went back to the bedroom door and draped it around my head and shoulders, tucking the front corners under my hips so that they wouldn't catch in my wheels.

"There's *got* to be another way!" Sam insisted.

"When it occurs to you, go for it," I said, trying unsuccessfully to smile. "When I go out, close this door and put the wet towel back as fast as you can, okay?"

"No!"

"Sam, it's got to be now, before the ceiling out there starts coming down. Look at me, I'm about as flammable as the water bed mattress. Come on, I'll be throwing a concrete patio block at you before you know it."

I placed my hand on the door before turning the knob. I couldn't remember how to tell what was too hot, but it seemed academic at the time. Sam came up behind and took the wet towel I'd picked up off the floor.

"Okay, but don't stop until you're either outside or back here."

"Deal. Here goes."

I almost turned back before Sam got the bedroom door closed; but as strange as it seemed to me afterwards, I could almost hear my late father's voice, quoting, I think, from the eighteenth chapter of Proverbs. "A man's courage can sustain his broken body, but when courage dies, what hope is left?"

Drywall doesn't burn well, but there was obviously no lack of ready fuel at the other end of the hallway. The heat hurt my eyes, but I could see that someone had made a substantial pile of Danny's wood scraps, and the wall of flames they were supporting had nearly burned a hole in the drywall ceiling. The thickest smoke was now halfway to the floor, swirling just above my head. Wishing suddenly that I'd taken the time to put on my socks, I slid the wet towel further down my lap so that the dripping end of it touched the pennies on my shoes. In a flush of optimism about saving our big computers, our files, and my fantasy novel, I closed the door to our smoky office across the hall before taking a big breath and charging the bonfire with as much speed as the distance and my soggy wardrobe allowed.

I suspect that even a sturdy tepee camp fire, built with progressively larger and larger sticks of native timber, would have scattered before my steaming wheelchair locomotive. A radial-arm saw, however, is a different matter altogether. I'm not always known for my instantaneous clarity of thought, but even as I careened through the flames and ran chest first into Danny's favorite shop tool, I thanked God for small blessings. Had the arsonist chosen the table saw instead of the radial-arm saw, I would have burned to death on the spot, stranded in the blazing rubble. With its squat legs and lower center of gravity, Danny's table saw would have easily withstood my suicidal onslaught. A radial-arm saw is no lighter, of course, but is, by comparison, taller and altogether more top-heavy. I flew out of my wheelchair when it stopped abruptly in the middle of the fire, and literally rode the scalding hot power tool as it toppled away from the fire and into the living room beyond. I prayed that the nasty sizzling sound around me was just the wet bedspread and not an unfortunate patch of my own skin.

I hit hard, rolled away in a disheveled heap, and lay, still holding my breath, in a tangle of steaming, wet linen and overturned equipment. The back door was closer, and I tried crawling in that direction, anxious to drag my lifeless legs away from the blaze. The effort made me dizzy. I sucked for air, and the smoky breath stuck solidly in my chest, but I made some progress before I passed out. The last thing I remember was clutching at the portable Sony telephone on the floor next to me and sweeping a frightened brown cat under the wet bedspread with my other arm. Through the dizzying fog in my brain, I thought I heard the gunfire-like sound of my high-pressure wheelchair tires exploding in the flames behind me . . . but my chair had only *two* air-filled tires.

THE LAW OFFICES OF

Ketchum, Latham & Bennet, P. A.

221 Lake Eola Drive
Orlando, Florida 32801
(407)555-1975 - FAX (407)555-1999

Rosemary I. Latham   William P. Graham
Robert G. Bennet   H. Russell White
Bernard R. Ketchum   Robert W. Albright
Rebecca H. Forest   Samantha Wagner-Foster
Charles D. Young   Paul W. Kilpatrick

16

Day's light was well on its way when I woke up on the back lawn, halfway down to the lake shore, with a clear plastic oxygen mask covering my nose and mouth. My voice was muffled, but the paramedic fire fighter understood me well enough.

"Sam!" I sat up instinctively and started dragging myself toward the house.

"Your wife?" the young man asked, restraining me with a sure hand on my shoulder.

"I've got to get her out!"

"Relax," the medic said with a laugh. He removed the mask from my face and began packing up the breathing equipment. "Sam's fine. She was out here hauling your sorry butt across the lawn when we arrived."

"She what?"

"She dragged you out somehow. Did you really try to roll through the primary fire in your wheelchair? That was dumb. We did save the chair, though, sort of." He motioned to his right, and there was what remained of my blue light-weight folder. The sew-up Continental tires—or what was left of them—were melted to the alloy rims, and the nylon seat fabric was mostly gone, with only melty strands here and there to bear witness to its former existence. The chair's electric blue paint was cracked and peeling in several places, but the frame seemed fine. Sixty-four aluminum spokes were warped and twisted, and the wet back upholstery was seared here and there, but mostly intact. My backpack still hung on it, a soggy and soot-stained blob of black canvas twill.

"So my hero's awake, eh?" I looked back up the lawn and saw Sam rolling toward us with my orange, rigid-frame sports chair upside down on her lap. "Thought you might want this."

"Thanks," I said. "And thanks for pulling my fat out of the fire. How'd *you* get out?" As I took the chair from her, set it upright next to me, and prepared to climb into it with the paramedic's help, I looked at our house for the first time. The fire fighters presently rolling up their hoses had clearly saved it, but not before the flames had torn themselves a chimney hole through the middle of the roof.

"Shot my way out."

Sam's answer jerked my attention back in a hurry, but my newly oxygenated brain puzzled it out almost immediately.

"The Beretta! Why didn't I think of that?"

"Billy Simpson said he asked you the same thing when you were both nearly eaten by Constance Galliger's alligator last year. I'd say it's a mental block."

The 9mm semiautomatic pistol was sort of a gift; that is, when Butch Grady "liberated" the handgun from a dead security guard's apartment, thus keeping it out of the hands of the Salvation Army—well, never mind, it's a long story. The thing is, she left it in my backpack that day and told me it was mine. I never bought into all that, of course, forgot about it really, but then it came in *very* handy and I just sort of hung on to it.

"Where was it?" I asked.

"I found it in a drawer under your side of the water bed," Sam said. "I was kinda freaked, looking for anything that might break the patio door, and it was rolled up in a University of Kansas painter's cap that I don't remember seeing before."

Mmm.

"How are the cars?" I asked to change the subject.

"Safe and sound. What about your computer?"

"Oh! I didn't even think . . ." I grabbed the sodden bag off the damaged wheelchair and found that both parts of the plastic snap fastener were melted into a black misshapen ball. I couldn't imagine what shape the laptop must be in, but I could picture the look on the computer repair guy's face. "Got a knife?" I asked the paramedic as he stood up to leave. He grinned and produced a stainless steel scalpel from the sleeve of his multizippered uniform.

"Will this do?"

"Great," I said. "Cut here. Thanks—for everything."

"You bet," the young man said as he turned to join his crew. "But don't try anything like that again, okay?"

"I promise."

The already battered case of my precious laptop computer was newly misshapen, its lines running away here and there like a Salvador Dalí clock that wasn't fully committed to its art form, but the latches came undone with some prompting and, though stiff, the lid-screen not only opened but lit up when I flipped on the tiny switch.

"For a gimp," Sam said, "you sure land on your feet a lot. Do you realize how lucky you are?"

Yes, ma'am.

The sun came up across the lake as it always did, but this month it was over the small weedy bay between the prep school and the wildlife refuge. In the good old days, people kept track of the months by how far north or south the sun rose and set. I was just glad to be alive to see it come up at all. The four of us sat on the patio drinking coffee from the convenience store up on the corner in Goldenrod.

"We're close," James Henderson said, dropping a handful of drywall screws back into the arson investigator's meaty palm. "Too close."

"One or two of these would have wedged up that slider quite sufficiently," said the rotund man in the wrinkled blue uniform. His name tag was conspicuously absent, but he'd introduced himself as Scott Barry. Neither the Orlando detective nor the Maitland arson investigator was looking his best, having been roused before dawn, but both were thoroughly tuned in to the drama at hand. "Whoever screwed all these into the track around that patio door wanted to be sure, dead sure."

"A comforting thought," Sam said, gently stroking the sleeping Tonkinese cat on her lap. Butkis knows exactly how to deal with trauma, and he wastes no time with postcrisis analysis.

Detective Henderson questioned Lieutenant Barry about the fire, and I absentmindedly pushed the button on the Sony cordless phone I'd apparently been clutching when Sam dragged me out the back door by my belt. The tiny light came on obediently and ran back and forth across the ten optional channel selection positions in vain. There was no power to the base unit in our living room, so the poor little light would keep scanning until I turned it off, or until the battery ran down, whichever came first.

"This thing is really escalating," Detective Henderson said when the fire investigator left. "Industrial sabotage to involuntary manslaughter—maybe felony murder—, then an outright murder, and now an unsuccessful attempt at a multiple murder. These people are serious."

"They are," I agreed, "but why? Can one lawsuit, one loss in court, be so important? This stretches the limits even of *my* distaste for lawyers."

"Hey!" Sam said, backhanding me with conviction. "Did you see that movie about the woman who set her abusive husband on fire while he slept? I pulled you out of it, but I can sure enough put you back in it, bub."

"Did you get that down, James?" I asked the grinning detective. "After I'm gone, your notes on this conversation will be the key evidence that sends this cold-blooded husband killer up the river."

Not to be left out of the posttrauma, tension-relieving fun,

James Henderson tore a page out of his small notebook, crumpled it up in one deft hand, and—to all appearances—popped it in his mouth, swallowing dramatically.

"I owe you one," Sam said to James. To me she said, "You lose."

"That's it, isn't it? I mean, really, it's all about winning and losing."

"And lawyers *hate* to lose," Sam said with some resignation. "It's drilled into us from the moment we take our first tentative look at the profession. Getting into law school is just the first of many battles, and the level of intensiveness of the competition goes up geometrically from there on out, always more at stake than the last time."

James Henderson's grin disappeared. We sat in uneasy stillness for several long seconds before the detective carried that pleasant thought to its present real-world application. "This isn't my 'hood, and even though your mailing address is Maitland, this is probably an unincorporated area. That means the cops aren't responsible, so I'll talk to the Orange County Sheriff. If they won't leave somebody," he said firmly, "I'll work something else out."

"Thanks, " I said, "but I think we'll be well watched over. The cavalry just arrived. Detective James Henderson, I'd like you to meet Brenda Grady."

"It's Butch," she said, extending her hand as the Orlando cop turned and stood up. "Sit. Looks like I missed all the excitement this time. What happened?"

Danny Kincade was appalled, first and foremost because we'd nearly been killed, but his intense dislike of drywall work was right there in the wings.

"I *hate* hanging Sheetrock," he said, after asking all the appropriate questions about Sam and me, and looking properly impressed by our answers. "*Especially* ceilings. I do it because it's part of the job, the good with the bad and all that, but to have to do it twice on the same house—now, that's a crime."

"How long before we can get back in?" Sam asked.

"Tonight if you really want to," Danny said. "I can tarp up the roof and replace the slider this morning, have the damaged crap out this afternoon, and if I can catch Don and Esther, we might-could clean up the insides enough by bedtime. I'll need a dumpster sled; it'll be too much for my pickup."

"Don and Esther?" I said. "They aren't that cute preppy couple who remodel houses together on PBS, are they?"

"No," Danny said with a chuckle, "they're my neighbors. They own a Service Master franchise, and if they can't clean up the mess and get rid of the stink, nobody can."

"Make it so," Sam said. "I won't be driven out of my new home that easily."

Aye-aye, Captain. Full ahead, warp three.

A redheaded and athletic-looking sheriff's deputy came and went, making out a report and apologizing that the department couldn't possibly leave someone but promising that they would step up their patrol of our neighborhood. I watched her walk away, glad that Sam had already left for the office. The freckled deputy reminded me of someone, the same someone who'd given me the KU painter's cap. Life is fraught with dangers, but Katie Newman—whoever and wherever she was—wasn't one of them anymore.

I tore my eyes away from the vanishing patrol car and went back to the patio. It was time to start writing real news. The hard drive in the melty-looking laptop sounded slightly asthmatic, but the word processing software came up okay, and my files seemed to be intact. As I began the article that would barely make the evening edition, it occurred to me with some mixed feelings that the nine-pound computer *might* have broken the safety glass in the patio door behind me . . . had I thought of it.

THE LAW OFFICES OF

Ketchum, Latham & Bennet, P. A.

221 Lake Eola Drive
Orlando, Florida 32801
(407)555-1975 - FAX (407)555-1999

Rosemary I. Latham	William P. Graham
Robert G. Bennet	H. Russell White
Bernard R. Ketchum	Robert W. Albright
Rebecca H. Forest	Samantha Wagner-Foster
Charles D. Young	Paul W. Kilpatrick

17

"REEBOKS," BUTCH SAID, stretching out in the redwood lounge chair across the patio.

"What?" Danny had the electric and the phone going again, and the computer on the redwood table was hooked to the bedroom phone jack and dumping my story directly into Ben "Good News" Dawson's desktop computer at the *Sentinel.* It was front-page stuff, but I doubted whether Ben would allow it to go there.

"Reeboks, you know, the sneakers? The firebug was wearing Reebok Pumps. You can see the round imprint of the basketball on the sole—there, coming through the roses, and there, going back out."

"So you're a tracker too," I said. "You never cease to amaze me, Butch. Can you tell me the weight, height, and sex of our friend as well?"

"Maybe," Butch said with a coy smile. "I'd say it's a he because Reebok Pumps are primarily a guy shoe and nine or nine and a half is primarily a guy size. He weighs more than I do," she went on, getting up and making a flamingolike one-footed imprint in the garden, "say, sixty or seventy pounds or so. Let's put him at about two hundred. Height? Well, there are two initial clues. First, there's the length of his stride, but that's a little shaky considering the circumstances. Next hint is better. He used a screwdriver to put two of those drywall screws up there along the top of the sliding door, without moving any patio furniture to stand on, so we know he's not short and fat."

"How do you know he didn't move the chair and then put it back?"

"Elementary, my dear Stick." Butch walked over to the redwood chair beside me and tipped it back on its rear legs. "Look. Every time it rains, a little of the weathered redwood and a little of the stain runs down the legs of these things and makes this pattern on the concrete blocks. I doubt that our torch ninja would have even thought about putting it back exactly where it was, especially in the dark."

"You're good."

"Of course I am. I'd put our boy at between six and six-three."

"What about the color of his eyes and his hair, Sherlock?" I said, bound and determined to stop Butch in her impressive tracks.

"Don't know yet." She stretched back out in the lounge chair and locked her fingers together behind her neck. "But he was wearing blue nylon sweatpants."

"Get out!"

"He snagged them on the roses," she said, proudly displaying the abandoned threads, which she had pulled from behind her right ear. "Stick with me, Stick. I'll make a detective out of you yet!"

"Is there a Pulitzer Prize for private investigators?"

"No, not yet."

"Then I'm not interested."

By the time Danny's neighbors arrived in their yellow van, our industrious handyman had replaced a sizable section of the pressed-wood subfloor, torn out most of the ruined drywall, and was nearly finished removing the charred framing lumber. It was depressing to watch, so I thanked Don and

Esther Callahan for fitting us in, excused myself, and went to the Palmetto Plaza for some lunch. The red light on my car phone was flashing when I transferred into the Monte, so after releasing the pop-off axles and stashing first the wheels and then the light orange chair frame in the back, I called the service. It became apparent that I would need to take notes, so I asked the young man on the other end of the line to wait while I grabbed the small notepad on the dashboard.

One call was Peter, and three were from other central Florida reporters, all hoping to scoop me on my own house fire. One call was Stanley Fredericks, another, Detective Henderson, and the last was Eleanor Algretto. I swear I know precisely what Pavlov's laboratory puppies must have felt like when the test bell rang. Just hearing the service operator say Ellie's name made my throat tighten, and no matter where I was when that name came up, I could always smell her perfume just as if she were seated next to me sipping on a lemon-lime soda, resting her left hand on my thigh.

I made all the calls but that one. Maybe it would be easier after lunch. Peter was ready, as it turned out, to tell me all about Shortshire, Ltd. and linear induction motors. I'd forgotten to call him and gloat about finding that out myself, so I let him enjoy his report and thanked him profusely for his efforts. James gave me the real name that went with John Dough and the mailbox place, but said the other telephone research would take a while longer. As it was, the John Dough news was enough for one morning.

"How should I approach this?" I asked the pro over pizza. Agent Stanley Fredericks had agreed to meet me at the mall food court and was thoroughly outraged at the attack on our house and our lives and genuinely intrigued at the latest letterhead revelation.

"Very carefully," he said. "If you had the motor thing, that would help. Even without it, you can still establish delivery. Surely the gizmo had to be signed for. I doubt he's got it at his house, but if he signed off on it, that's almost as good. Who is this Chuck Young guy anyway?"

"Fred MacMurray," I said, handing Stanley my doodled-up copy of the firm's letterhead.

"What?"

"You know, 'My Three Sons'? This guy is the perfect father and husband. Everybody likes him, he works hard without complaining, and he never misses his kids' soccer games."

"Well, I guess that explains why he doesn't have a check mark here on your official suspects list. Just goes to show, it's those nice guys that'll sneak up and get you."

For some reason that I would rather not try to analyze, I never just call Eleanor Algretto. From the moment I think seriously about picking up the car phone, some built-in autopilot system turns the old black Monte Carlo toward west Orlando. Good or bad, that's the way memories are.

"You didn't need to come all the way out."

"I know."

"I'm glad you did," Ellie said. "I've got some gossip for you."

"How's that?"

"The little Three Rs family," she said, unfolding what turned out to be the copy of the firm's letterhead that I'd given her. "I've been snooping around a bit."

Mmm.

"It's really kind of fun, luv, you know? I felt just like Angela Lansbury! I've never really been too comfortable hanging out with Daddy's golfing and tennis set, but if you want the inside story on Orlando's well-to-do, the Rosemont Country Club lounge is a veritable hydroponic hothouse of who's who. For example, did you know that Lester Brown, of Brown, Nealy, Howser & Columbine, and The Old Man were longtime golf buddies?"

I didn't know and shook my head. Small world.

Then Ellie took it from the top, starting with Rosemary Latham.

"Ran three rich husbands through the Big-D Cleaners years ago, Nick. The woman doesn't *need* to try another case, ever. She just gets jazzed by it, big time. If the rumors around the club are true, Rosemary climaxes her ecstatic courtroom foreplay by bedding the youngest, most virile studs she can find. I always wondered why the pool boy and the assistant golf pro smile so much. To hear the talk, you get the distinct impression that Ms. Latham's a legend among many of Rosemont's leisurely ladies of a certain age."

Ellie smiled at the puritanically shocked look on my face, then at the effect of her smile on my facial skin tone. "It's the nineties, luv, and women stopped waiting around for men to tell them what they want years ago!"

"I noticed."

"I'll give you that. Well, Bob Bennet is next. He's a straight arrow; faithful husband, good father, and totally unaware that he is a cuckold. His wife's affair sounds like gospel among the same grapevine stalwarts I've just mentioned."

"With whom was Mrs. Bennet supposedly doing time and a half?"

"I couldn't get a name, but I'm sure they all know. Whoever he was, he got around."

" Was? Got? Does the past tense mean it's over?"

"Could be. I don't know. I couldn't get anything much on Bernard Ketchum, except that he belongs to the Tuskawilla Country Club, out east, as far from his dad's hangout as possible. The rest have all been to functions at the club but aren't members—well, except one. Membership is a perk for partners, but associates have to pay something, I guess."

"That's right. Who's the other member?"

"Chuck Young. He coaches a soccer team—lots of the Rosemont kids—and the club lets him use one of the fields out there for their practices. Everybody speaks well of Chuck and his family, but with that 'they really haven't arrived yet' tone."

"I've heard that before. Well, thanks, Ellie," I said. "There's a bit of news at our end, I'm afraid. It'll be in tonight's paper, but I thought you'd want to know."

Ellie covered her mouth with her hand, and her big brown

eyes watered up in horror as I described our evening in the fiery lakeside money pit.

"Are you both okay?"

"Yes," I said, moved by her deep concern. I slid up one pant leg and showed her the bright red skin where I should have been wearing wet socks. "About like a bad sunburn, that's all."

"That's all? Someone's trying to kill you!"

"So it seems."

"Nick, you've got to go somewhere, both of you."

"We've both got jobs to do. Mine, right now, is to find out who's behind all this. Thanks for helping. It means a lot."

Ellie took my hands in both of hers. Tears ran freely down her cheeks as she fought for control. I reached across the Monte's seat console and pulled her into my arms. With her head buried in my shoulder, she wept, clinging to my neck like a child. What is friendship? I suppose it can be lots of different things, but right there—no matter what else came and went in my life from that point on—I determined to be Eleanor Algretto's friend, whatever that meant. Sam would just have to understand.

THE LAW OFFICES OF

Ketchum, Latham & Bennet, P. A.

221 Lake Eola Drive
Orlando, Florida 32801
(407)555-1975 - FAX (407)555-1999

Rosemary I. Latham	William P. Graham
Robert G. Bennet	H. Russell White
Bernard R. Ketchum	Robert W. Albright
Rebecca H. Forest	Samantha Wagner-Foster
Charles D. Young	Paul W. Kilpatrick

18

"CHUCK?" SAM WAS visibly incredulous.

"Seems a little unlikely to me too," I said, "but you explain it away, counselor."

"I just can't believe it." Sam sat behind her desk, shaking her head. "There must be a mistake."

Through the glass wall across the hall, Paul Kilpatrick was carrying on an animated phone conversation, but the firm's acoustics were deliberately designed to prevent our being able to hear it. "It does explain why his wife got in my face when I called that number," I said. "Having a lawyer for a spouse is a lot like owning a biker or a pit bull."

"Watch it."

"No, really. Somebody calls and gives me grief, I'm just gonna sic you on 'em. Hey! Maybe I could start a new security-protection racket—trained attack lawyers!"

"Clever. So what do we do now?"

"James Henderson is on his way over. You want to sit in as counsel for the defense?"

"I never!" Chuck Young sounded more incredulous than Sam had.

"Mr. Young," Detective Henderson said calmly, "this is

your rental box number, is it not?"

"It certainly is not!" He was emphatic. "Stick . . . Sam," he said, looking at us pleadingly, "do you guys think I had anything to do with any of this?"

"It doesn't matter what we think, Chuck," Sam said sympathetically, "but there's some pretty nasty circumstantial evidence pointing your way. How do *you* explain it?"

"Well, wait," he said, making uncomfortable eye contact with each of us, "let me think. The drop box is easy. First, I do have a real post office box here in Orlando, and I had to fill out paperwork and sign it. Wouldn't these commercial mailbox places have something like that? And whoever runs this place doesn't know me from Adam. I've never even been there! This is nuts!"

"And how do you explain the calls to Shortshire? The order was placed from your home, Mr. Young."

"I don't know how to explain that," Chuck said seriously, "except to say that if I were behind all this, I damn well wouldn't order your what's-it device from my home. Give me some credit."

"I think he's telling the truth, James," I said. I picked up a stray document on the associate's desk and handed it to the detective. "Let's see the signature."

"I'm no expert," Detective Henderson said, "but I don't think this is a match." He placed a copy of the Mail Boxes R Us agreement on the desk next to the legal document I had offered.

"Of course it's not a match!" Chuck said, slapping his hand on the desk. "I've never even seen this form before!"

"So maybe you're not John Dough, but that is your address and phone number, Chuck," Sam said. "Still, I'm afraid I have to agree with you, buddy, you're just not that stupid. Reminds me of that guy who robbed a bank with the note to the teller written on one of his own deposit slips."

"Reminds me of the same guys who would have us believe that Steve Epstein hit himself on the head with a bronze statue," I said, "but the linear induction motor was definitely ordered from inside your house, Chuck. No matter what we may think of her, Ma Bell isn't taking sides in this mess. I'd bet on it. Any ideas about that?"

"We're away a lot," he said, spreading his hands helplessly. "I mean, with the boys' soccer leagues and all. Between Marla and me, we come and go with the boys all the time. We're practically away from the house more than we're there, but I can't see Lester letting a stranger mosey in and use the telephone."

"Lester?" we all said in unison.

"Our komondor," Chuck said. Seeing the blank looks on all our faces, he went on. "It's a big Hungarian sheep dog with fur that looks like braided wool. *Very* territorial. Lester thinks that we're his sheep and the house is his pasture, and I wouldn't want to be the intruder who wandered in on him without us. There's a story about a Komondor that held a burglar by the throat, pinned to the front walk, for almost twenty-four hours until his master came home."

Mmm.

"You want me to what?" I was caught completely off-guard.

"I want you to teach me how to shoot that pistol," Sam said firmly. "I mean, not like shooting out the patio door, but *really* shooting."

James Henderson winced, and I think I blinked stupidly. We were standing in the parking lot behind the firm, comparing notes on our chat with Chuck Young, when Sam's comment came out of the blue. The detective recovered before I did.

"There's an indoor range out in Pine Hills," he said. "It's called The Bullet Hole, and they teach special handgun defense courses just for women."

"Sam," I said, trying to adjust to yet another discovery about my wife, "you won't even kill mice. You're into world peace. I mean, there's an 'Imagine' bumper sticker on your Mustang."

"And look at John Lennon . . . he's dead! I never thought

about it before, but all the good guys end up getting victim-
ized eventually. I won't be a helpless victim! No offense,
James, but all the 'serve and protect' stuff is crap. The police
can't possibly protect us. It's all they can do to make it to the
crime scene when it's all over. I don't want to shoot anyone,
but somebody tried to kill us, and I'm not ready to roll over
and wait for them to get it right the next time. I like my life.
And now that someone's nearly succeeded in taking it away
from me, I'm considerably more inspired to protect it."

What could I say? I'd shot people in self-defense . . . killed
several. It's hard to live with, but *live* is the operative word,
after all. They're gone and I'm still here. If it were the other
way around, how many more murders would those terrorists
have committed in the name of their cause? As with many
of life's hard questions, there's no way of knowing. After Sam
and I ate an early (and peaceful) supper at Angelo's, we visited The Bullet Hole, put a box of 9mm rounds through the
Beretta just to familiarize Sam with its operation, and signed
her up for a handgun safety and self-defense class that met
on Tuesday, Thursday, and Saturday nights. God help the
guy in the Reeboks if he came around Sam's dream house
again.

The Body and Soul Club is downtown Orlando's hippest and
most exclusive health club. There is a minimall in the all-
glass lobby of the stylish skyscraper, and I dropped off a roll
of film at a two-hour processing shop near the elevator before
riding up to the health-food restaurant on the top floor.
Rosemary Latham told me that she takes a two-hour lunch
at Body and Soul every day that she's not in court, and it
was there that she had insisted we meet for the interview I'd
requested. An overly healthy-looking brunet met me the second the elevator doors opened.

"Why, hello, Mr. Foster," she said, flashing a perfect, pearly
smile. "Ms. Latham is expecting you. This way, please."

"Thanks," I said, pushing hard to match her youthful
stride.

The window at Rosemary's table faced west, and the blue peak of Cinderella's Castle at the end of Main Street, Disney World, was clearly visible out and to the south. I had been worried about appropriate dress and found that my fears were well founded, but not in any way I'd imagined. Most of the diners were outfitted for their workouts. Rosemary Latham waved me to the space across from her at the table, where a chair had already been removed. The firm's sexy semisenior partner wore white Nikes with electric blue and pink trim, black nylon shorts, and a skintight electric blue cotton minitop that obviously doubled as a sports bra. I don't think I let my eyes settle anywhere they shouldn't have, but her greeting made me wonder.

"Not bad for thirty-six."

"No," I said diplomatically, uncertain whether she was fantasizing about her age or telling me her bust size.

"I took the liberty of ordering for you," she said. "I'm on a tight schedule. Is marinated turkey breast all right?"

"Fine, thank you. I just wanted to ask you some questions about your firm, and about Brown, Nealy, Howser & Columbine."

"Ask away."

Our interview was, hands down, the most unusual and manipulative I've ever tried to conduct; and, for once, I wasn't the manipulator. Rosemary wolfed down her bean sprouts salad before I'd eaten three bites of my turkey sandwich. The multigrain bread, I was certain, would impact my teeth and my colon for days. We moved our conversation from the trendy dining suite to a private workout room one floor down, where a Stairmaster and a Techtron treadmill faced video screens on opposite walls. A windowed wall between them looked south out at the SunBank building and downtown Orlando.

The shapely shark started with the high-tech treadmill and answered my questions while we "walked" through a wildlife preserve in Kenya to strains from the *Out of Africa* sound track, which came, as nearly as I could tell, out of invisible Surround Sound speakers in the ceiling. The incline of the machine rose and fell beneath her feet automatically as the terrain on the wall screen changed. We moseyed by a herd of curious wildebeest and trekked through a lounging pride of lions who watched us with interest but would not be stirred from their African sunbeams. Rosemary was only slightly flushed when she moved to the Stairmaster and began her trip up a long flight of stone steps that led to a mountaintop German castle. I thought the background music from *Die Walküre* was a bit much. Both workout machines, I noticed, had computers built onto their consoles for the workaholics, but Rosemary Latham seemed perfectly willing to stick to touring and talking and sweating.

"Brown, Nealy, Howser & Columbine is a big-money firm," she said breathlessly, pausing at a scenic overlook high above the Rhine River. "They're on retainer for several of the biggest insurance companies in the country. Sure, they'd do almost anything to win a big one like the Fraiser case. Who wouldn't?"

Mmm.

We never reached Valhalla, but the fourth stage of our interview was altogether too distracting, and Ms. Latham knew it. She'd been looking forward to it, no doubt, and enjoyed every second of my discomfort. At Rosemary's request, I followed her through a nearby door where she stepped behind a small folding room-divider screen and disrobed while she kept talking. She came out dressed only in a white sheet and pushed a button on the wall before climbing onto the table in the middle of the room and lying facedown in front of me.

"I wouldn't put a break-in past them," she went on, "but murder seems pretty unlikely."

Hans arrived promptly, and despite their outwardly discreet greeting, I'd have bet money that Rosemary knew considerably more about the bodybuilding masseur than the fact that he had powerful and talented hands. Neither of them was overly concerned about the shifting sheet, and despite my earnest attempts to keep my nose in my notebook, it was soon clear that Ms. Latham's body was extremely well kept and toned . . . everywhere. And she was visibly pleased that I knew it.

"If you had to guess, who'd most likely be behind a sabotage maneuver?" I asked, wondering what kept Hans's polo shirt from bursting apart at the seams.

"Mad Malcolm Nealy's the firm's wild-boy partner," she said, raising herself up on her elbows and making no attempt to hide her firm breasts, "but they've got dozens of associates. Who knows? They're original equipment," she said with a wink. "Not that I won't help things a bit when the time comes."

"What?" I said stupidly, before the frank change of subject registered fully.

She laughed. At some unseen prompting from Hans, Rosemary turned over on her back, taking far too long to pull the sheet across her perfect nipples. "I love my body," she said, deliberately turning her head to see and enjoy my embarrassed expression. "Especially the effect it has on younger men! Isn't that right, Hans?"

"Yes it is, Ms. Latham."

One of Ellie's favorite K. T. Oslin songs came to mind: "Younger Men Are Starting to Catch My Eye." The room was way too warm, and the pungent smell of tiger oil and sweat did little to help me focus on the last of my questions.

"I was a late bloomer, Stick, and a bookworm," she said. "The boys weren't interested in me back then, and I don't have forever, so I'm enjoying now."

"I can see that," I said. "Now, about a possible accomplice at your firm . . ."

"That's ridiculous. But come, we'll talk more while I shower."

Not!

THE LAW OFFICES OF

Ketchum, Latham & Bennet, P. A.

221 Lake Eola Drive
Orlando, Florida 32801
(407)555-1975 - FAX (407)555-1999

Rosemary I. Latham   William P. Graham
Robert G. Bennet   H. Russell White
Bernard R. Ketchum   Robert W. Albright
Rebecca H. Forest   Samantha Wagner-Foster
Charles D. Young   Paul W. Kilpatrick

19

THE PHOTOGRAPHS OF Steve Epstein's corpse were all too vivid and depressing, a stark metaphor about how life spirals out of control sometimes and sweeps innocent people into its ever-present, but not always visible, maelstrom of malevolence. There are dangers everywhere. Certainly the exhibitionist lawyer of a certain age in the shower a dozen or so floors above me was proof of that. Women in the nineties. It was a whole new ball game. As I rolled out to the Monte Carlo, I pondered the difference between today's ladies and those of the past. Upon reflection, I concluded that the contrasts were far more subtle than I might first have thought. Women could probably always kick men's butts in the end; it's just that they used to have the decency to *pretend* that they couldn't.

"Wagner-Foster."

"Isn't it awkward answering your phone like that?" I asked my favorite barrister.

"Sure," Sam said, "but I don't want you to feel left out. Where are you?"

"Just leaving the Body and Soul Club."

"How'd your talk with Rosemary go?"

"Hot."

"What?"

"Never mind. I'll explain later. Is Steve's wheelchair still around the office?"

"No. I think his sister from Miami took it away the day of his funeral. Why?"

"I don't know for sure. The pictures I took are back, and I'm wishing that I'd looked it over more carefully that day when the cops were done."

"Well, where are we in all this, Sherlock? Any leads?"

"Not really. I'm on my way to an appointment with Lester Brown before I polish off and turn in my story. After that, things could get nasty."

"As if they're not nasty enough already. Well, Scully and I are working late, so hold down the fort until I get home."

"That's what we're paying Butch to do. I wonder if she's discovered anything more about our late-night visitor?"

Brown, Nealy, Howser & Columbine is a *big* law firm. Unlike the modest one-story brick building where Sam and her cronies held forth, the competition leased two floors of the First State Towers building on South Orange Avenue in the heart of downtown Orlando, just blocks, in fact, from Body and Soul. The center of both floors was taken up by reference library rooms, clerical personnel work space, a gaggle of paralegal offices, and a small block of rooms filled with copy machines that were operated not by firm personnel, according to Sam, but by full-time copy machine company employees. The attorneys all had window offices of varying size around the perimeter of each floor. Power Alley at Brown, Nealy, Howser & Columbine was at the corners of each floor. It was in the most resplendent of these corner offices that I found Lester Brown.

"Mr. Foster, come in! Close the door and make yourself comfortable. Coffee?" he asked, pointing to the machine on the window sill behind him.

"Thanks, I'm fine. I won't take much of your time, but you've probably guessed why I'm here."

"Yes indeed!" he said with a laugh. "Two unexplained

deaths at your wife's firm, the police asking questions . . . how could Orlando's favorite hometown sleuth *not* be investigating a newspaper story? But how is it you think I can help you?"

In one sense, the antithesis of Bernard Ketchum, Lester Brown was Santa Claus in a pin-striped suit. All smiles and howdies on the outside. Inside, I felt sure, he was as dangerous—no, I take that back—he was probably more dangerous than Silverspoon had yet dreamed of being. I'd get one shot at this . . . maybe.

"I think we both know the answer to that, Mr. Brown. The question is, *will* you help me? I believe someone or some*ones* at your firm initiated a seemingly harmless act of sabotage that was designed to render impotent the opposing firm's key videotaped presentation. A felony break-in maybe, but not so unusual, perhaps, in the shark-eat-shark world of jurisprudence. A young up-and-comer at your firm, maybe, who wanted to beat the odds and win both an important and lucrative case for the home team and hasten the climb up the firm's letterhead ladder. Maybe a wild-card junior partner, even. Does my story sound like something you want to be publicly associated with?"

He turned a little red in the face and started to respond, but I pushed my wheelchair up alongside his desk—just enough to make him uneasy—and held up my hand.

"Don't answer yet. Hear me out. So this ambitious counselor hatches a truly ingenious plan to erase every videotape in the enemy's library when he or she learns about a compact but high-powered Canadian electromagnet that can be hidden inside the other firm's library. This young lawyer has an almost sophomoric genius for this sort of thing, I think, and actually rigs the device to go off when the other firm's senior partner unknowingly trips the unseen switch. Sort of an ivy league kind of irony, wouldn't you say?"

I rolled up closer, until my knees were next to Lester's and my right elbow rested on his desk while I continued my tale. Santa Claus looked stressed.

"Well," I said, spreading my hands in a gesture of help-lessness at life's harder fates, "did this brilliant tactician also know that the supermagnet would stop a pacemaker in its electronic tracks and drop the other firm's senior partner like a British law tome off a high shelf? Doesn't much matter. Dead is dead, and the sophisticated corporate prank turned into murder, felony manslaughter at the very least. Good story, huh? Wait, there's more."

I pushed my chair up until we were side by side and low-ered my voice. "Well," I went on, placing my right hand on his silk coat sleeve in feigned familiarity, "our worried hero suddenly has some serious track covering to do and endeav-ors to get the magnet right out of Dodge before the marshall returns, and wouldn't you know it, Festus—in the person of a meddling quadriplegic attorney—rolls in and spoils the midnight cover-up. Here is, in my opinion, where we sepa-rate the ivy league law school whiz kids from the professional blue-collar criminals: our preppy prankster panics and bashes in the crippled man's skull. But could you or I have done better in such a pinch? I doubt it," I said, patting his arm as if we were consoling ourselves over the Orlando Magics' loss of a good draft pick. "Bad stuff happens some-times . . . like Watergate, only worse."

Usually it bothers me that an inanimate object like a wheelchair can make some people so uncomfortable. In this case, as it had occasionally in the past, this unfortunate fact of life delighted me. And Scheherazade would have been proud; a lesser storyteller would have long since been thrown out of Lester Brown's spacious corner office.

"What happens next goes way beyond panic, Lester. May I call you Lester? I mean, when our flustered would-be legal eagle legend barricades a nosy reporter and his wife in their home and sets the place on fire, well, Lester, let's be candid, we're talking about a very disturbed individual here. One who's gone so far out on life's dark limb that he or she has not only become a hazard to themselves and others but is on the verge of bringing the wrath of Tallahassee down on the firm in a big, and perhaps unsurvivable, way. Certainly any reputable insurance company, for example, would not wish to be associated with a calamity of this magnitude—at least not one that might be construed to have been in any way condoned by the firm's top partners."

Lester Brown looked like a trapped animal. The pile of accordian file folders on the floor to his left and my bright orange wheelchair on his right walled him in, but I thought for a second that he might actually be considering a spider-like escape across his desk. It was my guess that nobody but a judge talks to a top lawyer like that and gets away with it. Then, even as I paused to catch my breath, the old pro gathered himself up, sloughed off the Santa suit, and started to let his sizable dorsal fin show above the water.

"Do not threaten me, Mr. Foster," he said. "I told the police—"

"Oh, come on, call me Stick. I know exactly what you told the police, Lester. Anyone in your position would certainly deny any knowledge about the linear induction motor and the break-in at Ketchum, Latham and Bennet, and that's all fine and dandy. You have legitimate interests to protect here, after all," I said, waving my hand at the panoramic view of Orlando, "but between you and me, I think you're going to have to act pretty quickly on this. You know, take sides. I understand that it's customary to deny everything, let things die down, and then quietly drop the offending associate's name from the firm's letterhead, but that just won't get it this time, Lester. This time, somebody tried to kill *me*. But it's up to you, Lester. I think Spike Lee said it best: 'Do the right thing.' "

Life's not a movie, and Lester Brown is not the kind of individual who would in this or any other lifetime spill his guts to a pushy reporter, even a pushy reporter in a wheelchair. All I could do was hope that he'd make up his mind to do the right thing—at least as much of the right thing as any lawyer can. Anyway, when he told me that if my theory was

correct (and he hastened to add that he "wasn't admitting
that it was"), he would not protect the party or parties responsible, I believed him. For the moment.

On my way home I called Detective Henderson and shared
what little new information I had, particularly Rosemary
Latham's comment about Malcolm Nealy.

"In the end," I said, "she and Brown are going to protect
their firms' reputations by cutting the guilty parties loose,
but they're certainly not going to work overtime turning over
the necessary rocks to find them. It's up to you and me,
James."

"I think the D.A. can establish enough probable cause
with Butch's footprints and sweat suit fibers to get us some
search warrants," the detective said, "but I'd rather narrow
down the field some. Of course, it could be a team deal, I
mean more than just one person at each law firm. And I've
been thinking," he went on, "we've been sitting on this, but
didn't you say you were turning in a story today?"

"On my way," I said. "Be in tomorrow's paper."

"Well, how about I try to hold a news conference here in
the morning, about the same time the paper comes out? No
intimate details, but enough so whoever tried to toast you
and Sam can see that it's too late to cover it all up by dis-
posing of one pesky reporter."

"Good idea, James. I'm for anything that might take these
red and white circles off our backs."

"Okay, that's settled then. Now, have you come up with
anything on the picture taker?"

"No. Actually, I forgot about that in all the high drama of
late."

"Well, it's a very disconcerting loose end because it just
doesn't seem to fit in to the scheme of things anywhere. And
as you say, other more menacing perils demand priority at
the moment, but I just don't like these incongruous little
fun facts."

"You're a tidy guy, James. What can I say?"

*　*　*

Shortshire, Ltd., faxed us pictures and illustrations of the linear induction motor, which enhanced my Saturday morning story about Old Man Ketchum's death rather nicely. Without mentioning any particular case or any other firm's name, I made it clear that there must have been outside and inside collusion involved. The morning paper and Detective Henderson's news conference brought the media magnifying glass down on the whole drama, and as the choices were relatively narrow, and the stakes were so high, I had little doubt that the berserker sharks would be caught. Even though it was a weekend, the local television stations had a field day with the videotape destruction angle, and interviewed several heart specialists about pacemaker technology and its relationship to electromagnets.

All in all, it was a great scoop with great potential; still, I wanted the guy who tried to kill us. It was personal. I put myself in his place. The day's media circus would have been more than enough to make me run, fast and far. I could almost picture the conspirators frantically making their getaway plans. If only I could listen in . . .

Good night, nurse!

I dropped the paper, turned off the TV, and dug the pictures of Steve Epstein out of my new backpack. Yes! I suddenly knew what the tiny but strangely familiar gray object protruding out of the side pocket on Steve's electric wheelchair was—the tip of a rubber-coated antenna. Snatching up the portaphone, I rolled out the front door and down the driveway to the street. When I was two houses away, I pushed the button and watched the little red scanner light dance across the ten-channel selector once, then lock on and give me a dial tone. I held the phone against my ear with my shoulder and pushed my wheelchair farther down the street. By the next mailbox, there was noticeable static, and by the next driveway, the dial tone cut out. I turned the phone off, rolled back to my neighbor's mailbox, and pushed the button again. The red light searched a little longer this time, but eventually locked on and produced a dial tone. I called the firm, where the F team had been at it since dawn.

"Sam!" I said when she eventually picked up her extension. "I'm calling from the Pattersons'!"

"Well, gee, Stick, that's wonderful. Why are you interrupting us to tell me that? Are our phones out again?"

"No," I said triumphantly, "I'm calling you with *our* phone!"

"That's terrific, babe, now can I go back to work?"

"You don't get it, do you? I'm out in the street in front of the Pattersons', calling you on our portable phone, the same phone every stinkin' member of your firm got in the mail a few months ago. If I were sitting down the street from Chuck Young's house right now, I could be calling you, or Canada, on his line. See? Whoever bought these phones could make calls on any of our lines without ever coming into our houses. He just needed to park down the street!"

"Oh."

"Good comeback, Sam. Now, think about this. Right now, with the media coverage and all, the bad apples are probably getting ready to bail out of the bushel basket and roll for their lives, and if we're lucky we can use their own technology against them. It's time to rally the troops!"

589 SOUTH PALM WAY
POST OFFICE BOX 13272
DAYTONA BEACH, FL 32122
(904)555-7623
FAX (904)555-2267

4218 BISCAYNE BLVD.
POST OFFICE BOX 69912
MIAMI, FL 33116
(305)555-2011
FAX (305)555-4144

255 S. ORANGE AVE.
POST OFFICE BOX 2234
ORLANDO, FL 32801
(407)555-0078
FAX (407)555-6601

Warren B. Adams
J. Leslie Baker
Lester M. Brown
John B. Columbine
Susan D. Cramer
William T. Croft
David S. Forrester
Adam W. Goldenbaum
David J. Howser

Sarah M. Hunter
Andrew S. Johnson
F. Stanley Larson
Howard C. Madison
Jay A. McKnight
David B. Maine
Sandy E. Martin
C. Wayne Milroy
Elizabeth D. More

Malcolm W. Nealy
Arthur F. Orser
Nancy B. Peterson
H. Mark Petrakis
Anne M. Porter
David A. Roberts
Jonathan T. Rude
Michael H. Seidman
Sally T. Solomon

J.D. Tanner
William D. Toomey
John W. Tucker
Peter W. VanHorn
Ramsey L. Walker
Gow J. Wang
Mary L. Wayne
Francis C. Wills
Toni R. Young

20

I CALLED SEVERAL members of the Orlando Orange Wheels wheelchair basketball team, Danny Kincade, Ernest Boyle, and—almost as an afterthought—Eleanor Algretto. All of them volunteered immediately, and yes, Ellie could get me the address for the "mad" man at Brown, Nealy, Howser & Columbine. After giving them instructions about where to meet me, I called a number of local electronic appliance stores while I drove and stopped at one of them on my way into town. Even Stanley Fredericks agreed that if my telephone theory was correct, it was an FBI matter. He promised to run the names and get back to me. The *Sentinel* called me on my car phone to say that a mysterious "someone" had dropped an envelope on my desk with "important" written under my name. I detoured to retrieve it and was rewarded for my efforts. The single sheet inside had six words typed across the center: *You should have been a lawyer.*

More significant than the unsigned commentary was the fact that the paper itself was a piece of Brown, Nealy, Howser & Columbine stationery. I noticed right away that this firm did not use its letterhead to advertise the rank of its partners and associates, though certainly every shark down the line knew exactly where they swam. Instead, their names were listed alphabetically. At first, there appeared to be nothing else of note on the big firm's extensive letterhead, but closer examination revealed faint question marks written very lightly with a sharp pencil next to three of the names on the list . . . Malcolm W. Nealy, C. Wayne Milroy, and Jonathan T. Rude. Lester Brown was doing the right thing.

"How do you know?" Detective Henderson asked when I got him on the phone.

"I can't tell you, James, but get these search warrants if you can."

"I need something, Stick, some evidence to give a judge. Any other day, maybe. But it's Saturday morning and they're all probably watching cartoons. I can't just interrupt something that important because Stick Foster says so!"

"You're a riot, you are," I said, realizing, of course, that he was right. "Any chance you'll give me your pager number?"

"Sure, why?"

"I may need to reach you in a hurry."

"Care to tell me what you're up to, Stick?"

"I'd better not, just in case it's illegal."

"You're right. I don't want to know."

James Henderson gave me his pager number and hung up, but not before saying, "Good luck."

My next call was to Sam. She wasn't happy about being interrupted again and didn't think it was a good idea that I stop by. The Fraiser team was terribly busy. Monday morning's settlement conference, she reminded me curtly, was coming up fast. Considering the fact that I was already pulling into a parking space in the firm's lot, her opinion on the matter seemed academic. She reluctantly agreed to bring Scully and meet me at the car.

"Tell them I need Scully's help with my chair," I said. "And be cool."

Scully knew I was up to something and could barely control the grin that threatened to break out across his face. He lumbered to my trunk and went through the motions of retrieving my toolbox and fiddling with the axles and spokes of one of my wheels while I sat behind the Monte's steering wheel and outlined my plan.

"I'll try to keep Silverspoon and Rosemary busy for a few minutes," I said. "You guys get on the phones and try to locate each of the other seven—Bob Bennet and the other associates. If they answer their phones, just hang up. We only want to know where they are right now. Think of a legitimate question to ask if you have to talk to wives or husbands. You know, 'I need to talk to Becky about the Bilge-water Brief,' whatever. Make it nonthreatening, okay? As soon as you're done, put a list in my car and let me know somehow, so I can wrap it up with Beauty and the Beast and get out of here. Oh, and I need everybody's street address."

"What's going on?" Scully said. "I have the feeling I'm gonna miss something fun today, eh?"

"Maybe," I said, "but if either or both of those two get a phone call and bug out of here in a hurry, try to follow them discreetly and let me know. I'll be in the car."

Suddenly Scully laughed as he glanced past me at the pile of boxes on the floor in front of the passenger seat. "Rip off the phone store, Stick?" he said with a chuckle. Then recognition spread across his face. "Hey! It's that phone we all got in the mail! So you're the ones who sent them out. How come?"

"We didn't send them out, Scully, but I'm going to find out who did. When I do, odds are that I'll know who's responsible for The Old Man's death." I flipped over the orange rigid-framed wheelchair Scully had been tinkering with and transferred into it. "Let's go."

Rosemary and Silverspoon weren't happy about my interruption either, but neither wanted to appear overtly rude and/or evasive in front of the other.

"Someone high up at Brown, Nealy, Howser & Columbine is spilling their guts," I began, hoping that by focusing on the enemy camp first, I might get a better look at the defenses here at Sam's firm. "Three possible saboteurs have been named, and warrants shouldn't be far behind. But, unless I miss my guess, there'll be a lot of buck passing going on if they get caught."

"And?" Rosemary said when I paused to watch their expressions.

"Well, apparently the partner's feeling was that if he assisted in the investigation, it would look lots better for the firm when things hit the fan. I understand lawyers rank pretty low in the popularity polls as it is, so a little good PR in a crisis couldn't hurt, right?"

"And you want us to spill our guts about the traitor in our firm," Bernard said with sarcasm. "Well, if we did know anything about it, we'd tell the police, not you."

"I might tell him," Rosemary said with a wink, "but honestly, we don't know who, if anyone, at our firm might be involved in this mess, and that someone here would kill either The Old Man or Stephen, even involuntarily, is unthinkable."

"I understand that's your official stand, but unofficially, surely you must have a gut feeling or two about who might sell you out on the Fraiser case?"

Rosemary Latham gave me a patronizing smile but remained silent. Bernard Ketchum's look of distaste actually softened.

"Look, Mr. Foster, I'm sorry that someone burned your house—"

"Tried to kill us!"

"Okay, tried to kill you. And though I hate to admit it, I think you're right about that magnetic device killing my old man. Certainly Stephen Epstein was murdered. And when the police figure out who's responsible, I'll see to it that they're prosecuted to the full extent of the law—*especially* anybody at this firm who's involved. But I will *not* speculate about it to you."

Mmm. Why wasn't I surprised? "Have it your way," I said, trying to think of relevant time-killing conversation to throw at the stone wall before me. I was about to ask something really lame about golfing partners when Scully saved me.

"We have real jobs here, Foster," he boomed as he barged into the conference room. "I ain't your mechanic, and my esteemed colleagues, though far too benevolent toward the physically challenged to say so to your face, would like you to go away now. *Comprende?*"

"*Comprendo*," I said trying to shrug instead of sighing with relief. "Even if you guys don't want to talk to me," I said as I turned my wheelchair back toward the door, "think about what I said. The Fraiser case isn't the only important thing that happens at this firm. Maybe nobody's trying to kill the two of you, but they're sure compromising the day-lights out of your firm." As I rolled out past Mrs. Lady Luck Sulla, I reached up and polished her cool right breast, once for The Old Man whose heart she'd broken, and once for the young quadriplegic for whom she'd fallen in a big way.

Sam and I passed in the hall, where I got an un-enthusiastic thumbs up, and she got my whispered thanks. On the passenger seat of the Monte I found two scribbled-up sheets of firm stationery. Targets acquired.

"Hey, Stick!" a wheelchair basketballer hollered as I drove into the lot at the Steak & Shake on East Colonial Drive. "Haven't we done this before? Déjà vu all over again!"

"Well, now that you mention it," I called back, pulling the Monte into a space near the knot of familiar cars, "I guess maybe we did."

My memories of that team effort suddenly came back full force. I caught up with the two killers I was looking for that day and, in a gunfight that still occasionally haunts my dreams in tediously slow motion, I shot them both . . . but not before I took a .38 slug in the leg and Peter Stilles's brother, Phil, was shot to death. Today's drama, I hoped, would fall far short of that.

THE LAW OFFICES OF

Ketchum, Latham & Bennet, P. A.

221 Lake Eola Drive
Orlando, Florida 32801
(407)555-1975 - FAX (407)555-1999

Rosemary I. Latham	William P. Graham
Robert G. Bennet	H. Russell White
Bernard R. Ketchum	Robert W. Albright
Rebecca H. Forest	Samantha Wagner-Foster
Charles D. Young	Paul W. Kilpatrick

21

In THE IMMORTAL words of Hannibal Smith, I love it when a plan comes together. But then, don't we all? Past glories aside, this particular plan didn't get off to a very promising start. In my haste and excitement, I overlooked a key ingredient in making my ingenious stratagem work. No sooner had I handed out the portable phones and demonstrated the scanner feature, than my helpful squad members began to pipe up.

"Park between eighty and one hundred feet away," I was saying, "and make sure the ringer is turned on. Any call they get will buzz you. Otherwise, scan them briefly every couple of minutes to see if they're calling out."

"Hey, Stick," Danny Kincade said, "did you charge these batteries?"

"What's that?"

"Yeah," Ernest Boyle added with a laugh, "the instructions say you've got to charge up these batteries for several hours before you can use these things. Mine's dead!"

"Mine too! Good goin', Stick!" called Joe Stetler, the Wheels' double-amputee player-coach. "Another shot, another brick!"

Amid the laughter and the catcalls, I remembered that,

indeed, Sam and I had not been able to use our mystery gift phone until one of its two rechargeable batteries had been juiced up in the Sony's base unit. Well, I can drop back and punt as well as the next guy, so as Ellie, Ernest, and Danny collected the telephones and returned them to my car, I briefed everyone on their destinations and promised to bring them each a phone as soon as the batteries were charged up.

"In the meantime, if your target person leaves their location, follow them if you can—discreetly—and call me at your first opportunity. I'll be around in a couple of hours."

I got more ribbing as the motorcade poured out of the Steak & Shake lot. Ernest was assigned to Malcolm Nealy's house, so I gave him my phone. Danny took a phone with no battery and said he'd drive by our house and pull the fully charged battery out of our base unit in the living room before heading out to Jon Rude's neighborhood. As I watched them leave, a cold chill ran down my back and I shuddered one of those shudders that rattles your teeth, but you try not to let anyone see. Some of these same people followed me out of this parking lot once before. I screwed up that day too . . . and one of them died.

"It's okay," Ellie said as she pulled by me on her way to Chuck Young's street. "It's a great idea, even if it is probably illegal. I'd never have thought of it. Wait, didn't you say that Chuck's a low-odds priority? Why not let me help you get these hooked up and cooking? Then, when they're ready, I'll help you pass them out before I head west."

I had to swallow hard and catch a breath before I could respond. Even then it was difficult. "Good thinking, El," I managed. "Thanks."

"It'll be okay," she said, reaching across the space between our cars to touch my arm. "I'll follow you."

Keep your head down.

We stopped briefly at the hardware store on our way to the armory where the Orlando Orange Wheels held their weekly practices. There, I bought several of those multiplug outlet expanders. I used Sam's key to the armory gym, and Ellie and

I then got eight base unit rechargers going, four at one location and four at another. Little red lights soon announced that the battery charging had officially commenced. Eight additional batteries—gray, each about the size of one of those miniature matchboxes—sat stacked nearby, awaiting their turn in the recharger.

"A minor setback," Ellie said, resting her hand on my shoulder before lowering herself to the lobby floor and leaning back against the wall. "No big deal."

"Thanks, but I should have thought of it . . . you know, when everything else fails, read the instructions?"

"You're preoccupied," Ellie said.

"An attempt on your life can do that," I said. "I *really* want these guys, whoever they are. Think about it, El. Lawyers aren't generally known for their integrity, of course, but this? Sam once told me, 'It doesn't matter what's right or wrong so much as what you can convince a jury they *must* do under the circumstances.' That sucks. And these guys wanted to win so badly—worse, they wanted to protect a negligent manufacturer and its insurance carrier so badly—they were willing to kill four people in the process! They just can't get away with it."

We sat in silence for several minutes, watching the little red charging indicator lights and thinking our own thoughts. I remembered a verse my dad quoted often when he was faced with dishonesty, and I repeated it out loud.

" 'I said in my haste, All men are liars.' "

"It sure seems that way," Ellie said softly. "Where's that from?"

"The Book of Psalms somewhere."

"Ever read any of Molière's plays? In *Le Misanthrope*," she said without waiting for an answer, "there's a great line that I used to know. Let's see. 'If everyone were clothed with integrity, if every heart were just, frank, kindly, the other virtues would be well-nigh useless, since their chief purpose is to make us bear with patience the injustice of our fellows.' "

Ouch.

*   *   *

There'd been no signs of panicked activity at any of the target acquisition sites by the time Ellie and I delivered the half-charged batteries. (The second set, we decided, would be fully charged before the first ones gave out.) Ernest reported that Malcolm Nealy had arrived home from somewhere a short while after the mall maintenance man had taken up his position down the street in the well-manicured west Orlando neighborhood. Jon Rude, according to Danny Kincade's report, had just finished mowing his Winter Park lawn. Hardly a sign of guilt and panic. Wayne Milroy answered his phone when I'd placed a bogus sales call earlier in the morning, but Joe Stetler hadn't seen hide nor proverbial hair of him outside his Tudor-style Londonderry Hills home. Something was wrong.

No names other than that of Sam's firm and those now departed members of it had been used, but my article and all the subsequent media attention had laid out the evidence pretty clearly. Orlando's famous Saturday radio call-in show was buzzing with calls about the bizarre tale of sabotage, evidence tampering, and murder.

"What do you think, Dave?" Orlando radio personality Barry Norringer asked his latest caller. "Would a lawyer in our fair city kill two people and try to kill two others just to win a case in court?"

"Well, Barry, it's like they say: What do you do if you've got Charlie Manson, Saddam Hussein, and a lawyer all against the firing wall, but your gun's only got two bullets in it?"

The talk show host played along. "I don't know. What *do* you do if you've got Charlie Manson, Saddam Hussein, and a lawyer all against the firing wall, but your gun's only got two bullets in it?"

"You shoot the lawyer twice."

"I take that as a yes vote," Barry said with a laugh. "Thanks for your call. Hello, Sarah? You're on Week's End Talk. If you'd just turn down your radio, we'll see if we can't hash out this crooked lawyer stuff . . ."

I hadn't heard too many calls, but one thing was obvious: none of the talk radio crowd seemed to doubt for a minute that a lawyer would cross the lines that had been crossed at the law offices of Ketchum, Latham & Bennet. Though the public knew nothing about the specific case involved and had no idea what firm had gone to such great lengths to beat a lawsuit, everyone in the know was watching Brown, Nealy, Howser & Columbine to see which way the dorsal fins would scatter. I pulled into Heardon Airport and drove out toward the back hangars, hoping I wasn't too late.

I was relieved to find that Brown, Nealy's new Beech 400A Jayhawk business jet was getting a bath when I pulled up. The sleek flying machine, a Mitsubishi design, had been purchased by Beech back in the eighties. I knew a Beech crew chief who was part of the acquisition team that went to visit the Japanese factory when the transfer took place, and his analysis of the whole affair was sadly hilarious.

"Beech wants a business jet, right?" he said. "So do they design one? No, too easy. They buy one the Japanese want to quit production on for reasons that I'm sure will become painfully clear to us all too soon. And our polite little hosts," the six-foot-six Wichita native went on, "had one heck of a good time at our expense. I didn't want to go in the first place, and I never want to go back. These guys' idea of rip-roaring fun was feeding the stupid Americans live and/or raw fish by-products, pouring sake down our throats, and making us sing for the natives at their juvenile karaoke bars. You don't have to understand Japanese to know how little they think of us, especially of our lazy-ass workers."

"Hi," I said to the high school–aged girl who was using a pole-handled scrub brush to soap down the jet's starboard side. "Somebody taking this baby out today?"

"Not that I know of," she said. "I wash planes every Saturday."

"Does this one fly much?"

"I don't know, really. Sometimes a bunch of wire-rimmed preppy types take it to the islands over the weekend, so it's not here to wash. Mackie, the guy who manages this hangar, says it goes to Miami a lot during the week, but I wouldn't know about that."

I left her to her work, drove the Monte several hundred feet, and pulled up under a shade tree near the chain-link fence that runs along the small airport's east boundary. If the young woman felt awkward about my surveillance, she didn't let it affect her work. So I waited, and I watched, and I thought. At least two people were in very big trouble. The kind of trouble that could not only destroy a legal career but likely land a body on death row. Even a body with competent legal representation.

Between telephone checks with my motley surveillance team, arranging for evening shift changes, and circulating freshly charged batteries, the rest of the day went pretty quickly. Sunday was another matter. The idea of catching bad guys, especially lawyer bad guys, was fun and exciting for a while, but by TV sports time on Sunday afternoon, the thrill of the hunt was wearing thin for most of my troops. This was especially true in light of the fact that none of our suspects did or said anything out of the ordinary all weekend. My cinematic visions of racing my Monte Carlo SS down the runway after the escaping corporate jet gave way to grave doubts not only about my logic but about my understanding of human nature.

THE LAW OFFICES OF

Ketchum, Latham & Bennet, P. A.

221 Lake Eola Drive
Orlando, Florida 32801
(407)555-1975 - FAX (407)555-1999

Rosemary I. Latham	William P. Graham
Robert G. Bennet	H. Russell White
Bernard R. Ketchum	Robert W. Albright
Rebecca H. Forest	Samantha Wagner-Foster
Charles D. Young	Paul W. Kilpatrick

22

"**N**O WAY!"

"Yes way, babe. They'll be here. You can bank on it."

It was a weary Monday morning, and James Henderson, Scully, Danny Kincade, Ernest Boyle, and Butch Grady all looked on sympathetically while Sam patiently explained the meaning of life to her well-intentioned but cognizantly impaired husband. We were sitting in the courthouse hallway, waiting for the rest of the Fraiser team and, more importantly, their counterparts from Brown, Nealy, Howser & Columbine. We civilians *might* be allowed to sit in, we were told, as we were material witnesses in the related destruction of evidence matter—something about "improper conduct collateral to the case." Sam was in full agreement that the guilty party or parties from Brown, Nealy were most likely members of that firm's Fraiser team, but we'd parted company radically on the issue of whether or not said perpetrators would show up, business as usual, for the pretrial settlement conference with the Honorable Vinnie "the Dragon" Baker presiding.

"These guys aren't suicidal," I insisted. "First, they screwed up their sabotage—"

"They don't know that," Sam said.

"Maybe not, but they know we know what they did. Their magnet's been in the paper and on TV, for Pete's sake!"

"An illustration of *a* magnet," Sam corrected me. "Not *their* magnet. It's all about evidence, babe, and we don't got none."

She was right about that. I knew it and I hated it. But did *they* know it? I still couldn't believe that anyone, even a lawyer, would have the brass to march into court after what had happened in and around this case thus far. Naturally, I was wrong.

The minute he swept into the hallway, I knew he was Malcolm Nealy. And I knew he was the one. Associates, paralegals, and related vassals washed along in his wake, and he spoke down to all of them at once as he issued commands with terse words and definitive snapping gestures of his left hand. The air around the man seemed to hover apologetically, begging his mercy should it somehow inconvenience him by its very existence in his space. He flashed a not-quite-civil smile at Silverspoon, ignored Rosemary Latham altogether, and made an almost imperceptible appraisal of my wife as he breezed past. The corners of his mouth and eyes turned up in the subtlest of grins as he glided into the judge's chambers through a door that had somehow magically opened before him.

Growing up with a good man, a man whose heart was as pure and guileless as any human being's can be, made me sensitive to what Obi-Wan Kenobi would call "the dark side of the force." Men and women who have no moral substance in their souls make my skin crawl, even from a distance, and I can usually look into their eyes and tell what isn't inside almost at once. I'd shot men who weren't nearly as evil as this man, and if the appropriate opportunity arose, I felt certain that I wouldn't hesitate to shoot Malcolm Nealy. This man had tried to kill us while we slept. I was sure of it. If there had been any doubt in my mind or heart about my snap judgment, Ernest Boyle would have erased it. He grabbed my shoulder and held me back until everyone else had followed Nealy's team into the Dragon's lair.

"He's dangerous," Ernest whispered. "I saw men like that in 'Nam who'd cut their buddies' throats while they slept, just because they were pissed off about the weather."

"Thanks, Ernest," I said, turning my wheelchair toward the door. "I feel lots better now."

Judge Vinnie "the Dragon" Baker is dangerous too. A relaxed-looking man with a quick wit, he knows the law, knows its failings, and does his best to make it work, at least when it tries to run amok in his courtroom. The nickname had been given him by a long-ago lawyer I might have liked—another fan of J.R.R. Tolkien. In *The Hobbit*, Bilbo Baggins used a ring that made him invisible to sneak into the lair of Smaug, a dragon of great renown and incredible wealth. The young hobbit learned the hard way that just because a dragon's eyes are closed, it is never safe to assume that he is sleeping. Many lawyers learned that same lesson in Judge Baker's courtroom. Though their hair was not actually singed by flaming dragon's breath like Bilbo Baggins's, it's rumored that the painful tongue-lashings Judge Vinnie Baker inflicted made them wince nonetheless.

"I wasn't aware we would have Ringling Brothers, Barnum & Bailey all here with us today," the Dragon was saying when I tried to squeeze my wheelchair into his chambers. "Let's move into the conference room next door, people."

Everyone but Malcolm Nealy shuffled, nudged, and excused their way around the judge's desk and followed him through the dark, paneled door in the back of his office. Nealy's minions cleared a path for their demigod, of course, and had they gone a step further, spreading palm fronds in his path, I wouldn't have been the least bit surprised. Judge Baker motioned to places around the long oval table and, as he did so, noticed me for the first time.

"Mr. Foster," he said with a firmness that brooked no familiarity, "I understand that you are here as a witness of sorts, and I read your article in the paper, but I must insist that everything you hear in this settlement conference be considered strictly confidential. Is that understood?"

"Yes, Your Honor."

"Good. Now, Bernard, before I ask you to introduce the rest of your menagerie and present your angle on this thing, I want to say a few words about your dad. He was a fine attorney. A bit too theatrical at times for my taste, but he did his homework and he served his clients well. I'm really sorry about what happened, whether Mr. Foster's spin on the tragedy is correct or not. You've got some big shoes to fill, Bernard, and I wish you luck. Now, in as far as the matter of Fraiser et al., I understand that it is your position that evidence has been destroyed?"

"Potential evidence, Your Honor," Silverspoon said. "The video presentation destroyed by the electromagnetic device discovered in our office wouldn't necessarily be admitted as evidence in court. Unless, of course, Brown, Nealy attempted to coach the defendants into changing their stories."

"I object to these groundless insinuations," Malcolm Nealy said with precision, dismissing everything Bernard had said with a distinctive twitch of his wrist. "It's clear to me that Junior doesn't have a case. And, unlike his illustrious father, he can't seem to conjure one up out of smoke and mirrors. I don't know what, if anything, actually happened inside their firm, or what mischief a disgruntled employee might loose there on any given day, but if there is any further suggestion that our firm has acted outside the law, I will file charges both in civil court and before the Florida bar."

"Don't get your dander up, Malcolm," the Dragon said softly. "You'll get your turn."

"I'm sorry, Your Honor, but you yourself just acknowledged that Ketchum, Latham & Bennet has a history of showboating, and I suggest that this elaborate yet clumsy fiasco is just more of the same."

"Your observation is so noted," Judge Baker said with a sigh. "Now shut up until I give you the floor. Bernard?"

The man's demeanor was as cool, calm, calculated, and collected as any I'd ever seen. He had just announced to everyone in the room that the death of The Old Man and the murder of Stephen Epstein were, as far as he was concerned, no more than gimmicks, scenarios orchestrated somehow to enhance the plaintiff firm's case . . . and no one had batted an eye.

I looked for some sign of a response on Silverspoon's face, but there was none. He was totally focused on his presentation. After briefly introducing those of us in his entourage, Bernard Ketchum took a videotape out of his briefcase and walked over to the television monitor in the corner.

"Your Honor," he said, "despite the fact that a person or persons illegally entered the firm of Ketchum, Latham & Bennet, installing a hidden electromagnetic device, which killed my father and erased several months' worth of work on Anthony Fraiser's case, and despite the fact that these unnamed individuals later returned, removing the device and murdering Stephen Epstein, I am pleased to report that it will not be necessary to bury you in documents at this time. Fortunately, the studio where this video was produced and edited had not yet destroyed all the individual dubbing copies. Our staff and theirs' have worked around the clock to reassemble this presentation. It will speak for itself."

And speak it did. This time I was watching Mad Malcolm Nealy's face. There should have been a flicker of surprise when the videotape he'd so cleverly eliminated reappeared before his eyes. But there wasn't. If he was surprised, troubled, disappointed, and/or pissed off, there was no sign of it on Malcolm's face; in fact, it was difficult to tell whether he was listening to Silverspoon or watching the video at all. His posture, his composure, his presence, all said there was no cause for alarm. He might have been looking at the judge, but it seemed to me more like Malcolm was daydreaming about the weekend just past.

His compatriots were not so aloof. They sat still enough, obviously ordered. upon pain of death to do so, but as the devastating tape graphically played out the chilling story of the young family man whose life had been cut short by their client's negligence and greed, their eyes told anyone watching that they didn't want to try this case. They didn't want to be in the room. Their eyes also told me that they knew it didn't matter what they wanted or didn't want. The moment Lester Brown and the other partners at Brown, Nealy, Howser & Columbine assigned this case to Mad Malcolm and them to his team, their fates had been sealed. These, ironically enough, were rats who could not jump ship. Their little rat ankles were shackled to the rowing bench, and Mad Malcolm was resolutely beating out the ramming cadence. The frail wooden galley of their present corporate lives was about to run into a modern battleship. So why was Malcolm so unconcerned?

"The Battle Hymn of the Republic" played softly while a huge American flag blew regally in the wind, superimposed in the sky behind the decorated grave that marked Anthony Fraiser as a veteran reservist who had served his country in Granada, Panama, Iraq, and Somalia. Pictures from his family photo album flashed and then faded around the dead man's headstone, and then it was over. There was a long silence in the courthouse conference room after the video-taped case summary ended. The television screen crackled and hissed softly as a maelstrom of bluish snow tried futilely to drift into the warm, still room. I fought the urge to shut off the VCR, aware that Silverspoon was milking the long seconds for all they were worth. The members of Mad Malcolm's defense team were sweating, profusely. All of them, of course, except the firm's number two partner and present defense team leader.

"The man's death is most unfortunate," Mad Malcolm said as he rose, casually flicked off the video equipment, and addressed the Dragon directly, "but it has little or nothing to do with my client or the alleged difficulties on the assembly line, regardless of what the preceding *cinéma noir* might suggest. The production is truly inspiring; worthy, I am sure, of consideration at this year's Cannes film festival. It is, I submit, like most quote/unquote *reality* television, primarily a work of fiction. As is the case with most tabloid journalism, there is just enough truth buried within to allow the viewer to suspend belief, at least momentarily. Were it to be viewed by a jury in a public courtroom, however, this video would be required to display the same disclaimer that precedes any novel and/or film: 'All the characters and events portrayed in this work are fictitious. Any similarity to actual individuals or events is purely coincidental.' It lacks, Your Honor, what Paul Harvey might call 'the rest of the story.'

"As my esteemed colleagues at Ketchum, Latham & Bennet have rightly pointed out, an assembly problem was caught by my client's quality-control department. We will show, however, that the testimony of the assembly-line employees is false. Further, we will provide definitive testimony from considerably more representative and reliable company employees that those same disgruntled line workers whose testimony you have just seen and heard actually discussed, planned, and then carried out an act of industrial sabotage as a means of protest following an unsuccessful vote to unionize the company's work force. Additionally," Malcolm went on smoothly as his minions handed documents to Judge Baker, "what my colleagues failed to show you, Your Honor, is the testimony and the documentation showing that the mechanical complication caused by the malicious actions of these former employees was carefully and completely corrected before the exerccycle ever left the factory."

Mad Malcolm was mesmerizing. He was as good as the video—better. He was real. Standing there in the flesh, playing on our natural cynicism toward the boob tube and everything on it, he was turning the plaintiff's case inside out, effortlessly. His team rallied visibly at the very sound of his voice. I hated him. I wanted to stand and shut his lying mouth—permanently. Judge Baker probably hated Malcolm too (who wouldn't?), but he was nodding his head, taking the foul documents being offered him and nodding his confounded head. If, for one moment, he gave credence to even one word from this devil's mouth, then justice was as blind as the poets allege. I was livid. I wanted to shout, to break the spell. Then, when I noticed the look of awe and professional respect in Sam's eyes as she watched her "colleague" weave his spell, I wanted to cry. Cry, and rip Mad Malcolm's lungs out. Not necessarily in that order.

THE LAW OFFICES OF

Ketchum, Latham & Bennet, P. A.

221 Lake Eola Drive
Orlando, Florida 32801
(407)555-1975 - FAX (407)555-1999

Rosemary I. Latham
Robert G. Bennet
Bernard R. Ketchum
Rebecca H. Forest
Charles D. Young

William P. Graham
H. Russell White
Robert W. Albright
Samantha Wagner-Foster
Paul W. Kilpatrick

23

Scully RECOVERED FIRST. In retrospect, it was ironic, almost funny, a grizzly bear of a paralegal jerking to his feet and lumbering to intercept one of Malcolm's rats—who had, by this time, fully recovered her zeal for rowing. At the time, however, my emotions were too far gone to recognize the humor. Scully ripped several documents from his startled counterpart's hands and waved them at the judge.

"This *evidence*," he said, his deep voice booming in the glass-and-mahogany room, "*if* it is genuine, was not surrendered during discovery. We specifically requested, and were assured we had been provided with, *all* company records relating to the manufacture and sale of their last year's product line. I respectfully request that you strike their defense."

"Mr., ah, Scully?" the Dragon said, glancing at the legal pad on the table in front of him. "Your zeal is most commendable, and your point is well taken, but I would remind you that this is not a courtroom. We're just having a friendly chat in order to see whether we can settle this business *without* going to court, so, until you pass the bar, how about we leave the lawyering to the lawyers?"

The limping bear grimaced as he returned to his seat. "I'm sorry, Your Honor."

"That's quite all right," Judge Baker went on, turning his attention to Silverspoon. "Bernard? Is this true?"

"Yes it is, Your Honor. No information of this nature exists anywhere in the company records we were given."

"Malcolm?"

"Your Honor, the plaintiff's attorneys have had complete access to everything we have, photocopies of every production and quality-control record for that assembly plant during the year in question. To be fair, however, we nearly missed these documents ourselves. These reports were incorrectly stored—filed, as I recall, with records about an eighteen-speed mountain bike with a similar model number. You will find them," he said, ignoring Scully and handing a slip of paper to Silverspoon, "in the same place we found them."

Silverspoon passed the paper wordlessly to Scully, who rose again and dragged his bum leg out of the conference room and presumably to the telephone in the hallway. The way I read it, someone back at the office was going to check out this bombshell posthaste. Sam was looking at Rosemary and shaking her head resolutely. She, Scully, and Stephen Epstein had, I knew, personally combed through every sheet of paper, in every file, for every model, for every possible loophole. If she said the documents were not there, they were not there. When Scully returned, moments later, the dismayed look on his face and the weak shrug of his large shoulders told everyone present that the file was, indeed, exactly where Mad Malcolm had said it would be.

"Your Honor," Sam said, her face the same color red it gets when she thinks the wheelchair basketball referee has just charged her with a bogus personal foul, "I was one of several individuals who read *every* document provided to us by the defense. That includes *every* document pertaining to the one-three-eight-seven Rock Hound five-fifty mountain bikes that came off the assembly line last year. I assure you that these documents—though they appear to be included in that file at the present time—were not there as of Tuesday or Wednesday of last week."

"Be careful what you say, Ms. Wagner-Foster," Malcolm said softly. "You are playing with fire."

Playing with fire? I hurtled away from the table and went after the man then and there. I was beyond reason or common sense. Mad Malcolm wasn't a man to choose his words carelessly. The unmitigated gall . . .

Scully's strong right arm shot out and he grabbed the back of my chair, stopping it so suddenly that my momentum nearly catapulted me out onto my face. Then the Dragon roared.

"Enough! Mr. Nealy, you will take your team to my chambers and wait for me there. If you cannot be sensitive, then I would suggest that you be careful—very careful—what you say."

I counted to something and tried to take long, deep, and steady breaths as I watched Mad Malcolm and his minions leave the room. I was almost under control when he turned to close the door, making eye contact with me as he did so, with a contemptuous gesture of dismissal and a malicious smirk I would never forget . . . or forgive.

"Well, fans," the Dragon said, his brown eyes sparkling under white, bushy brows, "this is more fun than a cat on a sharp stick. Any more surprises and I might have to scuttle a settlement just so some lucky judge can watch the fur fly from the bench. Okay, let's get this out of the way first . . . Malcolm Nealy is a prick. That make you feel better?"

He could see by the smiles at the table that it did.

"Good. Now that you know that I know, let's face facts. Mad Malcolm is one of the hottest young guns in town. He's moved up faster and farther than anyone before him at Brown, Nealy, and he's supposedly breathing down Lester's neck for top-gun status everywhere but on the letterhead. He didn't get there by being stupid, and he certainly didn't get there on his charm. What does that leave, you might ask? A fair question. Young Malcolm might be the best trial lawyer I've ever seen in my courtroom. He might also be the most amoral, but to date no one's provided a shred of evi-

dence to prove that. As far as the ancillary skullduggery surrounding this case, I want you to understand that my sus-
picions one way or the other have no bearing if this matter
goes to court . . . and Malcolm Nealy wants to try this case.
Make no mistake about that."

It was a little morality play with no sign of morality. Vinnie
Baker wandered back and forth between our room and theirs,
listening to and trying to sort through enough of the crap so
that everyone would get some idea of whether a settlement
deal was possible. When he discussed our case with us, his
focus was clearly on the theme that a "good case is not
necessarily a winnable case." The truth of that was finally
bulldozing its way through my own personal denial. It was
as if acknowledging this cornerstone principle of the American judicial system might somehow lend it legitimacy; I
didn't want to be an accessory after the fact.

I did want to hear what the Dragon was saying to Mad
Malcolm. As ludicrous as it sounds, I was reasonably certain
that eavesdropping under the circumstances was a violation
of some lawyer ethics thing, but considering the magnitude
of *that* oxymoron and the comforting fact that I wasn't a
lawyer, I didn't let the notion stop me. It is, after all, a very
common practice among wheelchair users to lean back
against a wall, lock their brakes, and relax their backs. Sitting all day in a low-backed, ultralight wheelchair, after all,
is more strenuous on one's spinal column than most "able-
bodied" folks might imagine, and if I happened to be leaning
back with my head against the wall that separated us from
the judge's chambers . . . well, sue me.

"Yes," Vinnie Baker was saying when I finally got my left
ear in just the right spot, "you might be able to win this case,
Malcolm, but win or lose, the media coverage will hurt your
client for years to come . . . *especially* in this town. Your new
friend Stick Foster will see to that. If the national and international wire services pick up his coverage, or if it ends up
on CBS "This Morning" and "Good Morning America,"

God help you. There's nothing the public hates more than seeing the big ol' bad guys getting away—literally *and* figuratively—with murder."

"There is no evidence to support any of the ridiculous accusations they are making," Malcolm said indignantly. "I object to—"

"Save your objections for someone who's being paid to care," the Dragon said, cutting him off. "As I said, you *might* win this case in the courtroom, but trust me, the public wants nothing more than to believe the story Mr. Foster is going to tell them. And, given his track record, it wouldn't surprise me a bit if he nailed your Teflon ass to the wall. Is this client worth your career and, perhaps, your freedom? Think about it while I go next door."

Why did I suddenly feel the red and white target rings on my back again? I let my chair drop back onto all four wheels and tried to look like I was enthralled with Silverspoon's whispered discourse. Judge Baker came through the door, closed it behind him, and sat heavily at the head of the long table.

"This is way too personal for him," he said, pointing his thumb over his shoulder. "If my guess is correct, he's got some heavy-hitting insurance companies in the wings as potential clients, all waiting to see whether Malcolm's the miracle worker they need to have on retainer. They've been hit hard in recent years, like the exploding pickup truck affair, for example. This case has the potential of making it possible for Malcolm to write his own ticket, and he knows it. With that much at stake," the judge said, turning to look at me, "your scenario is more plausible than I'd care to admit. And to win this case," the Dragon said to Silverspoon, "you might just have to prove that Mad Malcolm dove off the deep end, and I certainly wouldn't want to attempt that, and screw up."

Making the sabotage and murder part and parcel of the Fraiser trial meant, in essence, accusing Malcolm of a felony, sort of like officially pressing charges. Failing to prove those charges would lead to a lawsuit even an incompetent attorney could win. And if I was learning anything in all this, it was that Mad Malcolm was about as competent as they come. It just goes to show that sleaze knows no intellectual bounds. Actually, the more I thought about it, the sleaze ratio theory might actually function on an upwardly sliding scale. The smarter you are, the richer you are, the sleazier you can afford to be . . . and still get away with it. One sleaze-ball I knew, however, was about to start rolling back toward the sewer from which he had emerged. I would see to it personally.

THE LAW OFFICES OF
Ketchum, Latham & Bennet, P. A.
221 Lake Eola Drive
Orlando, Florida 32801
(407)555-1975 - FAX (407)555-1999

Rosemary I. Latham	William P. Graham
Robert G. Bennet	H. Russell White
Bernard R. Ketchum	Robert W. Albright
Rebecca H. Forest	Samantha Wagner-Foster
Charles D. Young	Paul W. Kilpatrick

24

To KNOW HIM, I hoped, would be to own him. By Tuesday afternoon, I was well on my way to becoming an expert on Malcolm W. Nealy. True to his word, Mad Malcolm had rejected every effort to settle the Fraiser case. The last number bandied about was under twenty million dollars, more than *eighty* million dollars *below* the amount a jury had awarded a mother and father who'd lost their son when his pickup truck exploded after a drunk driver hit him broadside. The defense wasn't having any of it. The Fraiser case, it seemed, would go to a jury.

Leaving the legal work to the lawyers, I turned all my efforts toward finding out everything I could about the man who not only thought he was above the law but acted as if he were the law personified. By noon I had spoken to five of his former teachers; by four in the afternoon, I had several faxed pages from his Lincoln High School and Boston College yearbooks; and by 10:05 P.M., my wheelchair and I were aboard the last flight north out of Orlando, headed, ultimately, for Harvard Law School. By the time I got back on Friday morning, I had a pretty consistent picture of this man who would be god.

"So?"

"So, yourself. You just got off the plane. What's happening in the Ivy League?"

"It's a bore, but you called me, El," I said. "I take it you've been snooping around some more."

"I prefer to call it fact-finding," she said. I tried not to stare into her soft brown eyes, afraid that I would drown in the depths of their compassion. "Something you said when we talked about the gang at Ketchum, Latham and Bennet stuck with me—you know, about who was sleeping with Robert Bennet's wife."

"Well?" I said, casting a glance around the multiplex movie theater parking lot where we had agreed to meet. I didn't see anyone in the distance with a big-lensed camera; but then, anyone in the distance with a big-lensed camera wouldn't have any reason to let me see them.

"Well, your question about the past tense got me thinking, and I assumed you were inferring that The Old Man might have been a contender in the matter."

"I said no such thing. But now that you mention it, it did cross my mind briefly. I mean, any man who would feel unfulfilled by a young vixen like Anastasia Ketchum could just as easily feel it necessary to supplement the good heart surgeon's loving as well. But what do I know about the life of the American stud?"

"I've had wonderfully erotic dreams about that very question," Ellie said with a laugh. And while I turned red and chided myself for having a big mouth, she went merrily on. "And, as I recall, you showed lots of promise! Anyway, as it turns out, your instincts about Bennet's wife were calling out to you. The Old Man was, in fact, nothing less than a legend in his own time. Once I primed the right pumps, the saga poured out at a rather alarming rate. I won't bore you with all the names dropped in his wake, but Delta Bennet was definitely one name and, it seems, even bragged about making the list."

"List? Women who slept with him certainly wouldn't be aware that they were just more names on a list? I mean, Dr.

Sanderlin struck me as a woman who would have been devastated to know that."

"You may be right, but whether they all knew doesn't matter. As far as an actual list goes, there were at least two. The exclusive club set society ladies actually compared notes on one list—who The Old Man hit on, whether they said yes, and how they liked the experience. I don't mean to shock your gentle sensibilities, Nick, but apparently Rodney Ketchum's capacity for creativity and endurance rivaled that of a Greek god, maybe Zeus himself."

"Get out! With his heart?"

"According to the women I talked to, it had nothing to do with his heart, trust me. But then there was another list. I had to work my dad for this, but it turns out that there is an *extremely* exclusive club among a very select number of top Orlando executives called the Leftover Club."

"No way!"

"Yep. To join the Leftover Club, you had to sleep with one of The Old Man's conquests . . . the more recent the better. The last Dad knew, the club had no president because in order to qualify, you had to sleep with a woman The Old Man was still seeing. Apparently, getting leftovers on the rebound was occasionally possible, but distracting a current target of Zeus's affections proved impossible. And then the legend died."

I didn't know what to say. I sat in stunned silence, contemplating the whole sordid soap opera. It gave a whole new meaning to the "old boys' club." The more I thought about it, the more significant both lists became. The first list might prove interesting in several ways, but the second was a potential mine field. I handed Ellie my notebook.

"Write. I want names."

"These ladies might brag amongst themselves," Ellie said, "but this isn't something to spread around. If they want to trash their marriages, that's their business. We shouldn't help, okay?"

"My lips are sealed."

Two names on the ladies' list popped: Delta Bennet, of course, was one. The other was Victoria Mann, the firm's curvaceous receptionist. Why wasn't I surprised? The rest—Jane Morgan, Erin Langford, Sally Brown, Lois Faulk, Alice Marie Crawford, Miranda Esposito, Dori Mickelson, Joan Long, and Darla Meredith—were just unfaithful wives whose stories I really didn't want to know.

"What about the other list?" I said, looking up from the returned notebook. "Only two guys?"

"Dad says there's more, but those are the only ones he knows by name. You want more, you can investigate those slimeballs yourself!"

"Fair enough. Do you know anything about these two?"

"An insurance company CEO and an investment banker. That's all Dad said. He says he's never met either of them but plays racquetball with a VP under the insurance guy."

"Okay. Thanks, El."

"You're welcome. *Now* will you tell me about your trip?"

It paled by comparison, but I outlined my discoveries, none of them too surprising. After I had set them at ease by telling them why I suspected the phantom n'er-do-well of murder and promising them anonymity, each person I interviewed—from old professors to academic deans to several old frat house buddies who still lived in the area—all told different stories with very familiar similarities.

"Basically," I told Ellie, "it always went something like this. Something happens. A prank, vandalism, and, in one case, a mysterious and plagiarized critical paper in a prestigious law journal that left a Harvard professor's reputation in tatters. Everyone always suspected Mad Malcolm, but there was never a shred of evidence pointing to him, only dubious evidence pointing to others, but never strong enough to convict. In high school he supposedly tore the head off a little girl's doll because the girl had accidentally brushed him as she pushed her toy stroller down the sidewalk in front of her house. Even his high school and college acquaintances said he never confirmed or denied his involvement, but they did say that the Ph.D. whose byline appeared on the plagiarized article was the only professor at the Harvard School of Law to give Malcolm a B for a semester's work. It blew his four-point-oh GPA, of course, and threw him out of the running for class valedictorian."

"And he's never slipped up?"

"Apparently not. Malcolm has a spotless record," I said, laughing as I recalled one of the judge's remarks that I'd overheard through the wall. "Judge Baker said he had a Teflon ass!"

"So what are you going to do about it?"

"I'm going to scramble some eggs while they're cooking . . . with a metal fork."

THE LAW OFFICES OF

Ketchum, Latham & Bennet, P. A.

221 Lake Eola Drive
Orlando, Florida 32801
(407)555-1975 - FAX (407)555-1999

Rosemary I. Latham	William P. Graham
Robert G. Bennet	H. Russell White
Bernard R. Ketchum	Robert W. Albright
Rebecca H. Forest	Samantha Wagner-Foster
Charles D. Young	Paul W. Kilpatrick

25

I T WASN'T TOO surprising to find that when the police located the Reeboks and the nylon sweatpants, they didn't belong to Malcolm Nealy. They didn't even belong to the same person. The sneakers were Paul Kilpatrick's and the sweats belonged to Russ White; and of course, neither man had any notion of where the errant sportswear had been, how it had gotten there, or who might have removed it from, then returned it to, their homes. Both men, as it happens, had ironclad, witness-enhanced alibis for their whereabouts on the night our house was torched. So what else was new?

Nor was it surprising to discover that nearly everyone at Sam's firm had reported erroneous phone charges to Mother Bell. The gift telephones had not only proved useful in their mischief, but it appeared by the sheer number of calls placed on others' lines that they may well have paid for themselves. Agent Stanley Fredericks had a clerk working up a list of those calls and trying desperately to tie them to our elusive shyster. Malcolm was at the top of his compulsive-obsessive game, but I was learning how he played, and it was only a matter of time before he slipped up. Then he was mine.

"The trial's been set for August," Sam told me over a late, squeezed-in dinner at Lorenzo's. After our long-awaited and somewhat traumatic return to Angelo's, I'd concluded that aside from Angelo's famous chicken parmesan, the fare was pretty much comparable at both restaurants. Other considerations, however, were noteworthy. Lorenzo's prices were roughly half those of the north Orlando competition. I can live with the red-and-white checkered plastic tablecloths. But it was the hot breadsticks that made me insist we return to the lower-rent South Orange Avenue restaurant on this evening. They were always freshly baked, with just the right amount of salt, garlic, and Romano cheese; and long after you'd forgotten what entreé you ordered the last time you were there, you would think fondly about those bread sticks.

"What about the bogus photocopies?"

"We're having them tested," Sam said, "but it's the originals we need. If somebody manufactured them, there are experts who can track the ink to the manufacturer's original batch date. It's never good to have those guys swear in front of the jury that the document you introduced as having been signed in 1980 was signed with a pen manufactured in 1993!"

"I wouldn't think so. What if you can't invalidate the documents? Can you still win the case?"

"That depends a lot on Scully. He's interviewing every past and present employee he can find, in person. There was a union vote we weren't aware of, and there were disgruntled employees when the vote failed, of course, but as long as the line workers we videotaped before can't be linked to actual threats of sabotage, we still have a chance."

I ate another bread stick. That this case, which seemed so obviously one-sided and winnable at first, could almost overnight turn into *we still have a chance* was unnerving on some very basic level. Sam seemed to know what I was thinking.

"It's like this more often than not, babe. With or without Malcolm Nealy. Quote-unquote facts come and go. Believable evidence is all that really matters in the end."

"So you've said."

We finished our minestrone in silence, and I was well into an otherwise marvelous ten-dollar steak and manicotti combination platter before I could figuratively cleanse my palate of the distaste that rose every time I was forced to deal with my wife's capacity to embrace the rules of legal engagement so placidly. I wanted her conscience to squirm. I wanted her to rail against the basic immorality of it all. Instead, Sam had learned the rules, accepted them, and demonstrated her considerable ability to play ball with the big boys. I consoled myself with the fact that she—unlike Malcolm Nealy—represented people who'd been seriously injured, people whose only hope for just compensation came from having counsel who knew the knotted ropes and how to climb them. Still, I didn't have to like it.

What would it take for Sam to cross the kind of lines Mad Malcolm had been crossing freely for most of his life? I didn't like thinking about that. First, of course, because when I looked hard into the stern face of reality, I suspected that I knew the answer. Sam hates to lose. Period. More to the point, I realized to my own amazement, I was really wondering about myself. How far would I go to make something nasty stick to Malcolm's slippery buttocks? When Sam interrupted my disquieting reverie, I was staring at the restaurant's watercolor mural of Venice, a half-eaten breadstick in my left hand and a forkful of manicotti suspended halfway to my mouth in my right.

"You okay?" she said, gently tapping me on the elbow.

"Huh? Oh, sure. Just thinking. What would it take to nail Malcolm, Sam? I mean, not just for the Fraiser case, but to get his license to practice law yanked by the Florida bar?"

"A felony would do it," Sam said. "You gonna be the man to bring him in, Marshal Dillon?"

"Yes, Miss Kitty, I am."

Nothing more threatening than a covey of quail had crossed our property line since the night of the fire. Butch and Ernest would have known. Butch did most of the baby-sitting, but Ernest spelled her whenever he could.

"It's just a game to him, isn't it?" Butch Grady said while

the three of us sat on the back patio watching the morning sun sparkle on the lake.

"In the army," Ernest said, "we called guys like that remotes. They're like land mines you don't have to step on, and you never know what might set them off. My theory is that people like that figured out early on in their lives that there's really no reason not to have or do anything they want. Most of them end up dead or in jail, I suppose. The rest of them probably become lawyers."

"Or politicians," Butch added.

"Or politicians."

"I want to nail him," I said quietly.

"I know," Butch said, "but what if he doesn't come back? I mean, he had his fun, he made his point, and maybe he's moved on to a different game."

"I don't mean here, necessarily. You're right, he moves from game to game so fast nobody's ever been able to catch up. But what if we offer him some enticement to play a game *we* arrange?" I told them about the Harvard Law professor. "Suppose we could anger him enough to make him respond, then catch him in the act when he does?"

"Sounds like entrapment," Sam said, sticking her head out through sliding screen door. "I'm leaving for work."

"Sounds like fun," Butch added when Sam disappeared.

We spent the morning tossing around and rejecting ideas. Several were workable enough, I thought, but crossed some invisible line I couldn't quite put my finger on. Ideally, I wanted Mad Malcolm to become ensnared in a trap of his own making, but it wasn't an ideal world, after all, and I was in a hurry. By lunchtime we still didn't have a plan, but we had decided that instead of watching my house, we would take turns watching Malcolm's. Couldn't hurt.

I had arranged to meet Victoria Mann for lunch at a quiet all-natural bistro around the corner from Rosie O'Grady's. There were delicate questions I had to ask about her alleged affair with The Old Man, but that wasn't the worst of it.

Were there members of the Leftover Club who owed their induction to Miss Mann's wide-eyed sexual generosity? Was it too much of a stretch to place Mad Malcolm in that category? It would certainly answer a lot of questions; foremost among them the matter of how he had gained access to the firm. Judging by Victoria Mann's reaction to Stephen Epstein's death, I found it hard to believe that she had willingly, or even knowingly, been a party to Malcolm's malicious madness, but making a pressing of her key while she slept was no hill for a stepper.

"Been here long?" the smiling police detective asked as he leaned down and looked in the driver's window.

"Hi, James. No, I just pulled up. Where'd you park?"

"I walked over from the station."

"There's no sign of Miss Mann yet," I said. "You don't suppose I spooked her, do you?"

"Did you tell her that I'd be here?"

"No. I arranged the meeting before I called you."

"Good. Well, let's just hang out and hope. Wait," he said, pushing something on his pager. "Hand me your phone. Thanks."

After saying "Yes," "I see," and "I'll be right there," James returned my cellular phone and headed around the Monte at a run.

"Crank this bad boy up and get us over to Lake Eola," he said as he got in the passenger door and fastened the seat belt. "Victoria Mann won't be joining us for lunch, I'm afraid. She's dead."

THE LAW OFFICES OF

Ketchum, Latham & Bennet, P. A.

221 Lake Eola Drive
Orlando, Florida 32801
(407)555-1975 - FAX (407)555-1999

Rosemary I. Latham	William P. Graham
Robert G. Bennet	H. Russell White
Bernard R. Ketchum	Robert W. Albright
Rebecca H. Forest	Samantha Wagner-Foster
Charles D. Young	Paul W. Kilpatrick

26

DUCKS, GEESE, AND humans were gathered around the crime scene at the west end of Lake Eola Park. Yellow tape stretched from the rear seats at the band shell, out around a park bench, almost to the rest rooms, and back. Several uniformed officers encouraged folks and fowl to stand clear and let the police do their jobs. While an ambulance waited for permission to remove Victoria Mann's Varga-esque body, a homicide team took pictures and combed the nearby Bahia grass for something more incriminating than marble-colored goose pies. A detective and a uniform were talking to possible witnesses over near the band shell, and one particular face stood out from the small crowd waiting to be interviewed. Detective Henderson was allowed in under the tape by a young female officer who deferred to him while ignoring me altogether. That was just as well, because Victoria Mann wasn't going to tell me anything anyway.

The brightly dressed young woman being detained for questioning and fidgeting impatiently at the rear of the small crowd looked as if she might bolt at any moment. Whether the middle school several blocks east on Robinson Avenue allowed students to leave for lunch or not, it was clear that this student was late for class.

"Emily," I said, rolling up beside her and holding out the flat of my hand. "Sappnin'?"

"Hi, Stick!" she said, slapping my hand with her own. Her big brown eyes were as pretty and as caring as Eleanor Algretto's, and they brightened considerably at my arrival. "Some guy did that lady with the centerfold bod over there, right in broad daylight. I saw him running away, so the cops want to talk to me, but I'm gonna get busted for sneakin' out at lunch. What time is it?"

"Quarter till."

"Crap! I missed fifth period. Well, I guess it doesn't matter now," she said, plopping herself down in one of the park seats.

Emily Warner was one of my mall rats, a teenager I'd met and befriended while doing a summer feature story about life at the Palmetto Plaza shopping mall. She and her ragged compatriots had helped me solve two different murders, and the bond of friendship we'd developed held a very special place in my heart.

"You saw the guy who did it?"

"Well, maybe. I mean, like, I noticed her, ya know, talkin' to a silk suit, see? I kept walking, but then there was this, like, commotion after I passed them. By the time I looked back, Boobs there was down and out, and the suit was duckin' out—there in the bushes behind the bathrooms."

"How long ago?"

"I dunno, like, fifteen minutes maybe?"

Detective Henderson came by on his way to the officers conducting interviews, and I motioned him to sit. "James Henderson," I said, "I'd like you to meet my very good friend, Emily Warner."

"Hi, Emily," he said. To me he added, "I see you're assisting Detective Huston and Officer Beard."

"They don't need any help from me. Emily just happened to be telling me about the guy in a silk suit who was talking to Miss Mann just prior to her demise, and whom she saw making a hasty exit over there behind the rest rooms."

"Did you get a good look at him?" James asked with new interest.

"Only from the back, like both times. White guy, fair skin. His hair was brown, moussed maybe—every hair in place like. And he had sunglasses too."

"What color was his suit?"

"Grayish, I think. Real faint pinstripes maybe."

"You've got a good eye," James told her. "Was he taller than the lady?"

"Yeah, he was, but not by much."

"What'd he do to her, by the way?" I asked the young detective.

"We don't know; no immediately visible wounds, anyway. Maybe he scared her to death."

"She suffocated," Emily said with certainty. "I watched her eyes bug out and everything, and then she, like, turned a nasty blue. That lady over there in the yellow sundress," she said, pointing toward the detective's current interviewee, "tried to do the CPR thing, but it just wasn't happnin'."

"Let me get someone on the escape route," James said, getting up and slapping Emily on the back. "You were a big help, Emily. Thanks."

"It's okay. Can I go back to school now?"

"Does Stick know where you live?"

"Sure."

"Okay. It was nice to meet you, Emily."

"Same here."

After he left, I offered Emily a ride back to school, but she said that would put her there too early for sixth period. It was something about timing her arrival to the next break between classes. We said good-bye and I watched as she skirted the tape and the crowd on her way back around the downtown lake. Emily Warner was a bright and lovely young woman. She came from what a politically correct social worker might call a functionally challenged home, but, from what I could see, she was still stroking strongly in the river of life. I desperately wanted her to make it. There was something about the mall rats that made you want to wrap up a better life, complete with a long and happy future, and present it to them with a reassuring hug. Unfortunately, I hadn't learned how to do that yet, so I offered up a silent prayer to the Creator my dad had always assured me would handle all such matters in His own good time.

After James assured me that one of his badge buddies would take him back to the station, I drove several blocks to the library, bracing myself for the pheromone cloud that surrounded Jennifer Creacy. It's never good for my ego to have to admit to myself that someone's very presence has that kind of an effect on me. I always wonder what kind of sexist, perverted, dinosaur-type that makes me, and I always try to psych myself into believing that *this* time I won't even notice. I *always* notice.

"This makes two! Two visits to the library in one month. Stick Foster, I'm so impressed. Let me see, does this mean we've worked through the denial *and* the fear? Why, acceptance is just around the corner!"

"Very funny. Hi, Jennifer. Where do I look to find out who's who in the Orlando business community? Is there a list of the heavy hitters in print anywhere?"

When she finished playing with her computer, Jennifer requested several magazines from the periodicals desk, hit me up for copier money, and started making photocopies. By the time I left, I was carrying several dozen sheets of paper, covered with data about Orlando's top executives, including Dan Dowdy and Raymond Devoe. Dowdy and Devoe, it sounded more like a morning radio team than a couple of old frat boys who saw and pursued women in much the same way a Kenyan poacher stalks an elephant with a fine pair of . . . tusks.

Dan Dowdy was CEO at Republic Insurance Protection Company. He was in his forties, married with children, and a level A racquetball player at the Body and Soul. He also owned and drove several expensive cars. Ray Devoe was the vice president of North American Investment, Inc.; and on the basis of the bio information on my photocopies, he had nothing at all in common with Dan Dowdy except money.

"Hello? Mr. Foster? How can I help you?"

"Hi, Mr. Devoe. Thanks for taking my call. It's about that time for the *Sentinel* to feature Orlando's first-string execs again—you know, make the tourists think that anybody who's anybody simply *has* to do business here. By the way, are you the Ray Devoe that Dan Dowdy was talking about?"

"Jeez. The bum draws to a straight, lucks out big time, and beats me out of a twelve-hundred-dollar pot, and now he's gotta brag to everybody in town."

Bingo!

After I set up appointments for the next day with both Devoe and Dowdy, I called Brown, Nealy, Howser & Columbine, told the receptionist I was calling from the attorney general's office in Tallahassee, and hung up as soon as she said she was connecting me to Malcolm Nealy. He was there. That was all that mattered. I circled the building several times and took my best guess about where Mad Malcolm would park his car. Unlike Sam's firm, this downtown glass high-rise didn't have its own parking lot out back. Real estate in the heart of Orlando is too valuable.

I found a parking spot on the street where I hoped the Monte Carlo SS wasn't too noticeable and over the next hour improved on that design several times, all without feeding a parking meter. A "handicapped" license plate has distinct advantages. Under the bucket seat somewhere was a black leather case. I dug blindly around in the crumpled napkins and green french fries with my left hand until I found and retrieved it. I knew the 100–300mm telephoto lens I had paid for so dearly would come in handy someday. I just hoped this was the day. When Mad Malcolm finally came out the front door, I discovered that I was right about which exit he'd use but wrong about the parking garage. He was coming my way.

Fortunately, he was on the opposite side of the street, but

still, my car was almost as well known as I was, and there was only one other like it in the area. I shot him several times from the front, counting his steps and watching his progress before sliding down on the seat and taking a picture of the *Sentinel*, with the day's date showing, that lay open on the floor. Dark gray suit, pinstripes, he was dressed just right, with every hair in place. I kept counting, trying to picture his movement on the sidewalk across the street in my mind. End of his building . . . another office building . . . deli on the corner coming up. When I thought he must have passed me, I sat up to get the shot I needed. Perfect! I got him three more times before he turned the corner at the sandwich shop. The third time my shutter fired, however, his eyes were looking squarely into mine. Had he noticed the car or did he have some evil sixth sense? No matter. I didn't have to develop the film to know that Malcolm wasn't smirking now. He was an unhappy camper when he disappeared around the corner.

Gotcha!

I immediately took the camera to a fast photo developing shop, calling James Henderson on the way. I had scoffed at the price and the usefulness of the Data Back feature the sales clerk had tried to talk me into when I bought the old Minolta 5000 some years back. On this particular day, however, it would have been quite useful to have the time and date imprinted automatically on each frame, but when Detective Henderson arrived with a notary from the police station, I did the next best thing. Everyone in the photo processing shop—employees and customers alike—watched me turn on the auto rewind, saw the little digital representation in the camera's program window mark the film's backward progress, and heard the whining stop when the task was completed.

They paid close (and somewhat fascinated) attention when I opened the back of the camera, removed the film, and handed it to the waiting technician, who fed it immediately into the long and complicated machine that stretched along the wall behind the counter, all the way to the front window where color photographs rode down a chain conveyor, right out in front of God and everybody. James took down their names, the notary witnessed their signatures, and I thanked them all profusely. At least there'd be no question about what silk suit Mad Malcolm had been wearing on the day Victoria Mann had died. And with any luck, Emily and some of the other nature lovers at Lake Eola Park would identify him from my photos, placing him at the scene. It seemed that Malcolm Nealy had finally slipped up.

THE LAW OFFICES OF

Ketchum, Latham & Bennet, P. A.

221 Lake Eola Drive
Orlando, Florida 32801
(407)555-1975 - FAX (407)555-1999

Rosemary I. Latham	William P. Graham
Robert G. Bennet	H. Russell White
Bernard R. Ketchum	Robert W. Albright
Rebecca H. Forest	Samantha Wagner-Foster
Charles D. Young	Paul W. Kilpatrick

27

MY NEXT STOP was Sam's office. I called to make sure my pugnacious bride still had her wheels to the grindstone but didn't stop to think that no one would have notified them about the death of their receptionist.

"Dead? How is she dead?"

"Dead, you know, the stopped living kind of dead. You mean nobody called? No police?"

"No. She just walked out for lunch like she does every other day but then didn't come back. How'd it happen?"

"I don't know, but I think we can place Mad Malcolm at the scene."

"Mad Malcolm? What does he have to do with Victoria?"

"Well, that's something we're just going to have to figure out. I'm on my way, Sam, but make sure nobody messes with her desk until I get there, okay?"

"Got it."

I placed yet another call to James Henderson. He was chasing down witnesses from the park and showing them Malcolm's picture.

"So far," he told me sadly when he returned my call, "your friend Emily's the only one who's relatively certain about seeing him there, but then she only saw him from the back."

"That's not good, is it?"

"No, that's not good at all."

James was chagrined that neither he nor the detective in charge at the scene of Victoria's death had thought about the possibility of evidence at her workplace, and he agreed to meet me once more.

While we waited, I explained the Leftover Club to Sam as I sifted through Victoria's desk and was dismayed to find that she actually thought it was a hoot.

"This is getting to be a habit," Detective Henderson said when he arrived and took his first gander at the huge scheduling planner lying open on the desk. "What have we got?"

"At first," I said, "I didn't think there was anything. But look. There's a note about meeting me at Zeto's for lunch. Everything's written in ink . . . tough to erase."

"If you walk into an empty office at lunchtime," Sam interjected, "how can you tell which of the secretaries are blond?"

James and I glanced at each other before looking at the striking blond in the wheelchair beside us. We shook our heads.

"Just look for the computer screens with white-out on them."

It seemed like an inappropriate time to laugh, but we did anyway. No disrespect intended. Still, Sam had taken my meaning immediately. Victoria recorded all the official stuff in various colored inks, and there were signs of white-out on every page.

"Anyway, as I was saying, it's all in ink. Except for these tiny initials that are almost hidden next to some of the dates. Here, between the one and the seven on the seventeenth. See it?"

"Looks like I.G.A.," Sam said. "Isn't that a grocery chain?"

"Maybe," I said. "But I'd bet against it. Look back through some of these other pages. The initials are different, but without meaning to sound sexist, I'd say there's a definite pattern."

Detective Henderson looked puzzled as I worked back several months, pointing out the various and sundry faint pencil notations, but Sam caught on after two months.

"One week out of every month there are no initials. Her period! That's what you're thinking, isn't it?"

"It crossed my mind. If she were a regular with the Leftover Club, that meant her dates weren't about a nice dinner and a deepening friendship. The slimeballs certainly weren't wining and dining her for her after-dinner conversation, and while she appeared to be a pretty ditzy individual, she wasn't stupid. Stupid people don't manage the comings and goings of a firm this size. Victoria Mann, I suspect, knew exactly what she was doing."

I turned back to the current two-week spread and pointed to the previous Saturday.

"Three guesses what the initials M.N. stand for."

"That was the weekend that somebody slipped those bogus documents into the Fraiser files, too!" Sam said. She immediately paged back to the week before The Old Man died. "Why would he need a key, though, if he already had one when he installed the linear induction motor?"

"A good question," I said. "Maybe he tossed the first key he copied. He's not noted for leaving incriminating evidence around."

"Or maybe he had a flunky do it the first time," the young police detective offered. "Who's I.B.D.?"

"Is that what that says?" Sam said, squinting at the faint, almost minuscule pencil marks. "I can't really make it out."

I pulled the Brown, Nealy stationery sample and the photocopies I got at the library from my backpack and looked for the initials I.B.D. The lawyer list jumped from Croft to Forrester, and the other pages were equally unhelpful. "Sorry. Nobody even close on my lists."

"Well," James said, straightening up and stretching his back, "it's not even good circumstantial evidence, but it is a start. If you want a list of those initials, you can copy them now, Stick. I'll have to take the planner back to the station with me."

"Thanks," I said. "By the way, how difficult is it for you to access a murder victim's bank records?"

"I'd need a judge to sign off. Why?"

"Again, not meaning to speak ill of the dead, but suppose that there were significant deposits immediately following the dates with initials by them?"

"Stick!" Sam said. "You're not suggesting that she's a, well, that she was—"

"Moonlighting?" I said. "Well, who knows? But think about it. What if Orlando's top wage earners suddenly started putting the moves on Victoria? We've agreed, I think, that she wasn't stupid, and so she finds out why. Okay, she's a liberal young woman, enjoys a high-class roll in the hay now and then, and maybe one or two of these guys get into the Leftover Club for free, but then it occurs to Ms. Mann that she can have fun and turn a profit at the same time. What's a few bucks' initiation fee to those preppies? They probably invest in similar business-related activities every time there's an out-of-town convention . . . and get a lot less for their money."

"That's a terrible thing to say!"

"Maybe, but the alternative isn't any better. Blackmail isn't exactly Camp Fire Girl behavior, but it *is* a motive for murder."

"I'd think that the dollar amount of the deposits would indicate one way or the other as far as those two options go," James said, "but let's wait and see. We're getting way ahead of ourselves."

"I just can't believe it," Sam said. "I mean sure, there were the occasional Jennifer Marlowe jokes, but this is hardly WKRP."

Mmm.

My meetings with Dowdy and Devoe didn't go the way I'd hoped. Friendly buddy chat just wasn't going to get me what I needed, so I had to resort to threats. Mentioning that Victoria Mann had been murdered didn't elicit the response I needed either. These guys were too cool for that. So I took another tack, and got both men's attention in a hurry.

"I'm not saying that I *have* to print the names of the Leftover Club members in the *Sentinel* or anything," I told Dan Dowdy when I visited his office, "but if I can't find out what I need to know about one particular member, then I'm going to have to turn over what I know about all the members to the police—like where you were on the night of the fourteenth, month before last."

That got a response, and if I didn't correct him when he assumed that his buddies had ratted on him, well, I'm sorry. Sue me. The long and short of it was that Mad Malcolm Nealy was not only a member of the Leftover Club but before The Old Man died, he was the hands-on favorite to make president. Ray Devoe thought it important to add that Malcolm was actually a better poker player than Rodney Ketchum. Like it mattered.

I hadn't heard anything from James Henderson that morning, but once I'd got them talking, I managed to get both Dowdy and Devoe to admit that they'd been pressured to slip Ms. Mann a sizable gratuity.

"Vicky was so fine," Ray Devoe said with heartfelt sincerity, "and we were right down to it, ready to do the deed, when she looked at me all innocent like and asked me what it was worth to me to get into the Leftover Club. I mean, come on! I'm only human. Well, I promised her whatever she wanted . . . time was of the essence. I wrote out a sizable check when we were finished, payable to cash, and have never regretted it."

"It was that good?"

"Trust me. That woman was Aphrodite, Venus, and Julia Roberts all wrapped up in one perfect package. Everybody thought Vicky was just a bimbo until she showed us all who was screwing who!"

"Did she ever try to blackmail you afterwards? Threaten to call your wife maybe?"

"My *ex*-wife? No, Vicky wasn't like that at all. She had real class. She used to call us her boys, and if we ran into her somewhere around town, she was genuinely friendly and perfectly discreet."

"Every horny Neanderthal's fantasy woman," I said sarcastically, but Ray Devoe didn't miss a beat.

"You got that right."

Both their stories agreed, and it didn't take a rocket scientist to see that Ms. Mann was the last woman on the face of the earth either man would want dead anytime soon. I left North American Investment, called ahead, then drove over to the Orlando police station. Detective Henderson met me at the generous row of wheelchair parking spaces provided by the city beautiful. I couldn't wait to tell him Victoria's secret, but he had already seen her bankbook.

"Nice pin money," he said after I told him about my conversations with Dowdy and Devoe. "Her average next-business-day deposit ran about twelve hundred dollars."

"Pin money?" I said with a laugh. I pulled the planner list out of my pocket, counted the initials, and multiplied by twelve hundred. "Good night, nurse! I'd say the Leftover Club was more like Ms. Mann's personal pension plan."

"Too bad she'll never get to enjoy it."

"Right. So what do we do now that we know?"

"I was about to get to that," James said. "Let's go visit the eggheads at the crime lab."

THE LAW OFFICES OF

Ketchum, Latham & Bennet, P. A.

221 Lake Eola Drive
Orlando, Florida 32801
(407)555-1975 - FAX (407)555-1999

Rosemary I. Latham
Robert G. Bennet
Bernard R. Ketchum
Rebecca H. Forest
Charles D. Young

William P. Graham
H. Russell White
Robert W. Albright
Samantha Wagner-Foster
Paul W. Kilpatrick

28

WE CROSSED THE parking lot to the squat red-brick building and stopped to gaze sadly at the front facade. The bizarre
silver wall sculpture glistened as the midday sun innocently
enhanced its grotesqueness.

"I was here the day your lady friend blew that abomination
off the wall with a fertilizer bomb, Stick. We all wanted to
give her the key to the city."

"Who knew the sculptor would rush back here from
where—Sweden?—and put it all back together? At least it's
kind of fitting that it be displayed here at the crime lab instead
of, say, at a museum somewhere, frightening schoolchildren."

"It's got crime written all over it for sure," James said. He
grabbed the door for me and then followed me inside. "But
I think we've got some media art here today that you're
gonna like just fine."

He was right. I liked it a lot. The videotape was your
typical tourist crap: Disney, Sea World, Universal Studios,
the works. In between were those silly things that only the
worst of tourists stop to record on videotape: roadside picnic
areas, billboards about area attractions, footage of an orange
grove, and even a shot of the resident alligator in the lake by
the airport. (His story made page one. Ben "Good News"

Dawson eats that stuff up.) Then there was Lake Eola Park. I watched the fountain, the paddle boats, and the waterfowl, knowing what was coming. Sure enough. There, dead center foreground—only slightly out of focus—in a clear, steady shot of the band shell, were Malcolm Nealy and Victoria Mann. As the view froze and locked on the outdoor stage, they stood face-to-face, talking in voices that the video camera couldn't possibly have picked up, while passersby stepped off the sidewalk and skirted them on both sides.

"Here, wait," James said. "You'll really love this." He punched the rewind button and we watched the crowds flow backward. When he pushed the Play button again, he held up a piece of yellow notebook paper and read aloud, matching his words to the movement of our subjects' mouths.

"Hi, Malcolm. How are you?"

"Fine."

James mimicked Malcolm's furtive glances, first left, then right.

"Well?" James said in a sorry falsetto as Victoria's lips moved. "What did you want to see me about?"

Malcolm did the glance dance again before speaking.

"Get off it! You wanted to see me. Don't waste my time. I have to get back for a meeting."

Victoria appeared uncertain about how to respond but was about to speak when Malcolm's left arm and hand moved with a sudden jerk. Then the pretty woman's eyes widened in alarm. She grabbed the right side of her neck, and her lovely eyebrows scrunched together.

"Ouch! Malcolm, what did you do?"

"Why are you doing this?" James and Malcolm said together. "For money? Didn't I give you what you wanted, you slut?"

Victoria seemed to waver slightly, and there was a pained and puzzled look on her face. Malcolm reacted instantly. Even as her knees began to buckle, he slipped adroitly into the passing crowd and was gone before her body hit the ground. The video camera operator chose that moment to use the zoom feature to examine various parts of the band shell and the flora and fauna around it before taking a final shot of the domed fountain out in the lake, oblivious to what had occurred right in front of his electronic eyes. The next shot was of children playing in a motel swimming pool. James turned off the VCR and set the piece of paper down on the counter next to the television set.

"Well, what do you think, reporter man?"

"I think that tourist gets the Oscar for best cinematographer. How'd you get it?"

"Came by cab. Can you believe it? Some tourist dad realized what he had just before he flew home with his family, so he hired a taxi to bring it here."

"No kidding? What's his name and where's he from? This'll make great copy!"

"We don't know anything about him. He just paid the cabbie and rushed back into the terminal to catch his plane. The lab gang says the tape was shot with a Dynomatic 508 camcorder . . . only a few million of those out there, and that's all we know."

"Thank God from whom all blessings flow."

"Whatever," James said with a good-natured laugh. "And for my next trick, step this way."

I followed him down the hallway and into a room that looked much like the high school bio-chem lab. Several white-coated occupants looked up and greeted us. A short black woman smiled as we approached.

"Good golly, Miss Molly!" James said with considerable gusto. "I'd like you to meet Orlando's ace reporter, Stick Foster. Stick, this is the woman who carries my heart in the palm of her hand—and wrings it like a sponge at every opportunity. My love, my master, my wife, the all-knowing, awe-inspiring Molly Henderson."

"Hi, Molly," I said, shaking the hand she offered. "Pleased to meet you."

"Same here. Don't mind Black Bozo here. When he thinks he's about to solve a big case he always gets like this. He's insufferable!"

"You'll sing a different tune when I'm featured on *Top Cops*," James said, "or when Stick and I move to Hollywood and detect for the stars."

"Foster and Henderson Investigations," I said. "It has kind of a ring to it, doesn't it?"

"I was thinking more of Henderson and Foster myself, but no matter. She'll come crawling when those big dollars start rolling in."

"In your dreams, cop!"

When the banter stopped, Molly showed me several blown-up stills of Victoria Mann's neck, just before she had reached up to touch it.

"Poison," Molly said. "The full report's not back, but it was definitely a cyanide compound. Now look at these close-ups. Here, nothing. Then in this shot, look." She handed me a large magnifying glass. "Now here in the last shot it's gone."

"You look just like Sherlock Holmes!" James chided as I peered through the glass.

"What is it?" I asked. "Looks almost like a splinter. Too big to be a bee stinger."

"You're right," Molly said. "It's a Middle Eastern innovation called the *ibrat al-maut*, the needle of death."

She picked up a normal-looking sewing needle with a long black thread run through its eye and a tiny ball of cotton impaled about an eighth of an inch up from its point. Molly looped the far end of the thread around her middle finger, gently picked up the needle by its head, using only her thumb and pointer finger, and dipped the needle's point briefly in a bottle of deep blue ink. The white cotton hungrily soaked up the ink, but Molly removed it from the bottle before it could take on enough of the blue liquid to make it drip.

"The assassin hides the thread and needle like this," she said, tipping up the point and turning her palm inward toward her side. "Then as he passes his target, he flicks his wrist like so."

I didn't notice that one of the papers posted on the overflowing bulletin board was blank until Molly's hand whipped forward and out, and the needle struck squarely in the middle of it and stuck there. Blue ink spread out across the fibrous veins of the paper in all directions, even as Molly took another step or two, giving the thread a tug as she did so. The *ibrat al-maut* came free in Molly's wake, and with another flick of her wrist she sent the whole contraption sailing across the room toward the wastebasket by the door.

"She shoots! She scores!" James shouted as needle, cotton, and thread disappeared into the trash. He clapped his hands along with the rest of us and made crowd noises with his breath.

"Don't let her fool you," said a young lab coat at the next workstation, "she's been practicing that for two hours!"

"I'm still impressed," I said. I looked back at the sheet of typing paper on the corkboard. The blue spot was already nearly the size of a quarter. "James, my man?"

"Yeah?"

"Have I ever steered you wrong?"

"Probably. Why?"

"Well, listen up, for I speak the truth. I would *never* dis this woman if I were you. Do you understand what I'm saying?"

"Amen, brother. I hear you."

Good night, nurse.

On our way back to my car, James told me the serendipitous tale of the tape. The sketchy synopsis of events had come that very morning from a rather confused Sikh cab driver. Apparently the video camera owner was watching the tape through the viewfinder while he and his family sat waiting to board their flight home. He had seen the brief TV news remote from Lake Eola the night before at the motel but never made the connection until he began reviewing his away-from-home movie.

"This fine man," James had mimicked the driver in a passable Ghandi voice, "he spoke very quickly indeed. He was very excited."

The cabbie understood the man to say that his plane was about to leave and that the tape just *had* to be rushed to the Orlando police station immediately. The tourist gave the cab driver a fifty-dollar bill and made him sign a piece of paper with his hack license number on it—his pledge to carry out the tourist's instructions without waiting for a fare. Who was the tourist? Where was he from? What flight was he taking? The apologetic cabbie didn't have any idea.

Did it matter? I didn't think so. An arrest warrant had already been issued for Malcolm W. Nealy, and a search warrant was on its way. I had mixed feelings about the whole affair, however. First, I was delighted to see Mad Malcolm go directly to jail. If he never passed "Go" or collected $200 an hour again, that was fine with me. But I had really wanted to be the guy who brought him down. To be beaten out by an unknown snowbird was what Emily Warner and her pals would call being "chowed." On a deeper level, I realized that I was disappointed. I suddenly thought about the relationship between Sherlock Holmes and the infamous Moriarity. Surely Holmes would have been disappointed too if his archenemy had blundered as badly as Malcolm. There is nothing brilliant or cunning about murdering a young woman in a public place. This was an impulsive crime of raw passion— anger, hatred, fear, and all those other emotional whirling dervishes that tend to suspend intelligent thought.

One other thing troubled me . . . a lot. If the average criminal consistently finds the key to the revolving door that is our court and penal system, how hard would it be for a smart lawyer like Malcolm Nealy to worm his way out? It was another one of life's nasty answers that I would have preferred not to know. And *when* he wormed his way out, whom might he hold responsible for the embarrassing inconvenience he had suffered? The target on my back was suddenly outlined in neon lights. Maybe I could find that tourist guy and slap the "Kick Me" sign on his back. . . .

THE LAW OFFICES OF

Ketchum, Latham & Bennet, P. A.

221 Lake Eola Drive
Orlando, Florida 32801
(407)555-1975 - FAX (407)555-1999

Rosemary I. Latham	William P. Graham
Robert G. Bennet	H. Russell White
Bernard R. Ketchum	Robert W. Albright
Rebecca H. Forest	Samantha Wagner-Foster
Charles D. Young	Paul W. Kilpatrick

29

As COWARDLY AS it sounds, that's exactly the way I wrote my article. Still, it was a good scoop. Careful to use "alleged" in all the right places when referring to Malcolm Nealy, I skipped over any part I might have had in the story and played up the damning videotape and the praiseworthy social conscience of the unknown tourist who had sacrificed his vacation film in an effort to help Orlando catch a murderer. I assumed the man would call when he arrived home, to see what had happened and to get his tape back. Orlando would then be able to acknowledge and thank him properly.

The story made the national wires, and within hours the phone calls began coming in from Hollywood. *Eyewitness Video, Inside Edition, A Current Affair,* and several "law enforcement" shows all wanted to cover it themselves. Local television coverage launched what became a nationwide search for the Unknown Tourist. One Orlando TV reporter went so far as to interview the cab driver and broadcast a list of eighteen airline flights due to take off at or around the time the Unknown Tourist risked missing his plane to "do the right thing." She took her viewers from one of the remote terminal boarding areas back down the long hallway to the monorail shuttle, carrying her microphone in one hand and a VHS tape dramatically in the other. We rode back to the main terminal with her and traversed the expansive lobby area to the front doors. Once outside, she actually hailed a cab by waving the videotape, demonstrating, I suppose, the great lengths to which the Unknown Tourist had inconvenienced himself to do a good deed for our town. Not to mention—though she did—the fifty bucks. Everyone was suitably impressed. It reminded me of something from the black-and-white reruns of my childhood.

Who was that masked man?

I was glad to hear that the judge had denied bail for Mad Malcolm, ordering instead that he be held over for trial. James said that the questions about the earlier deaths and the attempt on Sam's and my life probably helped.

"But," James said, two days after Malcolm's arrest, "if we could tie him more concretely to what happened at Ketchum, Latham & Bennet, it would sure help the whole case. Even if a jury buys the fact that the initials M.N. on Victoria Mann's planner stood for Malcolm Nealy, that still doesn't prove he slept with her or that she tried to blackmail him."

"You think that's what happened?"

"It sure looks like that's what Malcolm thought."

"Is he talking?"

"Only enough to deny killing her and threaten us with unlawful arrest and anything else he can think of."

"Surely he doesn't deny being there?"

"No, but he claims that he was set up. It's the national anthem of every criminal who's ever gotten caught. 'I was framed!' "

"Did the search warrant turn up anything helpful at his house?"

"Only a portable telephone like all the rest of you have. That should help. He claims he got it in the mail just like everyone else, but we checked *his* phone bills for the last year, and there's not a single charge that doesn't belong."

"Well, that's good, I guess."

I took my photographs of Mad Malcolm to the mailbox place and tried to verify that he was the man who had picked up the package from Canada. The lady had already spoken to the police on two different occasions but tolerated my persistence well. Still, as she pointed out, her memory of that day was pretty vague, and she handles a lot of large packages, and lots of businessmen have boxes here, and so on, and so on. The bottom line was that she didn't think she'd ever seen the man in my picture.

In a moment of inspiration, I took sneaky photographs of Jon Rude and Wayne Milroy when they left Brown, Nealy, Howser & Columbine that same afternoon. These two associates were said to be helping Malcolm with his defense "on their own time." I had the film processed in an hour and ran the pictures back out to the mailbox lady first thing the next morning. Nothing. I also remembered to look for the two associates' initials on Victoria's secret list. Nothing.

The police played the same game with the folks at First Orlando Trust, where the cashier's check that paid for the linear induction motor came from. Their records indicated that they received cash, as opposed to drawing the funds from someone's account, but the video record showed very little of a generic white man in sunglasses and a Pirates baseball cap, and the teller who prepared the check had no recollection of the transaction. She had prepared hundreds, maybe thousands of checks in the time since. Oh well.

In my kicking about to find some missing thread that would tie everything together, I almost went to see Lester Brown. He had promptly taken over the Fraiser case, spoken to both Judge Baker and Bernard Ketchum, and agreed on behalf of the bicycle company's insurance carrier to a sizable but quiet settlement. At first, I thought to thank him for his help and to ask him, hypothetically, how one would phony up factory records, but then realized that his firm was surely embarrassed enough, and being seen with me again would do nothing for his reputation. If he wanted people to know that he had suspected Malcolm Nealy of criminal activity, he could tell them himself. Still, no one had been able to provide the originals to the photocopies that mysteriously appeared at Sam's firm. Worse, no one seemed to care.

"The Fraiser case is over," Sam said simply. "We returned all the documentation as required, and there's new business to attend to."

"But that ties him to a break-in," I insisted.

"Then let the district attorney pursue it. It's not our business anymore."

I did speak with the D.A., who, it turned out, already had two investigators on the case full-time. He would, he assured me, prosecute this one personally. With half the television cameras in Hollywood and at least one news crew from every large city in the southeast camped in and around Orlando, why wasn't I surprised? James had already briefed him on my findings, the interviews in Boston and the Leftover Club in particular. After seeing just the partial list I had assembled from my conversations with Dowdy and Devoe, James told me the D.A. saw "no reason to drag these businessmen into this unless it is absolutely necessary." Right. As I sat chatting with him, I couldn't help wondering whether he might even be a member himself. I didn't ask.

I did ask him what kind of a case he thought he had.

"Without the video," he said, "I think I could convince a jury that he was guilty, but they might not have the courage to vote that conviction. After seeing the tape and Ms. Henderson's little demonstration of *ibrat al-maut,* they'll tie the hangman's knot for me."

It occurred to me as I left the D.A.'s office that he was going to enjoy this. Who wouldn't? Malcolm was just a high-class bully, after all; a prick, Judge Vinnie Baker had said; a thorn in everyone's side. "How are the mighty fallen in the midst of the battle!" Young David the shepherd-musician lamented over the death of two different men; one he loved like a brother, and one he had honored in the very face of death but would soon succeed as King of Israel. "How are the mighty fallen, and the weapons of war perished!" Who

would lament Malcolm Nealy if he were found guilty, disbarred, and sent to prison? Had he made one friend in all
his life? Could any thinking human ever trust a character
like Mad Malcolm for very long? How would a jury of regular
folks react to Malcolm's self-defense? Maybe Shakespeare
had someone like Malcolm Nealy in mind when he wrote
Henry VI: "The first thing we do, let's kill all the lawyers."
   And the people said: *Amen!*

It wasn't until late that night that my moldy mental alarms
went off. The past weeks' activities had been playing and
replaying on the projection screen in my brain, my rusty
mental calculator doing the adding and subtracting in place
of a sound track. Malcolm's malevolent face, Stephen Epstein's broken skull, Rosemary Latham's health club strip-
tease, and Eleanor Algretto's steadfast support. I could see
Scully limping through my subconscious and hear Judge
Baker talking about cats and sharp sticks; I scanned and
rescanned my various lists as if they were written on the
backs of my eyelids, and I watched the nervous flick of
Malcolm's hand in Lake Eola Park over and over in my mind.
Something was wrong, very wrong. But the minute I sat up
in bed and tried to think of what it was, the slowly forming
picture would vanish.
   I needed to say it all out loud, perhaps into a tape recorder.
No, I needed to talk to someone, sort out my jumbled
thoughts in front of a good listener. Turning toward the gentle rise and fall of Sam's back, I reached out to wake her. She
had to get up in a few hours anyway. As my hand touched
her shoulder, I knew it was a mistake. In my heart of hearts
I knew she would resent being awakened and would say so.
It was time I dumped the denial and came to grips with the
realities of the beautiful and talented woman I had married
in such a heated rush. With each passing month we talked
less, we made love less, and she worked more. The passion
with which she had once showered me almost daily was now
channeled into her work. It was fed by her desire to succeed

and rewarded in more ways than I could possibly count or compete with.

I transferred quietly into my wheelchair, piled my sweat-shirt, jeans, and penny loafers on my lap, and rolled out to the living room, where I dressed. I cleaned up in the kitchen, brushed my hair as best I could in the dark, and locked the front door behind me.

In the years since my spinal cord injury, I'd reached what might be considered an odd and/or illogical conclusion about people in wheelchairs. Conventional rehabilitation thought says that we replace our legs with our wheelchairs and we go on. I don't believe that for a minute. All one has to do is go to a state or regional wheelchair basketball tournament and scope out the parking lot. Or do the same thing at a regional meeting of the National Paraplegic Association or the Disabled Veterans of America. The younger generation favors two-door "muscle" coupes and four-wheel-drive Jeep Laredos, and the older folks seem to go for two-door Caddys and Continentals.

We use wheelchairs because we have to, but we replace our legs with our cars. Out there in traffic is the only place we can truly come and go on an equal footing with the rest of the world. The freedom and joy sometimes associated with driving fast are heightened for us, and we usually make the most of it whenever we can. Before I moved to Orlando and got married, I often had nights like this one, when my thoughts were unsettled or when my heart was troubled by matters I didn't fully understand. Back then, when I couldn't sleep, I drove.

Usually I cruised down A1A, catching glimpses of the Atlantic in the moonlight; but on other nights, depending on my mood, I'd take my old Z-28 Camaro out on Interstate 95 and let her loose. On some nights I'd do both. I picked up a ticket on I-95 once, from a rookie patrolman who didn't know me from Adam, but the rest of the guys only stopped me if they wanted some friendly wee-hour chat. Once I began sharing a bed with Sam, however, that behavior seemed somehow disloyal. Sneaking out in the middle of the night and driving away just doesn't sound like a "married" thing to do.

On this night, I had no choice in the matter. My old black Monte Carlo Super Sport and I hit the highway together, almost like old times, except this time I was in search of a friendly ear. I hardly needed to turn the steering wheel; this car always seemed to know which way was west.

THE LAW OFFICES OF

Ketchum, Latham & Bennet, P. A.

221 Lake Eola Drive
Orlando, Florida 32801
(407)555-1975 - FAX (407)555-1999

Rosemary I. Latham	William P. Graham
Robert G. Bennet	H. Russell White
Bernard R. Ketchum	Robert W. Albright
Rebecca H. Forest	Samantha Wagner-Foster
Charles D. Young	Paul W. Kilpatrick

30

I SAT AND sipped coffee at a table in the nearly deserted Denny's on West Colonial Drive until almost 2 A.M. My personal quest for the truth about life, the universe, and everything just sort of ran out of steam right there, about six blocks from Ellie's apartment complex. For the first half hour, I chided myself about wimping out. I spent another thirty minutes telling myself that I was a royal jerk if I thought I could marry someone else and then go knock on Ellie's door any time of the day or night. Stopping by her bookstore was one thing, but I'd never been to her apartment before . . . not that I hadn't been invited. By the time I'd finished speculating about what would happen if I called and woke her, only to find that she wasn't alone, I was thinking like a full-blown, basket-case neurotic.

It was that speculation that finally did me in. I'd watched that scene play out so many times on the movie screen, it already had a life of its own. At two o'clock, I decided, I would put down the nearly full cup of cold coffee, overtip the non-intrusive but worried-looking waitress, and go home. That's when Eleanor Algretto walked in the front door . . . alone.

"Hi, cowboy," she said, walking over to the table and sitting down across from me. "You come here often?"

"No, ma'am," I said, noticing that the approaching waitress didn't look nearly as nervous as she had the last time I
checked. "Never been here before. You?"

"For breakfast sometimes. No thanks," she said to the
waitress before the young woman could speak. "Me and the
cowboy here are goin' someplace where there's country
music playin'. It's that kind of night, don't you think?"

The waitress nodded uncertainly, but then grinned at me
when I left a five-dollar bill on the table, winked, and followed the lady in the western-cut shirt, blue jeans, and
pointy-toed boots to the door. "Thanks," I said to the re-
lieved-looking server.

"You're welcome, Mr. Foster."

I should *never* have agreed to let the *Sentinel* run my
photograph with my stories. And I *should* have left a twenty.

I followed Ellie's black Chevy short-bed pickup north to the
relatively new Pine Hills semi-high-rise apartment complex
where she lived and didn't manage to find my voice in either
the spacious common-room lobby, where the night watch-
man greeted her by name, or the close and quiet elevator that
carried us up to the top floor. Ellie's apartment, like Ellie's
bookshop, was decorated to make you feel at home. It was
attractive and comfortable without being house-and-garden-
magazine cute. The patio looked to the west, and through
the sliding glass door, I could see a handful of taillights, the
wee-hour traffic on Highway 50, stretching out toward
Ocoee and Wintergarden. I still couldn't think of anything
intelligent to say, but I'd never let that stop me in the past,
so I forged on.

"What just happened?"

"Fate." Ellie turned on the CD player, unwrapped the thin
package she'd carried in from her truck, and placed a new
disc in the changer tray. "I just took Rachael to the k. d. lang
concert down at the arena tonight. She actually surprised
herself and loved it. I saw your car at Denny's when I got on
West Colonial, and here we are. Fate."

Rachael Evans was the assistant manager, head salesclerk, and general bookkeeper in Ellie's shop, an extremely bright and gracious black woman who had once done me a great favor. She didn't strike me as a fan of country and western, or even pop soul, but rather more as a women who understood and loved the nuances shared by jazz, classical, and the blues.

"How did you get her to go?"

"It was a trade-off deal. I went with Rachael and her two sons to see Kris Kross last month."

"Mmm."

k. d. lang's Grammy Award–winning voice broke into "Constant Craving," and I tried not to look as uncomfortable as I felt.

"Well," Ellie said with a sad smile, "you're not the cheatin' kind, so let's go make some decent coffee and figure out why you're really here."

I followed her across the living room, pushed a stool aside, and rolled up under the breakfast counter. After crossing my arms on its chest-high fake butcher-block surface, I rested my chin on my forearm and just watched Ellie two-step gracefully around the small but efficient kitchen.

"And let's lose the embarrassment stuff, okay? You've got to get over feeling uncomfortable around me just because you're married, or we're gonna screw up this friendship . . . *again*."

Ouch.

"And I'm not ready to deal with that, understand?"

"Yes, ma'am."

"And another thing. I'm not your mother, so don't call me ma'am."

Yes, ma'am.

Once we got over most of the emotional hurdles and got down to business, it was wonderful—an easy friendship between two people who had always complemented each other's logic and conversation almost perfectly. We first experienced that rush when we met as high school freshmen. Ellie was going steady with a senior, but she and I were real buddies right from the start. Putting us on the same group project team was a guaranteed A+. The next year when we began dating, the friendship just got better—until, of course, I screwed it up. But now it was back. Ellie listened with genuine interest while I talked about the various scenes on my mental videotape of the Malcolm Nealy case. She stopped me, asked questions, and often made observations that I'd missed completely. I just knew that together we could nail Mad Malcolm's coffin closed for a very long time.

"So why do you think Lester Brown's office is important?"

"I don't know. I just keep flashing to my visit there, like I missed something important. Stupid, huh?"

"Probably not. Describe the office to me, in detail."

"I don't know, it was an office. A corner office. You know, big desk—"

"What kind of wood?"

"Come on, El, I don't know, walnut maybe, or dark maple. Why?"

"What was on the desk?"

"Paperwork—everywhere. Nothing I could read, even if I'd tried to."

"The walls? Pictures?"

"Bookshelves on the two inside walls, all glass on the other two. No. There was some shelving built into the big window section right behind Lester's desk. And there was a picture . . . no, two. One was a sailboat, a big one, and the other was, I suppose, his wife and two kids. Does he have two kids?"

"I don't even know him. Tell me about the family picture."

"Woman about Brown's age, brunet, good smile, actually very attractive. A boy and a girl, maybe fifteen and seventeen, looked like their mom. They were all standing outside—it was sunny—in front of a wall with letters running across it, just above their heads. Who cares?"

"What did the letters spell?"

I thought I remembered the picture pretty well, but I couldn't seem to make sense of the letters. "Nonsense, that's all. I just remember something like OSEMO. Skip it. Lester has a high-back swivel office chair, black Naugahyde and gray upholstery material. The floor was stacked with accordion-type file storage dealies. I don't know, El, let's try something else."

Ellie didn't respond. She was scribbling madly in the notebook on the floor in front of her. I was sprawled out on the sofa with my shoes off. Looking around the living room, I realized how much actual territory we'd covered in the past couple of hours. I'd been in and out of my wheelchair several times, had sat in at least two easy chairs as well as the sofa, and had been cross-legged on the floor at least twice. It occurred to me that Ellie and I had been physically and emotionally realigning ourselves all morning. And it all felt very right.

"I've got it!"

Ellie's exuberant shout caught me by surprise. I sat up with a jerk and reached for my chair before I realized that it wasn't necessarily a signal to start the unconscious musical chairs theme again. "You've got what?"

"OSEMO! I love word games, and this one was almost too obvious. Look, if the camera cropped out the first and last letter or letters, then we just had to experiment. The stupid thing is that I know that wall. It's the clubhouse wall at the Rosemont Country Club! Get it? Rosemont, R-O-S-E-M-O-N-T."

"That's really clever thinking, El, but what's the big deal about Rosemont?"

"So, I didn't know that the Sally Brown at Dad's club was *that* Mrs. Brown."

"Sally Brown? No, not the Sally Brown on the secret list you gave me? Good night, nurse. Oh, Ellie, I don't want to know this."

"And if your Lester found out . . ."

"Don't even think it, El. We're getting seriously sidetracked here over nothing."

"Nothing unless your Mr. Brown found out that our Mr. Ketchum was servicing his Mrs. Brown."

The words hung in the air between us. We stared at each other. I clutched my face in my hands and wanted to scream. Then I wanted to hold Ellie in my arms but scolded myself and put that thought away. I *really* wanted to make the last five minutes go away. Then it suddenly got worse. All I could do was sigh.

"I knew it was too easy," I said. "*Deus ex machina.*"

"Come again?"

"It's the old god-machine saves the day again thing."

"Whose god and what machine are we talking about exactly?"

"The tape, the irrefutable evidence we needed, dropped in our laps from heaven, at precisely the right moment. I should have known better. I *did* know better. But I really didn't want to know better."

"Of course. Could you elaborate on that a little?"

"He has a tic," I said.

"Who has ticks? Lester Brown?"

"Malcolm Nealy."

"Malcolm Nealy has ticks?"

"*A* tic, a nervous twitch, sort of. With his left hand."

"I'm sorry? What does that have to do with anything?"

"Malcolm Nealy is brilliant, a genius when it comes to plotting and carrying out evil. He's been doing it all his life. He would *never* put himself in a spot where he could get caught like this."

"And he has a tic. He twitches his left hand. Am I missing something here, Nick?"

"Lester Brown would know that."

"About the tic?"

"Exactly."

"I see. And?"

"And that's what I was seeing in the Unknown Tourist's vacation video. Just like at the courthouse. It was an unconscious twitch, not Malcolm Nealy throwing *ibrat al-maut*, the needle of death."

"Oh!" Ellie said, her mouth holding the shape long after the sound had turned to silence.

Reaching into my backpack, I retrieved the list I'd copied from Victoria's desk planner.

"Wouldn't you know it?" I said ruefully. "It was right there in black and white all the time: *LMB* . . . and a month before The Old Man died."

I *really* don't want to know this.

THE LAW OFFICES OF

Ketchum, Latham & Bennet, P. A.

221 Lake Eola Drive
Orlando, Florida 32801
(407)555-1975 - FAX (407)555-1999

Rosemary I. Latham	William P. Graham
Robert G. Bennet	H. Russell White
Bernard R. Ketchum	Robert W. Albright
Rebecca H. Forest	Samantha Wagner-Foster
Charles D. Young	Paul W. Kilpatrick

31

"OH, YES, GOOD SIR," said the cabbie. "This is most definitely the very man who gave me the tape on that most fateful of days. Did you see me, perhaps, on the television? I am to be on the television again, to tell my humble story to all of America? Very soon, yes indeed?"

"We all get fifteen minutes, my friend," I told him. "Thanks for your help."

So, the Unknown Tourist was really Lester Brown. *Inside Edition* and *A Current Affair* would eat this up . . . if they were ever to find out. But no one else knew. I might tell Ellie; but after that, things would get more complicated. Lester Brown had plenty of motive, to want both The Old Man dead and to set up Mad Malcolm. And Victoria Mann gave him ample opportunity, as well as ampleness in general. It put a whole new light on things. Instead of being a secondary and unexpected result of sabotage, it looked like The Old Man's death was the primary goal from the start. Then, of course, it was premeditated murder, not felony manslaughter after all. Erasing the videotape was just a convenient distraction that would serve to raise questions about the man heading up the defense team—Malcolm Nealy. The man Judge

Vinnie Baker said was "breathing down Lester's neck." And I thought Mad Malcolm was good.

I took the *Orlando Magazine* photo of Lester Brown, without its caption, to the Mail Boxes R Us lady next, and wasn't surprised when she recognized him.

"Yes," she said with confidence. "I do remember him now. That's the Mr. Dough who rented the mailbox here."

Right. And I'm Elvis, *thank ya vury much.*

I wasn't surprised by Butch Grady's call either. Without telling her why, I had asked her to do her phony Delta Force Exterminators routine and treat Lester and Sally Brown's Rosemont home for bugs—when there was no one home, of course. She phoned me the next morning to report that yes, there was a Dynomatic 508 camcorder and a 35mm SLR camera with a hefty telephoto lens at the Browns' house.

"Something you want to tell me, Stick?"

"Not yet, Butch, but thanks for your help. Can we keep this between us?"

"Keep what between us? That I illegally entered a rich lawyer's house? Heck no, I was hoping we could write it up in your newspaper. Maybe I could get my P.I. license suspended and go to jail. Look, Stick, we've been around the block a few times, you and me. You don't want to talk, don't talk. Let me talk instead. I think you helped put a very bad man away, but now you think maybe another bad man set him up. Am I close? So what? You gotta take care of your bad guys like you take care of the days of your life—one at a time."

"Where'd you get all that? Is there some knockoff book out there called *The Zen of Private Investigation*? Look, thanks, Butch. I appreciate all your help, and you'd better send me a bill this time, but until I sort out all the junk happening here, I'm not saying anything to anybody. No offense, but I've been wrong so many times in the last few weeks, I feel like a mouse in a maze with no exits."

"No sweat, Stick, you always seem to land on your wheels. Ciao!"

Ciao.

So Malcolm wasn't responsible for The Old Man's death, he hadn't killed Stephen Epstein, and he would have had no reason to set my house on fire—at least not back then. He was surely guilty of many things, including, I suspected, the most recent break-in and the manufacture of phony evidence in the now closed Fraiser case, but he was not in the county lockup for that. He had maliciously harmed the lives and property of any number of people since junior high school, including irrevocable damage to a Harvard law professor whose only crime was to set a higher standard for his students. Malcolm Nealy truly belonged behind bars. Probably more so than Lester Brown.

In another time, no one would have thought it out of place that a husband would kill the man who seduced his wife. In some cultures, the elders of the tribe would have helped him do it. And Lester's law firm, like his marriage, was also, quite arguably, a matter of territorial imperative. Lester Brown, unlike Malcolm Nealy, was just fighting back for what was his—a wife, two children, and a business he had built with his own proverbial two hands.

I needed time to think. I needed to look out at the Atlantic, smell the brine and the scent of faraway. Once the old Monte Carlo was back on Highway 50, it proved that it could go east almost as well as west, and in less than an hour, I was driving across the humpbacked intracoastal bridge near the Cape.

The sun was probably disappearing over the Gulf of Mexico, and had I been in Tampa or Clearwater, I would have enjoyed the sunset colors. Instead, I pulled into the small jetty park just east of the space center, parked under a palm tree that had never gotten a fix on whether it was growing up or across, and rolled my wheelchair over to the redwood picnic table where I'd sat and watched the waves break on the rocky man-made shoreline several times before. The sun was gone, but I would have the moon. No matter how many initials had been carved into that old table, new ones always managed to squeeze themselves in somewhere. I ran my fingers over the ones I remembered and wondered about the people who'd scratched their legacies here since the last time I looked.

I've always been attracted to good people. My job as a reporter has many advantages, but one of the most rewarding is that it lets me collect people, usually good people. I don't mean genius-type good people; rather, I mean solid, hardworking people who have spent time and energy to learn how to do their jobs well. My first years as a newspaper reporter were spent latching on to people like that all up and down central Florida's east coast. I worked side by side with them, sometimes for a week, sometimes longer. I met the people they met and tried to capture the essence of who they were and why they were doing what they were doing. Ambulance crews, highway patrolmen, hot dog vendors, and blue crab fishermen, I loved sharing their worlds. I always came away feeling richer for having been a part of their experience, and the friendships I made left me with a real-world Rolodex of good people . . . good people who could always bail me out when I wasn't quite able to handle some new adventure myself.

Basically, I was a leech. If I couldn't be good myself, then surrounding myself with others was a hedge against failing as a reporter. When my words failed me, I used their words. Somewhere, about the time we learn to write our names in cursive script, we are all introduced to the infamous bell curve. First our intelligence quotient is hung out on it; then our grades are wrung out on it; and then our vocational aptitude is strung out on it. Once we have seen our shadow as cast by this brilliant star of statistical science, we are forever caught in its looming pronouncement. And, though we would never willingly admit it to one another, the vast majority of us are terminally average.

Average. This sentence, once handed down in eternal judgment, hangs over our heads like Damocles' sword; at any given moment we might be justly struck down for crimes of mediocrity against mankind. In my own way, though, I think I've stumbled onto an escape route out from under the executioner's dull blade. Despite my lackluster high school and college careers, despite my spinal cord injury, and despite the raging mediocrity in nearly every area of my life, when I decided that I wanted to try writing professionally, I didn't have the sense to know just how ridiculous the idea really was. The odds of success are, after all, pretty slim . . . but then I was never much for numbers.

So, why am I a moderately successful newspaper reporter while so many smarter, better trained, best-o'-the-bell-curve-type aspiring journalists are not? I have a theory about that. When your typical Joe Average walks under a great church bell with a long, thick rope hanging down from it, he doesn't swagger by, secure in his understanding of such things as the physics of sound waves and the music theory behind percussion instruments. He can't calculate the pitch, the range, and the sustain qualities of the bell just by looking up at it. This is good because, like Joe, most of us terminally average types have to reach up and grab the rope. We have to experience the pulling and then hear the bell ringing for ourselves. And when *this* Joe Average can't even reach the bell rope, for example, he usually knows someone who will come and reach it for him. Except tonight.

This was a job I had to handle by myself. My dad always made right and wrong seem so distinct, so easy to identify and choose between. The tattered paperback *Living Proverbs* he carried around in his shirt pocket was his morning devotional, and he would pull it out and refer to its heavily underlined pages often throughout the day. Instead of meeting Sam at the Bullet Hole for the third practice session with her new Lady Smith .38 Special, I drove home, retrieved my dad's old book of Solomon's "nuggets of truth," and headed for the coast. Thumbing through its yellowed pages, I wondered whether Sam would be annoyed that I disappeared instead of keeping our date with the black-and-white man-shaped targets . . . or whether she simply and honestly wouldn't particularly care.

Pushing that thought away, I forced myself to think about Malcolm Nealy and Lester Brown/John Dough/cat burglar/arsonist/Unknown Tourist. It would be so easy to leave everything alone and walk away from the story. There were lots of other stories that I could write. Just by keeping my mouth closed and looking the other way, an evil man probably wouldn't be hurting anyone else for a very long time, and a family man pushed to extremes by two men with little or no moral character would probably never bother another soul. I opened Dad's old book of Proverbs in the middle, found the sixteenth chapter, and read a verse he had underlined with a blue pencil. "The Lord made everything for His own purposes—even the wicked, for punishment." There. It was Malcolm's destiny. Like Judas the traitor, it wasn't a matter of *if* he would ultimately hang himself, only a matter of when.

I turned back a page or two and came across a nugget that stood out because it *wasn't* underlined. "A witness who tells the truth saves good men from being sentenced to death, but a false witness is a traitor." Great. What if the guy you save by telling the truth isn't so good? What if he's bad to the bone? Would that still make you a traitor? Midway between those verses was one I remember Dad quoting on a number of occasions. "The Lord is watching everywhere and keeps His eye on both the evil and the good." That helped a lot.

I paged back and forth for hours, squinting in the light of one of the park's pole lamps, but none of Solomon's nuggets seemed to offer the critical mandate that I sought. In the end, it was a verse in chapter twenty that finally helped me make up my mind. "It is a wonderful heritage to have an honest father." That was true. My father's legacy was an example of what the world *could* be like if we honored character over success. He had always been the man I wanted to be, and now it was time to live up to the legacy.

THE LAW OFFICES OF

Ketchum, Latham & Bennet, P. A.

221 Lake Eola Drive
Orlando, Florida 32801
(407)555-1975 - FAX (407)555-1999

Rosemary I. Latham	William P. Graham
Robert G. Bennet	H. Russell White
Bernard R. Ketchum	Robert W. Albright
Rebecca H. Forest	Samantha Wagner-Foster
Charles D. Young	Paul W. Kilpatrick

32

I SPENT MOST of the night watching the moon sparkle on the waves and marking the slow steady progress of ships whose lights could be seen moving north and south out on the dark horizon. It was a warm, breezy night, perfect, really, and once my mind was made up about whether or not I could look the other way and let Malcolm Nealy take the fall for Victoria Mann's murder, my ability to think creatively seemed to improve significantly. Until the car phone rang at midnight.

I told Sam that I was sorry and explained where I was and that I was trying to sort out some personal stuff. Yes, I could have called. I said I was sorry. No, there was nothing else the matter. Yes, next time I would be more considerate. No, I hadn't eaten supper. Yes, I was alone. No, I wouldn't be home soon. Yes, I was thrilled that she had consistently placed four out of five shots in a group the size of a man's heart—precisely where a man's heart was allegedly located. No, of course I wasn't mad at her. God forbid!

It took me a while to get focused again, but by sunup I had a plan. Not a brilliant plan, maybe not even a good plan, but a perfectly solid Joe Average kind of plan that at least I hadn't borrowed from anyone else. The morning sun felt wonderful on my face, and as I loaded myself and my trusty wheelchair into the Monte and headed out in search of a hearty breakfast buffet, I was starting to get excited about the day ahead. After a leisurely repast, I used the return trip to Orlando to make phone calls.

"Hello?"

"Scully! How are you this fine morning?"

"Are you kidding? I'm a grunt at a law firm. How do you think I am? What's goin' on?"

"I need a little briefing on a legal technicality, and then I need a fast law library research job."

"Why aren't you asking Sam?"

"Because you're the best, Scully."

"Bullshit."

"Okay, well, it's really sort of a wrong-side-of-the-bed thing."

"Ah! *That* I believe. Well, fire away. I'll help if I can."

"First, tell me all about expectation of privacy."

"Now? You want to see the tape again, this morning?"

"It's important, James. Honest."

"Okay. Meet you at the crime lab in half an hour."

"Thanks."

"Yes, Mr. Foster, I *could* order those documents surrendered, but I can't see where they have any bearing on our case."

"I'll tell you what, you get me those documents, and I promise that I'll save the D.A.'s office from making the biggest and most embarrassing mistake in its history—and since you're the D.A., that should seem like a reasonably priced quid pro quo."

"You're not implying—"

"I'm not implying anything . . . yet. Will you get me those documents?"

"All right."

"Today?"

"Okay."

"Great! You won't regret it."

"I think I already regret it."

* * *

"Oh yes, that's a very common item here, of course. I'm sure you'll find exactly the kind you need. Is this for your daughter?"

"No. It's for a friend of mine in jail."

"Oh, my . . . I see. Well, my name is Margaret. Just ask for me when you get here."

"Thank you, Margaret. I'll see you in about ten minutes."

"Okay, watch. Panning, lots of panning. Then, right here, boom, steady as a rock. Our Unknown Tourist just set the camera down—probably on the edge of the hot dog stand—and walked away. There! Watch that ugly woman in the straw hat." I said.

"What?" asked Detective Henderson. "I can't even see her face. Who is she, Stick?"

"She is a he. Get a blowup of her nose, and that mole thing on her temple. Then make a list of the items she's wearing."

"Is this a joke?"

"No, it's not. Look. Now the camera's moving and shaking again. Feel like trading promises?"

"I'm already going steady, with my wife, but what did you have in mind?"

"You help me produce a little documentary—it might take a few days—and in return, I'll give you the Unknown Tourist, the ugly lady in the straw hat, John Dough, The Old Man's and Stephen Epstein's killer, and the person who *really* murdered Victoria Mann. And I further guarantee that both the cabbie and the Mail Boxes R Us lady will make positive identifications to verify my findings."

"We have the wrong man? Are you serious?"

"Dead."

"I don't have to make any deals, Stick. The law says you've got to tell me, regardless."

"I know."

"And you would?"

"Of course."

"You've got a deal. What can I do?"

33

IT WAS JUST like in the movies. The big room was split down the middle, lengthwise, by a wall of face-to-face cubicle-type desks with clear Plexiglas separating each desk from its mirror image. Each cubicle had its own telephone. There were six video cameras mounted near the ceiling, four at the corners of the room, and one each midway down the opposing long walls. One guard stood at each of the two doors. I had just rolled in through one door, the other led directly to jail. There were several visitors already talking to inmates on the black telephones, so I picked a spot equidistant between two of them, shoved the chair out of the way, and rolled up to the desk. Now came the hard part. I'd only get one shot at this, so I took a couple of deep breaths, let them out slowly, and tried to concentrate on my game plan.

It wasn't until Malcolm Nealy actually came through the other door and into his half of the big room that I knew it was a go. They would have told him who his visitor was, so he had a choice as to whether he wanted to see me or not. That he had come at all was a positive sign. If he were confident about his defense, he would waste no time on the likes of Stick Foster. But he had doubts. *He* knew he hadn't killed Victoria Mann, but Milroy and Rude would have told him

all about the receptionist's desk planner, the young witness
in the park, and the tourist's damning videotape, and now
he wasn't sure there was a way out of the snare that had
been so carefully set for him. And Mad Malcolm had tight-
ened the wire himself by running away from the scene. In
hindsight, he must have wished that he'd stayed in the park,
caught Victoria's slumping body, and called out for help. Too
late now for anything but regret . . . and doubt. I was bank-
ing on Malcolm's doubts. It was Tennyson, I think, who said:
"There lives more faith in honest doubt, believe me, than in
half the creeds." It was time to find out if that was true.

His composure was perfect Malcolm, the set of his shoulders and his confident stride, but as he lowered himself into
the chair and reached for his end of our private telephone
line, I thought I saw the questions in his eyes. Maybe it was
wishful thinking. It was hard not to gloat at him, Mr. High-
and-Mighty in his pale lime green, one-size-fits-all county
jail coveralls, but *my* composure had to be absolutely perfect.
There was no room for improvisation in the script I had
written by the light of the silvery moon.

"What do *you* want?" he said.

I didn't answer. Instead, I hugged the phone to my left ear
with my shoulder and flipped open my notebook while I
looked impassively at his face. Study him.

"I'm here. What do you want?"

I watched his eyes, distantly, and gave him nothing.

"Hey!" Malcolm said loudly. He banged the receiver
against the Plexiglas twice before returning it to the side of
his head. "Earth to jerkface! Do you hear me? Why did you
come here, reporter?"

He spat the title. I gave no indication that I had heard it.
I'd been practicing the impassive, unhearing look in front of
a mirror for several hours. It felt right. It was certainly having
an effect.

"You ignorant crip!" he whispered into the phone's
mouthpiece. "Is this some kind of game? I'm not amused.
Tell me why you're here or get out of my face!"

His left hand twitched, and he shoved it out of sight below the desktop. I made a casual note on my pad, glancing away for barely a second.

"Look, I didn't set your damn house on fire! I've never even seen your house, okay? I don't particularly care if you believe me or not, but that's the truth. Is that what this is all about?"

Long seconds passed. He started turning red, and veins stood out on his forehead. I wanted to see his jugular. I studied him impassively, my lips parted casually, my eyes studying his face in patient detail. He put his arms on the desk again, and I made another phony note when his left hand jerked.

"If you're looking for a confession, newspaperman, you're nuts. I didn't kill that woman. I didn't lay a hand on her, and I don't know anything about needles and poison. I was set up—framed! Are you listening to me? I didn't do it!"

It was difficult to concentrate, to remain unaffected by his mounting tirade. I studied the wrinkles around his eyes, refused to let my face react. Had he ever had doubts like this before? I didn't think so.

"I don't know who you think you are, but I don't have to waste my time putting on a show for you, you dumb gomer. If you had half a brain, you'd be out there finding the *real* murderer, not here gawking at me like I was a sideshow freak! What is it you want anyway?"

I made another notation. Malcolm's twitch was a fascinating barometer of his general level of stress. Perhaps his usually cool and commanding exterior was due in large part to a strange subliminal pressure-valve function of his left hand. It wasn't helping him much now.

"Look, you write whatever you want, but I'm innocent. And when I prove that, I'll sue you and your paper back into the age of movable type! What do you want from me anyway? Say something!"

He rose partway to his feet, then sat back down and looked at my eyes. This was going to be hard. I studied the tiny

blood vessels in his eyes, and then his cheekbones and his
nose, careful not to engage him eye-to-eye. He was getting
command of himself. Now he was studying me.

"You want me to storm off in a huff, don't you, Foster?
You're playing some smartass personal game with me, and
you just came to watch me lose it. Well, tough cookies, crippled boy. I was too cool for you even back when you were a
whole man. You were a whole man once, weren't you?"

Then he smirked. It was the very same smirk that kept
me out in the moonlight weighing my options far longer than
I might otherwise have lingered there. But I held on. I gave
him nothing whatsoever to make him think that I'd heard
him. Nothing even to verify his existence in the room. Oh,
I studied his face, but it might as well have been a painting
or a sleeping animal at the zoo. I willed his words to stream
past me, impotent and empty. Malcolm was not used to
being ignored. His hand twitched twice, and he clutched it
with his right hand, noticing, I think for the first time, that
I was making note of the action. He placed the phone on the
desk and sat back in his chair to consider me.

We sat there like that for some time. I tried to will myself
to look only slightly contemplative, perhaps a bit undecided,
but nothing more. Not yet. I was counting on Malcolm to
do the rest, to make the leap. He had to come to it by himself.
I marked another twitch, and this time all his bells and
whistles went off at once. He threw himself forward, his face
very nearly against the Plexiglas, swept up the telephone,
and shouted into my ear.

"You know! You already know perfectly well that I didn't
kill Victoria Mann! You know who did this to me! You son
of a bi—"

That was my cue. I gave him the look I'd been saving. My
first and only acknowledgment. My version of a smirk was
nothing so crass and blatant as Malcolm's. It was the very
essence of subtlety. It was the merest wisp of wind across
the petals of a tiny wildflower, it was a tightening of the lips
and a light in the eyes so faint that no one in the world could

have detected it . . . except Malcolm. For Mad Malcolm it was a searing beam of laser light, aimed, launched, and delivered right on target, just for him. Then I nonchalantly hung up the phone, put up my notebook, and rolled away. Behind me, Malcolm Nealy was furiously smashing the telephone receiver against the thick Plexiglas. Everyone in the room could hear him quite clearly.

"Come back here, you son of a bitch! You can't do this to me! Damn you, Foster! What have I ever done to you? You bastard!"

Detective James Henderson met me at the front door. He looked a little lost, a bit awed, and very anxious to chat.

"That was it?"

"That was exactly it," I said. "Man, I'm thirsty."

"I'll buy," James offered. "It took three guards to subdue him, Stick. What *exactly* was that you were doing?"

"Act One, my friend. That was Act One."

THE LAW OFFICES OF

Ketchum, Latham & Bennet, P. A.

221 Lake Eola Drive
Orlando, Florida 32801
(407)555-1975 - FAX (407)555-1999

Rosemary I. Latham	William P. Graham
Robert G. Bennet	H. Russell White
Bernard R. Ketchum	Robert W. Albright
Rebecca H. Forest	Samantha Wagner-Foster
Charles D. Young	Paul W. Kilpatrick

34

ACT TWO OF my debut as a playwright was all Mad Malcolm's. A soliloquy of anger, frustration, hope, and, above all, doubt. He had the six-by-eight-foot stage all to himself. This was experimental theater and performance art taken to the extreme; one actor, no script, no director on hand, and no audience. Thanks to Ernest Boyle, my ex–Green Beret stagehand, the Orange County Jail was experiencing difficulty with its outside telephone lines, and Ma Bell wouldn't be able to "find" and fix the problem until morning. Malcolm spent his long night playing to a tough room—stewing, if you will, in the juices of his personal dilemma. The irony was that I wanted to be his ray of hope; more than that, I wanted Malcolm to see me as his only hope.

By mid-morning the next day, Malcolm Nealy had commandeered the newly "repaired" telephone and, after sending his hapless associates out to search for me on foot if necessary, was relentlessly calling every conceivable number at which I might be reached: home, car, the paper, Sam's firm, the Orlando Police Department, he tried them all, again and again. By noon he had reached a point of frenzy that I thought might do. It was time for the curtain to rise on Act Three.

"How'd he do last night?" I asked Detective Henderson when we met in the jail's security control room. Television monitors covered one entire wall, six of them showing their slightly fish-eyed takes on the big visitation room.

"The guard said he was up all night pacing and talking to himself under his breath."

"Good."

"Are you sure you know what you're doing?"

"As much as I ever do," I said. "Thanks for the time, by the way. I just couldn't bear the thought of getting him off scot-free without at least trying to rattle his cage a bit."

"How'd you get by Milroy and Rude? They were camped out at the main entrance with a subpoena for you last time I looked."

"Came in through the garage and took the prisoners' elevator."

"Good thinking. Well, I can't wait to see what kind of psychodrama you've got, in store for the poor man today. Break a leg!"

Funny.

I had barely rolled up under the visitors' desk when Mad Malcolm stormed into the room and stalked to the seat across from me. He swept up the telephone, looking like he might shout, but I met his eyes before reaching for my receiver. The look meant Don't screw with me, I'm all you've got, and Malcolm understood. He hated me, but he understood. He sat down carefully and took a breath.

"Look, Foster, I'm sorry about yesterday. I know I'm a smartass, and it must be fun watching me squirm in this place. Okay, so I've got a bad attitude and I usually don't care much about what other people think of me. That doesn't mean I deserve a murder rap."

His eyes were bloodshot far worse than they had been the day before, and they sported dark circles that gave him almost a manic raccoon look. His normally perfect hair had not been combed. I listened to both the fear and the loathing in his voice and wondered what it must be like for someone like Mad Malcolm to grovel. The uncontrolled movement of his left hand suggested that it was a bitter psychological trauma, at the very least. I remained silent but met him eye-to-eye, waiting.

"Okay, you don't like me. Hell, nobody does. But you saw that tape, and you saw me supposedly throwing a poison needle at Victoria Mann. And you know it was just my stupid hand jerking, don't you? Okay, you're a smart reporter, you've got a reputation for getting to the bottom of things, and I can respect that, so help me get to the bottom of this. Who set me up? I've been up all night trying to figure out who it was and how you found out. Was it John Columbine and Davey Howser? They've hated me ever since I passed them on the ladder. Was it Bernard Ketchum? Does he really believe I killed his dad? Hell, he hated his dad. Or maybe Wayne or Jon? I've always ridden them pretty hard."

Fatigue and paranoia often share the same hot pillow, and Malcolm Nealy had plenty of sleepless shadows in his past. But the age-old question remains: if everybody really *does* hate you, and they really *are* all out to get you, then are you really paranoid or simply observant? I let him ramble, let the level of his anxiety rise freely.

"Okay, look, thanks for coming. I know you don't owe me anything, but a jury will eat up that phony tape. They'll put me away and take turns patting each other on the back, while the real killer gets off free as a bird. And I know you know who it is. I've read too many witnesses and too many jurors not to know. It's Sarah Hunter, isn't it? Never sleep with an associate who's down the ladder . . . I knew better than that! She really went off when I didn't call her again . . ."

I thought of Ellie. Next to a neurotic newspaper reporter, Randy Travis was probably her favorite fantasy man. I could hear him singing "Diggin' Up Bones" while Malcolm flipped through the list of those he filled with bitterness and hate. I felt a great sense of thankfulness welling up inside as I thought of all the wonderful friends I had—often despite myself. I didn't like Malcolm, but seeing him face-to-face with his own friendless existence, I couldn't help but pity him a little.

"Look, okay," he whispered as a new tack occurred to him. He looked around the room furtively before leaning in toward the Plexiglas between us. "I can pay you! I've got money stashed away that the IRS doesn't know anything about. I'd have to pay a private investigator anyway, and you've already done all the legwork. It would be found money! Name your price."

That was the cue. *Reporter smiles before speaking. A patient, sincere, yet slightly condescending smile.*

"You can't afford me, Malcolm."

My first words had a profound effect on Mad Malcolm. Even though I'd spurned his offer, he would see my response as a victory. He had opened the door, made me respond. He rallied, he was moving toward more familiar ground, making arguments, shifting emphasis—anything to reach the goal.

"Let's work with that! Look, I know that rag doesn't pay you that well. I'll give you three times your annual salary, cash on the qt, no W-2 forms, no hassles. You give over with what you know—just tell the truth—and you can call it a consulting fee. How's that?"

I shook my head *no*, but let my eyes say *maybe, but not yet.*

"Okay, I understand. How many times does a guy get somebody over a barrel like this? I need you, and good help doesn't come cheap. I know, I'm a lawyer. Look, I can sell some stuff and double that. Half now, half when I'm out!"

Right. And then you and I can be buds out at the country club. I kept my face noncommittal but tried to show signs of wanting to leave. Malcolm read me immediately.

"Wait! Don't go! Man, you must really want to see if I'll fry for this, don't you? Damn you, you're a cold bastard."

He regretted saying it immediately. He knew he couldn't afford to alienate me. He hated me more and more as the seconds ticked by, but his survival meant doing whatever it took. Until, of course, he got out.

"I'm sorry, Foster, look, I'll do anything . . . just don't let me take the heat for this. I'm innocent!"

He was teetering on the emotional brink, floundering in unfamiliar waters. Malcolm wasn't used to not being in control, and I was giving him all the times-up signals. His left hand was positively fluttering.

"Wait! Don't go! Isn't there anything I can do or say to make you help me here? Talk to me! Name your price!"

"You don't have enough."

"How do you know? I mean, why do you hate me so much? You don't even know me! You're willing to let me go down for a murder I didn't commit. Why?"

I was turning to leave, but I saw the moisture in his eyes. He was tired, frightened, and out of options. In other words, he was right where I wanted him. I pushed back up to the table, pulled the backpack off my wheelchair, and reached inside it. Malcolm was fighting with himself, juggling anger, fear, hatred, ignorance, and now confusion. I put the baby doll in the blue dress with white polka dots on the desk between us, keeping my hand on it while Malcolm stared dumbly, totally lost. After several seconds he looked up and met my eyes.

"What is it? Are you nuts? What does that mean?"

I released the doll, and the head dropped free of its body and rolled forward against the Plexiglas. The red-cheeked face smiled up at Malcolm, and the little hinged eyelids popped open together. Memory and recognition fought their way across Malcolm's face when I placed an old color photograph of a little Boston girl on the desk next to the doll. His mouth fell open, and he looked back and forth from the items in front of him to my face. I could see him fighting back the ghosts, struggling to regain control. Sweat beaded on his forehead and his upper lip, and his left hand looked like it was about to come off at the wrist. When he got hold of himself, and thought through the implications of my evidence against him, outrage won out over discretion.

"I don't believe this!" he said, surging to his feet and aiming an unstable yet accusatory left pointer finger at the doll. "You're screwing me over because I pulled the head off some spoiled little brat's doll?"

It was what Scully had called a *spontaneous declaration*. Malcolm's voice boomed through the large room, indignant and unbelieving.

"I was just a kid, for God's sake!"

Before he could sit down or think to lower his voice, I pulled the old law journal out of my pack and laid it down next to the doll, so that the title page of the article was facing him. His eyes went wide, and he let go of the phone altogether.

"Where do you get off, Foster?" he shouted, waving his arms expansively before pointing them both at the desk. "What are you, anyway, the self-appointed conscience of the whole world? So what?" he shouted, gesturing at the law journal again. "I phony up an article to pay back an anal-retentive old professor who screwed up ten years' worth of a perfect GPA, and you think you can threaten me with it now? Get real!"

It is also, Scully verified, called *giving up your expectation of privacy*. As long as Malcolm spoke softly, using the telephone, nothing he might have said would have been admissible in court. The moment he stood up in front of God, the video cameras, and everyone, he gave up that privilege. I placed the bogus Fraiser documents next to the law journal, along with copies of Victoria Mann's keys to the firm.

"I used a key, Foster!" Malcolm stalked back and forth, lecturing me in his vexation. "I walked into Ketchum, Latham & Bennet and slipped those in the files to shake up the plaintiff's case. So what? Everybody does it! Who are you to judge me for how I serve my clients' best interests? I didn't hurt a soul! You're going to let me take a murder rap because you don't like the way I practice law?"

"The way you *used* to practice law," I said to myself as the curtain came down on Act Three, and I packed up my props to leave. "I don't like the way you *used* to practice law."

THE LAW OFFICES OF

Ketchum, Latham & Bennet, P. A.

221 Lake Eola Drive
Orlando, Florida 32801
(407)555-1975 - FAX (407)555-1999

Bernard R. Ketchum	William P. Graham
Rosemary I. Latham	H. Russell White
Robert G. Bennet	Robert W. Albright
Rebecca H. Forest	Samantha Wagner-Foster
Charles D. Young	Paul W. Kilpatrick

35

I DIDN'T PARTICULARLY enjoy breaking the rest of the Unknown Tourist story. It was the biggest scoop I'd had since coming to Orlando, and the Hollywood crews already nosing into the affair were whipped into a frenzy by the new revelations, but I felt ambivalent. Malcolm Nealy was off the hook for the murder of Victoria Mann but would face a number of lesser charges, including felony breaking and entering, which, while they might not land him in prison, would certainly get him disbarred. Lester Brown would go to jail for a very long time. The evidence was overwhelming. His execution of the crime(s) was every bit as good as any of Malcolm's stunts, but his inability to cover his tracks adequately and dispose of evidence was his downfall. Hollywood loved that. The phone business was odd, though. Even after confessing everything else, he swore up and down that, apart from ordering the L.I.M., he'd never used the portable-phone gimmick to make illegal calls on anyone else's lines. Hollywood really loved that part, but the rest of us weren't particularly thrilled. There were movie offers coming from everywhere, and anyone having anything to do with the bizarre case was being offered tidy sums to "sign off" exclusive interview rights with the various production company representatives.

It is a sign of our times. Budding and talented novelists can't buy a literary agent. I knew because I'd been shopping my fantasy-in-progress around. And up-and-coming screen-writers have more chance of winning the lottery than they do of getting representation for their work in Hollywood. But you take out a contract on your boss, stab your husband to death with a pair of fabric scissors, or dress up like a woman and stick someone with a poison needle, and lawyers and agents will line up around the block to sign you up and sell your story. You and every Tom, Dick, and Harry who's ever had occasion to chat with you over the backyard fence.

Within forty-eight hours I'd received calls from eight literary agents and four paperback publishing houses. The tentative over-the-telephone advance numbers were pushing the mid-six figures, and all the agents insisted that if I signed on with them, that would simply be where the auction for rights would begin. I needed a lawyer.

"Do you want to write a true crime book?" Sam asked.

"I don't know," I said. "I'd never thought about it before."

We lay on the water bed together for the first time in several days. A lot had happened in that time. Outside our patio doors, the full moon sat smiling like a good-natured children's book illustration over Lake Martha, its light falling across Sam's face and catching in her golden hair. At first I thought that I wanted to kiss her, to make love to her until the moon was shining on another part of the world. But it came to me just before I reached out to take her in my arms that I didn't want that at all. What I *really* wanted was for Sam to make love to *me* . . . like she did so often during the early months of our marriage. There's a big difference.

"I think you'd do a great job," she said. "Especially in capturing the humanity behind the crimes. And a three-hundred-thousand-dollar book advance is not exactly small change—and that doesn't even include the money you'd get for a movie option."

"What's the difference between a movie option and a movie deal?"

"The option just gives one production company the exclusive right to the book for a limited period of time, say a year. They give you money not to make a deal with anyone else. At any time during the option period, if they decide to go ahead with the project, then a real movie contract is drawn up. You might get ten thousand dollars for the option on a deal like this, and then maybe eighty to one hundred and fifty thousand the day they start shooting. It all depends on how many companies want the project, and it looks like everybody and their sister wants this one."

"Mmm. Did you like any of the agents I made you talk to?" I'd started channeling all the calls to Sam, telling callers that "my lawyer would be handling everything."

"I'm having two of them checked out," she said. "If they don't make the cut, there's one other who sounded pretty together. What did you think?"

"I liked the young one with the sexy smile that you can see over the phone." I said.

I got an elbow in my ribs for my honesty. And then a soft sliding hand across my stomach. And then a long, wandering kiss about the head and shoulders.

"It's been awhile," I said.

"Since what?" Sam said, kissing behind my ear.

"Since you've been . . . here. Like this."

"It's just the job. I'll try to make it up to you."

And try she did. I suppose that's why I didn't notice the tall, dark figure of a man walk into our bedroom.

"I always wondered how you cripples did it, but I don't think I'll cancel my evening plans to watch."

The sinister shadow with the silenced handgun was Mad Malcolm Nealy, and his voice would have scared Freddy Krueger right off the street.

"I don't know exactly what you thought, Foster—or even if you thought—but you've merely inconvenienced me. If I lose my license, it will only be temporarily. But you have embarrassed me. You simply can't do that and expect to just go merrily back to your book deals and your movie contracts.

I won't permit it, certainly not from a half-man. I wonder? Do a half-man and a half-woman add up to a whole person? I seriously doubt it."

Sam slowly rolled off me, but not before I breathed "Floor when I poke you" into her ear.

"Easy," Malcolm said. "I'm not sure who to shoot first, Foster. Your wife? Or maybe gut-shoot you and make you lay there and watch while I screw her?"

As Sam sat back against her pillow, the moonlight fell across her breasts. Her nipples were full and hard, and her frightened breathing caused them to rise and fall dramatically in the shimmering light. I regretted having been so quick to slide the straps of her nightgown down and off her shoulders and her arms but then realized that Malcolm was staring at my wife's body with total concentration and pure lust. I poked Sam in the ribs, screamed to distract Mad Malcolm, and dove off my side of the bed.

The drawer in the base of our water bed hit my wheelchair's footrests when I yanked on its handle with my left hand but opened far enough to allow me to reach in with my right. It seemed to take forever, but I found the 9mm, shook loose the painter's cap in which it was wrapped, and released the safety before it had cleared the drawer. That's when I heard the shots, five of them.

"No!" I screamed, sitting up and pointing the Beretta at the evil shadow with the wide and dangerous eyes. I fired three times, but the 9mm rounds sailed through the empty place where Mad Malcolm had been standing and killed the medicine cabinet in the bathroom instead. Where had he gone?

I was shuffling along on the floor, making my way to the foot of the bed, when Sam's reading light came on.

"No! Don't give him a target! I can't see!"

I blinked stupidly against the light and fought to focus my startled eyes. I still couldn't see Malcolm, but Sam sat upright against her pillows like a Greek goddess with her beautiful breasts heaving steadily in the lamplight. The diminutive Golden Eagle she had had tattooed there seemed to be flying. I didn't see any blood but didn't let my eyes linger any longer. Mad Malcolm couldn't have gone far. I swept the room with the automatic.

"He's dead, Rambo," Sam said.

"What?" I scooted the rest of the way to the foot of the bed and looked. There he was. I reached up and flicked on the switch by the door, and the overhead light illuminated the body that lay bleeding on our bedroom carpet. His legs were crumpled up under him, but he had fallen backwards, clutching at his chest. I looked back at Sam.

"Are you okay?"

"Yes, I'm fine."

"*You* shot him?" I could now see the smoking hole in the bedspread. Of course she shot him.

"It looks that way, doesn't it?" Sam pulled the Lady Smith out from under the covers and placed it gingerly on the bed. "He looked just like one of those silhouette targets at the range," she said, her breathing a little more normal. "Only a *lot* closer."

My hands were shaking, and my knuckles were white from gripping the Beretta. "Call nine-one-one," I said, scooting toward Malcolm's body and pushing the silenced handgun farther away from him with the barrel of my 9mm. Of course that was Sam shooting; Malcolm's gun would have made only a raw spitting noise.

"Not a bad bit of shooting, eh, babe?" Sam said, straightening her nightgown and returning the straps to her shoulders.

"Glad they made you practice that sort of thing, aren't you?"

"Oh, yes," she said, picking up the telephone receiver and dialing the three famous numbers that spell *help* all across the country.

"Just for clarification," I said, leaning back against the chest of drawers, "we've been sleeping with that thirty-eight, haven't we?"

"You're darned straight we have."

"And you intend to go on sleeping with it?"

"What do you think?"

Mmm. Maybe Molly Henderson and her *ibrat al-maut* wasn't the most dangerous spouse in town after all.

While the first faint sounds of sirens echoed in the distance, I looked more closely at Mad Malcolm Nealy's corpse. He would never abuse another human being. Sam had practiced too diligently for that. Like everything else she put her hand to, Sam never played to lose. There were five bullet holes in Malcolm's chest, four of them in a group the size of a man's heart . . . precisely where the man's heart was allegedly located.